Cadence

Dianne J. Wilson

Cadence
COPYRIGHT 2019 by Dianne J. Wilson

Contact Information: titleadmin@pelicanbookgroup.com

All scripture quotations, unless otherwise indicated, are taken from the Holy Bible, New International Version(R), NIV(R), Copyright 1973, 1978, 1984, 2011 by Biblica, Inc.™ Used by permission of Zondervan. All rights reserved worldwide. www.zondervan.com

Cover Art by *Nicola Martinez*

Watershed Books, a division of Pelican Ventures, LLC
www.pelicanbookgroup.com PO Box 1738 *Aztec, NM * 87410

Watershed Books praise and splash logo is a trademark of Pelican Ventures, LLC

Publishing History
First Watershed Edition, 2019
Paperback Edition ISBN 978-1-5223-0029-8
Electronic Edition ISBN 978-1-5223-0027-4
Published in the United States of America

Dedication

To Dad, who made it easy for me to believe in a
Heavenly Father who loves me
and always has my back.

Spirit Walker Series

Affinity
Resonance
Cadence

1

Mist-fire burned across Kai's skin, so fierce it stole his breath away. Bree clung to him. Shivers wracked through her body.

Get out!

Turn back!

You're going to die!

A stubborn ball of resolve remained in the pit of his belly. He kept walking. One foot, then another. Bree's weight shifted, and she struggled against him.

"We're going to die! Let me go. Are you insane?"

"Just a bit more." Kai's arms throbbed from the mist and Bree's weight. She scrambled like a wildcat in his arms, but he held on. He held on for the time in the desert. He held on the way her father should have. Their feet hooked, and they came down hard. Kai kept his arms locked even as the blackness inched across his vision and claimed him.

~*~

"Kai."

Was that Bree's voice in his head? "Hmm?"

"You can let go now."

Bree's face hung over his, so close he could taste her breath. He craned his neck and squinted. A worn throw lay at his feet. He was on the couch in Torn's office. The pain from the mist lingered on his skin and

1

he cringed as he held up his hand, expecting to see charred flesh. No sign of damage. His skin was normal. Everything came into sharp focus, and he heard the blast of the air freshener. Green vapour curled through the air.

"Affinity enhancer. Don't breathe it in!" He shoved Bree aside and hunted for something to dislodge the canister. A chair. Kai swung it high and smashed it into the device mounted on the wall. It flew off and bounced on the floor. Lungs burning, he grabbed it and ran. Another two lined the walls down the passage. Kai stepped over sleeping bodies to hook them off too. He dashed to the kitchen, snatching breaths in short gasps. He threw open the chest freezer, tossed the canisters in, and shut it.

Bree peered around the door. "Is it safe to breathe yet?"

"Help me look for more. We need to get rid of them all."

They searched the building and found a dozen more. Once they'd all been stowed in the freezer, Kai slid to the floor and felt his muscles turn to jelly. Bree sank to the floor opposite him, drawing her knees up under her chin. Her face was pale in the frame of her fiery hair, dark rings under her eyes. Kai drank in the sight of her. She was the loveliest thing he'd ever laid eyes on. And this time, she was right here with him.

"You're here."

"Apparently I am. Where are we?"

"We are back in the natural realm." Kai struggled for words. "On earth."

Bree eyed him sideways. "You think I'm an alien?"

"No! I just don't know how to explain it." He shrugged. "I'm sorry for squishing you. I couldn't let you go and risk leaving you behind again."

"So, if we were going to burn to death, at least we'd die together. Is that it? Romeo and Juliet but without the family drama."

Kai squirmed. He'd discovered glimpses of enough family drama to put Shakespeare's stories to shame.

Bree shrugged. "It doesn't matter. What now?"

"They should be waking up soon. And then...I'm not sure. Who would have sabotaged us like that? Why?"

"I haven't been here, remember? We should make tea." She pushed off the floor and turned a slow circle to get her bearings. Wiping dust off the urn, she filled it and switched it on. While the water heated up, she dug through the cupboards to find teabags and mugs. She favoured her whole hand, keeping the damaged one pulled into her sleeve.

Kai watched her move, and it soothed him.

She handed him a mug full of steaming sweet tea and then slid down next to him on the floor, balancing her own tea. "That was painful."

Kai sipped and felt warmth return to his fingers. "The mist?"

Bree nodded. "How did you know it would bring us back?"

"I didn't. It was a gut feeling. You make good tea."

"I know. It's been a while since I could." Her cup clinked on the tiles as she put it down.

The sounds of moving people filtered through the doorway. "The rest of them are waking up." *Where was Runt?* "Did you see a little dark-haired girl anywhere in the building? And two kittens?"

Bree shook her head. Without warning, she flew

off the floor. "Elden!"

Elden, her brother, stood propped up by the doorway. He winced as Bree smacked into him, throwing her arms around him fiercely. He hugged her with his eyes shut, his breathing shuddery. After a long moment, he pushed her to arm's length before folding her into another hug.

"I didn't think I'd..."

Bree smacked his arm. "I know. I didn't think I'd see you again either. Why did you have to go and get involved with those people? Sometimes I swear you have no brain."

Elden held up his hands, blinking.

Evazee pushed past their reunion into the kitchen, her gaze slid over the boiling urn, the teacups, and finally rested on Kai. She sat down on the floor next to him, and the warmth of her seeped into his skin. He hadn't realized how cold he was.

"Well, that was quite something." Evazee kept her gaze on the ground, and her pale hair hung between them like a curtain.

A dry chuckle shook him. "Indeed. I want to hear your stories sometime. A lot happened after we were split up."

Evazee blinked and switched her intent focus to her fingernails. "Yeah, we can swap stories sometime." She glanced towards Elden and Bree, who were still hurling insults at each other. "You brought her back."

Kai nodded. Weariness crashed in on him, and the desire to be horizontal seemed overwhelming. Too many unanswered questions. He needed to think, and for that he needed time and space. None of which he'd get around here.

Evazee spoke softly, "You should come to the hall.

Everybody is waking up. They're going to need somebody to talk them through."

"You can do that. You're good at that."

"Oh, please. I'm not the only one who can talk, you know." She pushed off the floor, picked up a cloth, and started wiping counter tops furiously, as if they'd gotten dirty just to annoy her.

What was wrong with the girl? "You know I'm right. You are way better at that whole thing." He stretched his arms up, working the kinks out his back. Carrying Bree was one thing, but hanging on to her as she'd turned wildcat? That was enough to tie knots all down his spine.

Evazee frowned at his arm. "Boy? Is that a muscle I see?" She dropped the cloth, pushed up his T-shirt sleeve, and held up his arm. "Flex it." Her eyebrows shot up in disbelief. "It is! Look at that bump! Whoa!"

"Evazee, stop it." Kai grimaced as Bree and Elden came closer, looming over him to get a better look.

Bree reached out and squeezed. "Yep, that's a muscle." She took on a conspiratorial tone, whispering into Evazee's ear, "He carried me all the way through the mist."

Evazee's eyes sparkled. "For real?"

Bree grinned and nodded, her red curls creeping across her face each time her chin dipped.

"And who fought me every step of the way?" Kai yanked his arm away and pulled down his sleeve, cutting off any further opportunities for comment. They might as well be investigating a zit on his nose. "We should go. Apparently, everybody is waking up."

He stalked out of the kitchen, and Evazee followed him into the dark passages. The bodies that he'd hurdled over to get to the dispensers were beginning to show signs of life. Some had made it to half-sitting, others had made it all the way onto two feet, but most of them needed a wall to stay upright.

He couldn't help noticing that Evazee slipped past them all with her arms crossed over her chest. The Evazee he remembered, would be right in there, glowing and letting her hope rub off on everyone. Now she held back, pale and distant. As far as they walked, a sea of green surrounded them. It twisted his belly. So much was broken and bent out of shape in all of these kids.

By the time they'd picked their way through to the main meeting hall, acid-bile gathered at the back of Kai's throat. He swallowed the urge to throw up. Then he found a dark corner and sank to the floor with his knees drawn up. He shut his eyes and focussed on swallowing. His mind wandered, throwing up images of Grave Keepers, Shasta, and the vision he'd seen at the pools. It had just been a vision, but it was stuck in his mind on repeat. TrisTessa with an injured arm—he recognized her. But the baby who'd healed her and the man who'd taken the baby and left? There was nothing familiar about either of them. Even knowing that his name was Roland didn't help.

Peeping through his half-shut eyelids, he surveyed the room. Across the sea of green, a guy sat staring at him. Kai looked away, but soon found his gaze drawn back. From this distance, there was nothing remarkable about the shadowy figure across the room, but the fact that he was staring at Kai so blatantly made Kai's skin crawl. The green in the room assaulted his senses, and he flinched.

Bree found him and sank to the floor close enough that he could feel warmth from her leg on his. He tipped his head towards his silent fan. "Do you know that guy?"

Bree followed his gaze and shrugged. "There're lots of guys. Which one?"

Kai checked to see if she was messing with him, but her face was straight. He pointed to the man, but he wasn't there. "Oh, he's gone. He was right there, boring holes through me with his eyes."

Bree waggled fingers over her temples. "Probably just leftover from whatever was being pumped into these rooms."

"You're probably right."

"Elden wants to talk to you. He sent me to fetch you. He's waiting in the kitchen."

"Great. What now?" Kai's head ached. The pain started in his shoulders and spread over his scalp like a swimming cap a few sizes too small.

"He wouldn't say. Secret boy stuff I guess."

If Bree knew more, she wasn't saying. Dealing with Elden was the last thing he wanted to do right now. "Sure. Go tell him I'll be there soon."

Kai waited until Bree was out of sight, used the wall to push himself up, slipped from the room, and out onto the street.

~*~

Feeling useless, Evazee moved between those who were waking up. She should have words dancing in her, golden words, full of Jesus-life and power to work inside any who chose to listen. Her hand slipped to her throat to cover where her imprint used to be, and her belly twisted as if someone had scooped out her insides with a spoon. She glanced behind her.

Bree handed out steaming cups from a tea trolley.

What now, Jesus? What do we do with these kids?

Ruaan and Zap ran into the room and headed straight for her. "We need Kai. Where is he?"

"What's going on? He's around here." She searched the room where she'd seen him last, but he was nowhere. "What's the matter?"

Zap stepped in close enough that his words stayed between them. "It's his friend, the small one. Something's not right."

"Runt?" Evazee's hands grew cold. "Take me to her. Now."

She picked her way between the sprawled bodies to follow Ruaan and Zap from the room. Outside the passage was gloomy, shut off from any windows that would bring in natural light. A few of the overhead lights had blown, and Evazee's heart pinched at the thought of being back in thick darkness. "How far is she?" Evazee had left Peta sleeping under a soft blanket in the room, but she didn't relish the thought of leaving her in case the girl woke up and panicked.

"Basement. I think she's found something."

Evazee followed them to the lift and watched lights running in a straight line as the box took them into the belly of the building. The doors drew back with a hiss, and the air around them twisted with a strong sense of wrongness. It gathered in a ball of tension in the pit of her belly. Breathing was suddenly hard.

"She's behind there." Zap bounced on his toes, reluctant to lead the way.

Ruaan glared at him. "Well? Lead on, McZap. We'll be right behind you."

~*~

A sign hung on the doors to the SandSky Studio declaring it open in spite of the closed doors. Kai let himself in and instantly considered turning around and leaving. The vision he'd seen of the baby healing TrisTessa and being taken away by a man named Roland sat in the centre of his brain, overshadowing all other thoughts. All his other worries led back to this one. He had to know if the Pools of Resonance had been lying. Or worse, telling the truth.

Pockets of people ambled through the gallery, gathered in quiet clumps around the rooms. TrissTessa would be easy to spot with her shock of black hair that refused to be tamed. Kai ran a hand over his own rebellious spikes wondering if he should shave it all off. Before he had a chance to seriously consider that option, he saw her.

TrisTessa was dressed in worn jeans and an oversized white shirt with the sleeves rolled up past her elbows, her hair piled on top of her head in a semblance of a bun. She carried two containers of water with a paint mixing tray balanced precariously on top. Paintbrushes poked out from her armpit and her face pinched in intense concentration highlighting the fine lines around her eyes and mouth. Something about her defied time. *Mom. Mother. Mother dearest.* He settled on her name.

"TrisTessa!"

She turned, and her face glowed as she saw him.

Kai rubbed his neck. This was awkward. How would he even start this conversation? "Here, let me help you." He coaxed the paintbrushes out from under her arm and took the paint trays. Her cheeks flushed and she shot small, sideways glances at him as they walked down the airy corridor.

The building had been designed to use every scrap of natural light. Skylights let in just enough to make entire wall panels glow as if lit from inside.

Kai drank it all in, feeding off the simple beauty of reflected light.

TrisTessa cleared her throat. "Would you like to paint a bit? I've just had a client cancel. I've got it all set up. Unless you're busy, of course."

Kai shook his head. "I'm OK, thanks. It's not really my thing. I just want to ask you a few questions."

"Come on, it's this way." She led him to a small round room, a terrarium of glass in the middle of a jungle of plants. There was a single easel set up in the centre. A rocky water feature trickled outside an open window, filling the air with the music of running water.

"What are you going to paint?" Kai welcomed the distraction, the chance to put off asking her about what he'd seen.

She grinned at him and mischief danced in her eyes. "Oh, I'm not painting. I already know how." She opened a box of paints, set the water down on a small table, and waved him to his place in front of the blank canvas. "This is for you."

This was worse than asking her his question. "I'm not here for that. I just need to ask you something."

"We can talk while you paint. It will be easier."

"What would I paint? This is not my thing."

"It doesn't have to be. Wait, let me start you off." TrisTessa squeezed out coloured blobs onto the paint tray next to him.

For a moment Kai thought she would put brush to canvas, but instead she motioned towards him.

"Don't think. Just put colours on the canvas.

Abstract is what we are aiming for."

Kai didn't have energy to argue. He dipped the brush into the purple blob, smooshed it into the blue and painted a wavy line diagonally across the top corner. Without rinsing his brush, he dipped it into the yellow and swirled the yellow paint into the green. Another wavy line appeared below the first one, swirls of all four colours blending.

TrisTessa grinned at him, nodding her head. "Perfect. Keep going."

Kai decided to play her bluff. If she'd been hoping to avoid his questions by making him paint, he was about to prove her wrong.

His brush swooped up and down as he considered his words. What he would give to have Evazee's talent of saying the right thing. That would be great right now. "I had a vision. We can call it a dream if it's easier for you."

TrisTessa focussed on his painting, tilting her head this way and that, rubbing her chin thoughtfully. "A vision is a vision. Go on."

"You were in it." His hand shook and the line went skew. "There was also a baby." Kai felt her gaze on his face, but he stared fiercely ahead as if the canvas was the only thing in the world. He dabbed a thick blob of orange over the ruined line. "You had hurt yourself, but the baby grabbed your sore arm and his touch healed you." He cleared his throat against the tension threatening to choke him. "A man came in—"

"Roland."

"Yes, Roland. He took the baby away." Kai had switched from lines to circles. He painted another one, trying to figure out what he was actually asking TrisTessa. *Mom.*

"And you want to know if you were that baby, if Roland is your dad, and if that is what happened?"

His hand dropped to his side, brush splodging paint onto his jeans. For the first time since tackling the subject, he met her gaze.

"What you described is exactly what happened." She reached for him, as if to take his hand but folded her arms instead. "Don't hate him, Kai. He thought he was doing the right thing."

"It makes no sense."

"Very little in life does." She squinted at his canvas, a random mess of colours that could have been the work of a three-year-old. Grabbing his hand, brush and all, she dipped the tip into the black and guided his hand through a series of swift strokes. Kai couldn't quite make out what it was until the last few strokes landed.

Under the direction of her skill, his random mess became an eagle, soaring high against a backdrop of planet earth.

TrisTessa grinned at him, delight crinkling the skin at the corners of her eyes. "Good job."

The gallery doorbell rang. TrisTessa crossed to a small monitor mounted next to the door and pressed a button. The display lit up and showed three men and a woman at the front door of the gallery.

Kai was studying his, or rather *her* handiwork, but he heard her suck in air and a sliver of disquiet shot through him. She spun towards him.

"You have to go now." She bustled him towards the door and away from the main entrance. "Use the back exit. Go quickly."

"What's going on?"

"Nothing!" She forced a smile and her voice

softened. "Nothing, I just have an appointment that slipped my mind. I'm sorry, Kai. Please excuse me. Follow this passage, go left at the end, and you'll see the door. Go now." She was as jumpy as a lizard on a hot desert floor, torn between watching him leave and observing whoever had come into the gallery. With a quick wave, she turned her back on him and left.

Kai had half a mind to follow her and see what had rattled her so badly, but he was tired and hungry, and their conversation had left him more unsettled than before. Let her have her secrets.

2

Runt was in the basement. She lay flat on her back stretched out like a body in a coffin with her hands clasped around a glowing object, the light so strong it shone between her fingers, making her skin look transparent.

Evazee ran to her side and felt for a pulse. Her heartbeat was shallow and irregular. "Guys, get that thing out of her hands." She pulled back Runt's eyelids. Her eyes stared with little response from her pupils, which had stretched to inky black circles.

Ruaan and Zap knelt on either side of the small girl.

Zap prised her fingers back, but each time he got one free the rest would clamp down harder.

Ruaan swatted his hands. "Shove off. Let me try."

Zap tucked his hands in his armpits with his eyebrows cocked.

Ruaan held Runt's fingers in one hand and tried to wedge his other hand between her skin and the object. The tip of his finger slipped past hers and touched the glowing pendant. He shot back as if he'd stuck his finger in a live socket. He smacked into a wooden storage crate and fell to his knees groaning.

Evazee frowned at Ruaan on the floor. "It's no use. We have to take her upstairs."

Zap side-stepped along the wall, keeping as much

space between him and Runt as he could. He pulled Ruaan to his feet and shoved him towards Runt. They lifted Runt between them and carried her to the lift.

Evazee was about to push the button to close the door when she heard a thin growl. It raised the hairs on the back of her neck, even though it was a pitiful sound that held little promise behind its threat. She peered out of the lift, changed her mind about investigating and pushed the button quickly.

"We're taking her upstairs. Once she's settled, you two are coming back to find out what is growling down here in the dark."

3

Kai walked into chaos at the OS. A small Chinese girl sat just inside the front door, sobbing. Her blue-black hair was caught up in two ponytails that stuck out from the side of her head like paintbrushes and huge tears trailed down her cheeks and dripped off her chin. A green mess wrapped tight around her heart. He reached for her hand, helped her up, and she followed him, wiping her nose on her dirty sleeve.

A group of boys squared up in the passage, ready to pull each other's hair out. Kai could almost feel the green waves of altered testosterone rolling off them. The two taller boys seemed to be the main instigators. Kai pushed them apart. "Stop that rubbish and come." Kai walked on without looking back.

In the meeting hall, a skinny girl in jeans and tank top had taken over the drum set. The beats she played were random as if she were trying to avoid rhythm altogether. If that was indeed her goal, she was succeeding.

The discord rattled through Kai, and he walked over, took the sticks out of her hands and flicked his head for her to follow. Her cheeks flushed, but she left the drums and joined the group behind him. As he walked, he gathered them. All broken, twisted, messed up from the Obsidian Square Affinity training program. The group behind him swelled and doubled, then tripled.

He led his motley following towards the auditorium where he'd played to drunken crowds before, the same place they'd all been given their first good meal together. Each kid he spoke to came with him. His gut told him they would follow and they did.

He waved towards the chairs. While they filed in and settled, his mind raced. They all needed fixing, there was no doubt there. But where should he start? He had a hunch, but it was a long shot and if he was wrong, he could lose some of these kids. *Tau, what now?*

The little girl holding his hand tucked in close to his leg and sucked her thumb. Her tears had dried up and left two dirty tracks down her cheeks.

A side door flung open, and Zap rushed through. Sweat ran from his temples, and he breathed hard as if he'd run up hundreds of stairs. "Kai! Where have you been, man? Come quick. It's Runt." He bolted up the stage steps, grabbed Kai's arm, and halted. Then he spun in a slow circle. "I'm interrupting. I can come back."

Silence had fallen across the room, with the audience's attention shifting from Kai to Zap.

Kai had to tap Zap's arm to get his attention. "What about Runt?"

"She found something. A necklace. Kai, she's not conscious."

Kai pulled Zap close and whispered, "I can't leave this lot alone. They're trouble waiting to happen. Split them into groups of their gifting. By the time you're done I'll be back."

"And just how am I meant to do that? I don't even know—"

"You've been around this place longer than me. Figure it out. You can hear thoughts sometimes, right?"

"Yeah, but only under sim."

"That's the thing. That whole adventure we've just got back from? That wasn't a simulation. We were in the spiritual realm."

"Ah, man, I don't like that. I don't—"

"We don't have time. Look how restless they are. Don't over-think. Your brain will get in your way. Just trust Tau to show you. Now, where do I find Runt?"

~*~

Evazee stroked Runt's hair. Without her words, touch was the only comfort she could offer. Her loss stung keenly and grew into a lump in her chest that she struggled to draw breath around. Runt shivered so hard that her teeth rattled, but her forehead was too hot to touch. A convulsion twisted through her, and she cried out. A hot, helpless tear rolled down Evazee's cheek.

The necklace glowed between Runt's tightly clenched fingers, shooting out glowing beams that moved, tracing patterns on the walls and ceiling. It was all too much. Evazee shut her eyes and hunched over. *Jesus, help.*

The door swung open, and Kai rushed in with a small Chinese girl in tow. Kai glanced around before meeting her gaze. "What's going on?"

Evazee kept stroking Runt's hair. "We found her like this downstairs. We tried to take the necklace, but it's impossible. I don't know what to do. She's burning up."

Kai swung around, staring at the walls, the ceiling. "Do these images change? Or are they just repeats?"

"What images?"

Kai squinted at the ceiling and pointed.

Evazee followed his finger and gasped. "Whoa, I thought they were just patterns. Can't make out what it is, Runt's fingers are right across it all."

"It looks like the inside of a lab. Those men are wearing lab coats. Let's move her hand."

"Tried that already. Let me just say that it's not advisable."

"Maybe not." Kai studied Runt's hands and arms, his forehead creased. "There is some type of current flowing from the pendant. It's locked Runt's fingers and arms. Can you see it?"

It was a throwaway comment, but it stung. Evazee fought hard to keep her face neutral. "That's your thing, remember?"

Kai didn't answer. His full attention was on Runt. "Get ready to grab the necklace. I'll say when." He reached for her elbows and flinched as his skin touched Runt's. Grimacing as if he were holding a hot poker, he clenched his jaw and held on. Runt thrashed from side to side, a guttural moan escaped her lips. Kai kept holding.

"Any second now..."

Evazee's blood pounded so loud through her head that she had trouble hearing over it.

"Now! Take it."

Runt's fist popped open. Evazee shoved down the fear and reluctance that paralyzed her and grabbed the pendant. As it lifted off Runt's skin, it snapped shut, cutting off the images and throwing the room into darkness. Evazee lost balance and fell.

Runt yelled, convulsed once, and collapsed back onto the couch.

Evazee tried to slip the necklace off past her head, but her hands had closed around the chain as if it were super-glued to her skin. "I can't get it out of her hands. I'm scared of hurting her."

Something bumped and shuffled through the room. In a moment, lights flickered on overhead. Kai had found the light switch. "That's not quite what I had in mind."

He had dark rings beneath his eyes and his hair stood up in all directions. Seeing him so mussed up bent her insides a little. Evazee slipped a hand to Runt's forehead. It was cool to the touch, and the girl seemed to breathe normally again. Her eyelids fluttered open at Evazee's touch. She frowned hard and poked Evazee's cheek. "You real?"

"We're back." Evazee spoke softly, but the wariness lurking in Runt's eyes didn't budge. Shadows shifted across her face. She was a terrified little girl. Evazee kept her voice low and gentle, "You're safe now."

Runt's hands flew to the pendant around her neck and relief relaxed her muscles. "Took you long enough."

"I know, I know. At least we're here now."

Kai knelt next to her. "That's a nice necklace. Where did you get it?"

"I found it. It's mine now." Her jaw clamped shut, forcing her lips into a tight line.

"Are you being honest, Runt?" Kai fought to keep his face straight.

Runt was struggling not to blurt out everything. Deception was not in her nature.

"Oh, fine. That boy—Snitch—he gave it to me. It's just a present."

"Do you know what it's for? What the pictures mean?"

Runt rolled her eyes. "It's just for pretty. I'm tired now. Is there food?"

Evazee reached for her hand. "I'm sure we can find something for you. Come on."

~*~

Kai and the two girls walked into chaos in the auditorium.

Runt was licking ketchup off her fingers from the hotdog she'd eaten. She stopped dead and stared.

Zap and Ruaan argued on stage, while the kids down below stood behind crossed arms, shifting awkwardly from one foot to the other.

It only took a quick glance for Kai to see that their grouping was completely random, nothing to do with their gifting at all. He mounted the stage, two stairs at a time. "Guys, what is going on?"

Zap was red in the face from arguing. "This genius has been arranging kids according to their birth date. That's not even logical."

Kai tried to keep the frown off his face. "And you?"

Zap swung his hands in circles as if trying to coax the right words out. "Height. Tall ones over there and short ones on that side. Makes perfect sense."

"What about their gifting?"

"Oh, there's no way to tell that. None at all. We're just going to have to go according to height." Zap looked pleased with himself, then turned to Kai and grimaced. "I'm not a nitwit."

"I never said you were."

"But you *thought* it and that's just as bad."

Kai rubbed his chin as a thought budded. Maybe there was a simple way to do this. "Runt, go get a big piece of cardboard and a marker from the office. Don't sass me, just go." He pulled Zap close and whispered, "Walk through the crowd. As you go, repeat this in your head: *if you can hear this, sit down and put your hands on your head.*"

"I'm not going to do that."

Kai silently steel-eyed his friend.

Zap caved. "That's not fair. You can't order me around using your thoughts." He turned on his heel and harrumphed.

Kai turned to the kids in the hall, who were fast losing interest and getting rowdy. He cleared his throat and clapped his hands, but nobody noticed. He considered yelling, but nobody would hear him. Kai turned in a circle to check the stage and found a guitar. In a few seconds, he'd tweaked the tuning, plugged it into an amp and began to play. A wave of quiet rolled over the crowd, starting with those closest to the stage and washing through to the edges of the room.

Kai played until he had all their attention. "Right everybody, close your eyes. We will be giving instructions that you might hear. Or you might not. If you do hear them, do what they say. If you hear nothing, do nothing. Simple, yes?" He waved Zap towards the people.

At first, nothing happened. Giggling broke out as Zap passed a group of younger girls. Zap walked in a slow zig-zag, making sure to get within a few steps of each person in the room. He paused and then glared at Kai.

Then it happened. A tall African chap sat down and put his hands on his head. Then another, and another. By the time Zap had finished his circuit, there were at least twenty who had heard his instruction and sat on the floor with their legs crossed, hands on their heads.

Kai waited until Zap was back alongside him. "Open your eyes." Small chaos erupted as each one looked around. "Those who are sitting, please make your way to the front here. Zap will be teaching you how to use your gifting. It seems you are able to sense the thoughts of those around you. This is a form of discernment, and it's part of your gift. Please go with Zap."

Zap sidled over to Kai. "What are you doing? You can't make these kids my problem. I don't know how to teach them about this. I barely know when I'm doing it."

Kai patted him on the head. "You'll do great. Now go get on with whatever you think will work."

"You're forgetting that I don't even know how I'm doing this, let alone how to teach someone else. You can't make them my problem."

"And we can't afford to let them go without doing something to bring them back from the training they've just been through. Come on, Zap. Just go." Kai turned his back on Zap, hoping it would be enough to cut off the conversation. He didn't have anything else to say. Zap just had to get out there and figure it out.

Ruaan shoved Zap's shoulder. "Go on, Bru, do the right thing."

Kai patted Ruaan's back. "Ruaan, I'm glad you feel that way. You're up next." The effect on the boy was the same as whipping out a box of snakes in a kindergarten class.

Ruaan backed away so fast he nearly tripped on

his own feet.

Zap chuckled, pointing at Ruaan as he led his little band of broken souls out of the auditorium to find a quiet place.

Ruaan rubbed the back of his neck. "I don't even have a thing. Sorry man. Can't help you."

"Don't start with me. Today has been too long."

Runt came back with the cardboard and pen and shoved it into Kai's hands. He crouched on the floor and wrote in his neatest writing. *If you can read this, follow me.* The words squiggled across the page, worse than a spider dancing through an ink stain. Runt clucked her tongue, took the pen and card out of his hand, and settled on the floor. She turned the cardboard upside down. The tip of her tongue poked out the side of her mouth with concentration as she wrote out the same words and handed it over to Ruaan. "At least they might be able to read it now."

Ruaan's face was flinty. "Both of you are forgetting one big thing. This is not a sim, we're stuck in ordinary life. I could only see in sim-dark."

Kai grinned. "So you admit it then? You have a gift."

Ruaan's mouth worked open and closed like a goldfish. Eventually he got some words out. "Not exactly. Like I said, it's not going to work anyway."

Kai glanced around the room, chewing his bottom lip. "I think it's worth a shot. Runt, get the lights please."

The little girl jumped to do his bidding and the room plunged into darkness. A girl at the back screamed. Kai shut his eyes. His arm hairs stood on end as Ruaan brushed past. Somebody got the screaming girl to stop, and the quiet was broken by spells of nervous giggling. Kai couldn't see a thing but his heartbeat pounded loud in his ears as time dragged.

Ruaan cleared his throat. "Lights, please."

As the bulbs flickered to life, Kai stepped back in shock. Ruaan had gathered more followers than Zap had. Ruaan caught his eye and shrugged.

"They're yours for now. Go teach them."

Ruaan led his troupe out with hunched shoulders, scratching his head.

Bree hung back, chewing on a fingernail. Kai winked at her and turned to the group that was left. "Show of hands. If I put a paintbrush in your hand right now and told you to create a picture for me, who would be terrified?"

Half of those left sitting stuck up their hands.

Kai nodded, it was about the number he'd expected. He reached back for Bree's hand, drawing her forward. "Those of you with your hands down, this is Bree. She is your mentor." He led her forward, ignoring her hissing and gently guided her down the stairs to her group.

Runt sat on the edge of the stage, swinging her short legs.

Kai waved her over. "Your turn."

"What must I do?" Runt grinned at him and her face glowed.

"Dance. Right here on the stage. Will you do that?"

"Sure. What for?"

"Dance for Tau. I'm pretty sure He's watching."

"Oo, I like him. I need music." She twirled on the spot, swishing her dress this way and that.

Kai picked up his guitar and spoke to the

shrinking crowd, "Runt is going to dance. If you want to join her, come on up." He strummed a few chords, mulling over what to play. His fingers slid over the strings. The rough steel made his fingertips tingle. Shutting his eyes, he thought back to every encounter he'd had with the enigma of Tau, and his fingers moved in response. It was a melody he'd never heard or played before, a light bubbling of notes that dipped and twirled. Tau's kindness rippled through Kai and into the music he played.

When the piece ended, Kai opened his eyes to a small circle of girls gathered around Runt. They moved together in unison, taking turns to lead and follow. Runt grabbed hands and led her entourage off the stage with her eyes sparkling, chattering away to them like a chipmunk.

Kai and Evazee were the only two who hadn't claimed their groups yet. "Evazee, it's your turn." Where was the girl?

4

Evazee sat at the foot of Peta's mattress, watching her sleep. Her silvery hair fell across her face as soft as moonlight and Evazee resisted the urge to run her fingers through it. She didn't want to wake her small friend. The makeshift bedroom was a hollow, cold hall with a high ceiling and mattresses lined up all down one bare cement wall.

The scarf around her neck made her itchy, but taking it off was not an option. She adjusted it to cover where her imprint would have been and sighed. The door swung back and Runt led in, followed by a group of young girls. They didn't walk, they skipped and giggled.

Runt swung her arms around, twirling in between words. She saw Evazee and halted mid-twirl. Her gaze slid to Peta and she whipped around to her group with her hands flung out like fly swatters. "Shh! She's sleeping!" She tiptoed across the room to Evazee, hunkered down on her haunches and whispered, "We need somewhere to dance."

"There's plenty of space here. Go for it."

"But she's sleeping."

"It will be fi—" Evazee caught her breath. Runt's necklace had slipped out from beneath her shirt and hung swinging right in front of Evazee. A flash of images bombarded her mind as she watched it move.

A laboratory. Two men in white coats arguing. Harmless enough, but Evazee's stomach knotted.

Evazee watched as Runt spread her girls out in a circle. She twirled once in the centre, but the necklace swung up and smacked her on the chin. In one smooth move, Runt stripped off her jersey, taking the necklace with it. She dumped them in a heap and ran back to her girls.

Peta stretched in her sleep, rolled over, and curled up with her back to Evazee.

Runt had drawn her girls close around her, all deep in discussion. Evazee moved before she could change her mind. She sauntered past Runt's top. Then she bent down and fished out the necklace from the soft folds of the fabric and slipped it into her pocket, being careful not to touch the pendant.

One last glance at Peta confirmed that she likely wouldn't be waking up soon. Evazee tiptoed out and walked the OS flat until she found the room with the testing grass. The sense of being followed was overwhelming, but each time she checked, the hallway was deserted. With one last peep behind her, she slipped inside and closed the door. Just to be safe, she crossed the room and tried the sliding door. It was unlocked and slid back easily. The feeling of being watched washed over her again and she shivered. There was no turning back now.

Evazee padded out onto the lawn and sat down cross-legged. She took the necklace out of her pocket and watched it swing on the end of the delicate silver chain. Fine patterns traced the outside and there was a hinge on the left. Was it wise to open this thing by herself, hidden away where nobody would find her if things went pear-shaped? She adjusted the itchy scarf and curiosity won. She had nothing to lose.

Her fingers traced along the right edge and found a tiny raised bump. With the lightest push, the pendant popped open. It was empty inside. Evazee frowned and poked her finger in to feel if she'd missed something. As her skin touched the silver, an image appeared on the mirror-like surface. It grew and stretched, expanding outside the confines of the jewelry. Like a giant growing bubble, the image swelled with such force, Evazee was thrown back. It continued to stretch, expanding over her, settling onto her, enveloping her into the moving image. She was no longer outside the bubble, but inside—included in the story as it developed around her.

Unable to move, she lay there, pinned to the floor. In the vision, her back was glued to the wall. Her gaze flicked to take it all in. A laboratory stretched into the distance, the far wall almost too far to make out. All the labs Evazee had ever been in were brightly lit. This one was a mere fraction above darkness. What were they hiding?

Three men worked together at a table. One scribbled on a page, pen moving fast as he worked through calculations. One sweated over a test tube, dropping in infinitesimal quantities of different liquids. The other observed, rubbing his beard to give his hands something to do. They stopped every few minutes to confer in quiet voices.

Evazee heard the clap of a door shutting, and it echoed as if far away. Movement caught her eye, and her pulse raced. Elden walked into her vision. Sideways. Cool and collected as if walking on walls was a thing he always did.

"Elden! What are you doing?"

"Looking for you."

She knew he'd seen her when his jaw dropped open.

"What are you doing up there, all stuck to the wall? What is this? What's going on?"

"Get over here and hush." She gestured with her eyebrows, "Look."

Elden sauntered over to her and awkwardly got himself lined up on the wall next to her. He smelled of soap and something else that Evazee couldn't place.

A small sound escaped his lips.

"What's wrong with you?"

Elden blinked and squinted, tipping his head sideways. "It can't be."

Evazee crossed her arms and sighed as loud as she could manage.

"That's my dad."

"You mean the one whose grave we nearly fell into?"

"One and the same."

"Bree should see this." Evazee felt for his hand. It was cold between her fingers. She didn't dare say anything, but she could share the warmth of her skin.

Elden's fingers tightened around hers. "I don't understand what we're seeing. Is it a real place?"

Evazee shrugged, her lips stayed frozen in a tight line. If she said yes, she could spark a wild goose chase with no guarantee of success. If she said no, she'd crush his hopes. Either way, she'd be left feeling responsible for the mess.

A strange fire smouldered in his eyes as he studied the image of his father. "Don't tell Bree what we've seen. I'm going to find him."

"Elden—"

"Don't say anything. You can't stop me." He struggled against the pull of the wall, his arms and legs flaying like windmill blades. "How do I get out of here?"

"Well, I haven't quite figured that part out yet." She focussed on the scene playing out in front of her as if her life depended on her absorbing every detail, when really all she wanted to do was avoid looking him in the eye.

~*~

It was hours after sundown when Kai gathered his friends in Torn's office to discuss the day. Zap sat on the edge of his seat with his toes tapping, while Ruaan stretched out on the sofa with heavy eyelids. Supper had been simple, cornbread and sausages with mashed potato. Though simple, it had hit the spot with Ruaan and he was currently sliding into his post-food coma.

Runt sat at Kai's feet, leaning her head on his knee, cuddling his two kittens on her lap. Zap and Ruaan had gone back down to the basement on Evazee's orders to find the source of the growling. They had found the two kittens, spitting-hungry, and managed to catch them. They got them safely upstairs with only a few bleeding scratches to show for it. Now, with their bellies round and full, they were meek and sweet once more. Much like Ruaan.

Bree stood by the window looking as if she'd rather be anywhere else on the planet but here.

"You're expecting us to do the impossible, Kai. I don't know how to activate or develop gifting in myself, let alone others." Zap shrugged.

"And the rest of you?" Kai glanced at the others who all seemed intent on avoiding his question. "There has to be a way to undo the damage that's been done through dark Affinity training. Surely."

Ruaan peeped through one eye. The other was shut tight. "You need someone good with words to speak to them. Like Zee."

Kai's belly twisted. "Where is Evazee? I haven't seen her since yesterday. You guys? She shouldn't be gone for this long."

Zap shrugged. "Maybe she went home. She's been a bit out of it lately."

"She would have said something to me, I'm sure." Kai sat quiet, sorting through his thoughts that seemed more scattered than sheep after a lightning storm.

Runt stuck up her hand. "I saw her in the big bedroom this morning. I think she stole my necklace." Thunderclouds settled into her eyebrows at the thought.

"The necklace. That's not good." Kai patted Runt's soft hair.

Bree stirred from her post at the window. "I haven't seen Elden either."

A broad grin broke out on Zap's face, "Oh, I see what's going on." He elbowed fresh-air as nobody stood close enough to have their ribs poked.

"Zap, really?" Kai puckered his face. "How can you even think that? That necklace knocked Runt out until we found her and closed it. They could be stuck somewhere until we find them."

"Yeah and maybe they don't want to be found. I've watched them two together. More sparks than...oh I dunno. There's a lot of sparks."

Kai dismissed him with an eye roll and a wave. "Runt, can you remember what happened when you opened the necklace? Are you OK to talk about it?"

Runt was breaking up a play-fight between the two kittens. She admonished them both sternly with a stiff finger before separating them by putting one on either side of her legs. "When I opened the necklace, it was like watching a movie, but I got sucked in and got stuck."

"What do you mean *sucked in*?"

"It was like being part of the story, but I don't think the people in it could see me or hear me. But I could see them, hear what they were saying." She shuddered. "I could even smell that they all needed a bath." Her nose wrinkled at the memory.

"So if Evazee opened the locket, she would be stuck until someone closed it?" Kai asked.

"Maybe."

The door swung open, and Peta's small, shiny head poked in. "Evazee?"

"Hey, Peta. Come in. We're looking for her too. Any ideas?"

Runt's back stiffened as the small blonde girl pushed into the room on her tiptoes, pale and fragile. She crossed the room to Kai and sank to his feet opposite Runt.

Peta spoke in a voice like a silvery bell, "There is this one place..."

5

The sliding door to the testing grass was unlocked and slid back at Kai's touch. Evazee and Elden were on the ground next to each other, a bubble of vision played out above them. Kai threw himself on the ground and started a slow leopard crawl. He somehow managed to stay low enough to make it all the way to his friends. His hand shook as he reached for the pendant. It was lit up with green lines that criss-crossed the surface in harsh zigzags. Kai hesitated, but steeled himself and grabbed hold of the cold metal. The hinge was tight, but he snapped it shut on the second attempt. The bubble popped and winked out with a soft hiss. He tucked the pendant into his pocket. This thing was way too much trouble. It would be wise to destroy it.

Evazee and Elden stayed on the floor, barely breathing, skin icy to the touch.

"Help me get them into the lounge." Kai tucked his hands into Evazee's armpits and dragged. Ruaan and Zap groaned as they picked up Elden. Kai backed up into Bree as he tried to haul Evazee off the grass. She stood in the doorway, her spine stiff, not moving as he came closer.

"Didn't see you Bree, sorry. Help me."

Bree seemed deaf as she pushed past him onto the grass clutching her chest.

Kai dragged Evazee into the room. Peta held up one leg and Runt the other. With an enormous communal grunt, they lifted her onto the couch. Runt pulled a throw over to warm her. Kai waited for the boys to manhandle Elden through the doorway before squeezing out to get to Bree.

"Hey, what's up?" She didn't respond until he touched her arm.

She roused like a dreamer, trying to clear the fog between dream and reality. "I saw my dad."

"Could you see where your dad was?"

"A laboratory, I couldn't make out any other details. Kai, what is that necklace? What does it show?"

"I wish I knew."

"Do you think it could lead us to him?" Bree's voice was even, as if she were asking about the weather, but the pulse in her neck throbbed and gave her away.

The pendant had given her hope. Cynical Bree, who despised hope. How could he tell her that the pendant glowed green enough to seem radioactive? He couldn't. "It's possible. I think we need to run more tests before we trust it."

"He's nearly out of time."

"Come on. Let's go inside. It's getting cold out here."

Bree allowed him to lead her from the grass and into the deep folds of a soft couch.

Kai glanced around the room and felt a sinking in the pit of his belly. They were getting nowhere fast. Training the others had been a dismal failure for all of them. How would he even begin to undo the damage done so that he could send these kids home? Now he had this toxic necklace to worry about too.

His thoughts were interrupted by a pat on his leg. He looked down to see Runt staring at him, with her hand out. Peta slid in behind her and stared up at Kai too.

"What?"

"My necklace. I want it."

"Runt, I don't think it's a good idea. This thing is dangerous." He hunched down and eyeballed her. "Please trust me on this one. I will give it back to you, I just want to make sure it's safe."

Her nostrils flared as she glared at him. "It came to me. It's mine. I want it."

Kai stood up and towered over Runt, if only to remind himself that he was the mature one of the two. It didn't dent Runt's bravado one bit. "OK, tell me, why is it so important to you."

"I like seeing things. Useful things. Like her dad." Runt tipped her head towards Bree.

"We don't know if we can trust what it shows us. It could be lying."

"I don't think so. Maybe we can see things that will help all of us."

"Well, I'm not going to trust it until we can do more than *think* it's safe, and I'm not going to discuss it anymore so you can swallow your arguments."

Runt stomped out of the room, and Peta followed her.

~*~

Evazee lay on a couch, drifting in a fog between sleeping and dreaming. She heard the door open and judged by the soft footfall on the cold wooden slats that it wasn't Kai.

Bree's shock of red hair glowed in the low

lamplight. No matter how hard Bree tried to flatten it with her fingers, it had regained most of its curls.

"Hey. Are you feeling better?" Bree hovered over Evazee.

Evazee shrugged. "I'm good. Just tired, really. You?" This was awkward.

Bree breathed. Her gaze flicked to different parts of the room, relentlessly restless. "I need your help."

Evazee pushed herself upright on her pillows. "I don't think there is much I can do for you, but fire away."

"I need the necklace that Kai took from Runt."

"Wow, you sure get straight to the point. I'll be honest in return. He won't give it to you. He seemed pretty sure about that."

"That's why I need help."

"You're not suggesting we steal it, are you? I don't know Bree—"

"It's my dad." Bree dropped next to Evazee's couch. "He was one of the lab coat people." She ran fingers through her hair, it straightened for a moment before popping back into tight curls. "Here's the thing. You and me? We've never really had much to do with each other, but I've watched you and Elden. I know there's something going on. Don't deny it." She frowned at Evazee's waving hands. "It's his dad too. Please. I just need to try the necklace one more time. If I can just get a clue, maybe I can go find him. We can put it back straight after."

"But Kai said it could be tainted. He can see that kind of thing. How can you be sure that what you're seeing isn't a lie?"

"It's all I've got. I'm willing to take that chance. If you won't do it for me, do it for him." Bree glanced across to the couch opposite where Elden lay sleeping with his one foot propped up on the backrest, the other poking off the arm of the couch like a flagpole. She leaned in close, her voice dropping to a whisper, "Between you and me, I'm worried about him. I don't know how deep his connection with the other side goes. Finding his dad..." Bree stopped to take a breath. "That might be the thing that stops us losing him. It could literally save his life. I know you pretend you don't care for him, but I can see through that."

Evazee blinked rapidly, scrambling for something to say. Her mouth opened but nothing came out. She shut it and settled for a vague shrug. "OK, fine. What are you thinking?"

~*~

Kai blew into his cupped hands to warm them. He cracked his knuckles and picked up his guitar. A quick glance around the group that sat around him in a rough circle showed him more green than he had energy to deal with. This particular bunch had green flowing through their veins. How would he even begin to fix that?

He put the guitar down, tucked his jacket close around himself, and motioned for them all to follow him. They trailed behind him in single file, dragging their feet across the cold tiled floor. Kai led his group, feeling like a fraud. He had nothing to offer the five of them, yet they followed him without question, without hesitation.

As they drew near to the stairs that led to the rooftop, they passed one of the older girls trying to sweep the floor. Her hair was tucked into a scarf away from her face. She was using a vacuum cleaner pole and brush as a broom, but the dirt on the floor stayed put, and she grew redder in the face and sweatier as she tried harder.

Kai walked over, took the pipe from her hands, plugged the machine in, and hit the button. In seconds, the dirt she'd been sweating over was history.

"I thought it was broken. I didn't think to try again." The girl blushed to the roots of her hair. Kai grinned as he handed back the pipe. The poor girl pulled the scarf from her hair and hid behind it.

Kai patted her arm. "Good work." As he turned back to his group, he heard someone call his name. What now? Evazee and Bree crossed the room, speed walking as if racing each other. Evazee got to him first.

"You're up. How are you feeling?" Kai studied Evazee closely. A glint of green sparked from her every now and then, but never enough for him to pinpoint its exact location.

"I wanted to ask you about...er, training." Evazee squeezed her hands. Maybe she was nervous.

Kai waved his group to head upstairs. "Sure. I have a group ready for you to take, but only when you're ready. "

"Oh? Oh. Really? Why?" Evazee crinkled her nose and leaned on the cold metal balustrade.

"I need you to teach these kids what you know." Kai was ready to launch into his sales pitch, but Evazee's eyes rolled back in her head and she fell, slow and graceful.

Kai rushed forward, but his jacket hooked on the balustrade. He shrugged out of it and left it hanging as he bent over Evazee. Her head missed the stairs and landed gently on a cushion of her hair. It was the strangest fall Kai had ever seen. Her head rolled back, and she groaned.

"Evazee! Are you hurt?"

Evazee peered through her lashes, as limp as a ragdoll. Kai was about to call for help, when her eyes flicked open. She sat up, rubbing the back of her head.

"I don't know what happened." She shook her head, blinked twice, stretched as if she'd been sleeping for a week, and pushed herself onto her feet. She slowly rolled up and swung gently before steadying. "Sorry about that."

Bree swooped in from behind. "I think you need some tea. Don't worry Kai, I've got this. You go do your thing."

"But—"

"That was a good chat, Kai." Evazee leaned on Bree's arm, limping a little. "We'll finish up sometime. I really need that tea."

The two girls hobbled off, back the way they had come in, shooting little waves at Kai.

He would never figure girls out. Ever. He swung around looking for his jacket, unhooked it, and climbed the stairs to the rooftop. Between vacuum cleaners, his two friends, and all the kids he carried in his heart, he was ready to go back to bed.

~*~

"I'm *not* leaving you for longer than five minutes." Evazee had her hands on her hips, glaring at Bree who lay on the floor ready to open the pendant. They'd decided to hide away in the basement for their experiment but now that they were here in between all the stacked boxes, Evazee was getting cold feet. A dull ache lingered at the base of her head from her last pendant visit. It had left a residue of dread hanging over her and her skin felt cold. Her insides were empty and vague nausea sat at the back of her throat.

"Ten. You can't give me less than ten. I don't know what I'm looking for. It might take me a while to find these clues."

"Fine, eight."

"You've been watching too many cheap movies. This bargaining thing is old and tired. We should stop." Bree rolled on her side and rested her chin in her hands.

"I agree. Five it is." Evazee smiled sweetly.

Bree smiled back, fake as a plastic rose, then rolled onto her back, tracing the patterns on the pendant. "I could swear there's a paintbrush carved into this thing. It's beautiful. I wish I could keep it."

"Can you hurry up, please?"

"Fine." She took a deep breath, placed the pendant on her skin, and popped it open. Her finger slipped and touched the inside where there'd usually be an antique portrait of an old forgotten family member.

The image bubble began to grow and Evazee backed away fast to stay out of the story. She checked her watch. Just after 4:00 PM.

Bree twitched and shivered under the onslaught of images.

Evazee checked her watch. Thirty seconds had passed. She tucked her hand behind her back, determined to ignore it. Footsteps tapped across the wooden ceiling of the basement and Evazee felt her pulse double as someone pulled on the trapdoor. She couldn't let anyone in, not with Bree stuck to the floor like this.

She ran up the stairs two at a time, threw back the trapdoor, and stepped out of the basement to find

Elden.

His face lit up as he saw her. "I've been looking for you."

"You found me. What do you want?"

"Just to talk. Where is Bree? Is she OK? You two have been scarce."

Evazee fidgeted with the trapdoor catch. She had to get rid of Elden. Bree's time was running out. "Elden, Kai was looking for you. I think he went up to the rooftop."

"What would he want with me?" Elden drew back as if she'd told him she had a lice problem.

"I don't know, he didn't say." She shifted from one foot to the other.

"Is there something you don't want me to see down there?"

"Pardon?" Evazee's eyes grew wide. She blinked and tried to relax her face.

"Come on, Evazee. I've been trained to sniff out lies and half-truths."

"Like one of those dogs at the airport?" She forced a laugh.

"Aah, a joke." He gave one cold laugh. "That won't throw me off. What are you hiding? Move aside."

"Fine. Bree is down there. But you can't go down, it's private. Girl stuff. I need to get back to her, so if you don't mind moving off, I'd be grateful."

"You and my sister. That can only be trouble."

Evazee couldn't wait any longer. "Stop being a pain. I'm going down and you are staying up. Promise me."

Before Elden had a chance to respond, Evazee opened the trapdoor as low as she could manage and slipped through the gap. It shut on top of her, banging her head slightly. For some reason, this made her angry at Elden. How could he put her in such a spot? And his sister, too.

She flew down the stairs, throwing herself to the floor at the bottom. She leopard crawled below the vision bubble and reached for the pendant around Bree's neck. She squeezed the two halves, but it wouldn't close.

Shivers tore through Bree so hard that her teeth clacked.

Evazee rolled onto her back and tried again, but the angle was awkward. Tears ran down Bree's face. Should she call Elden?

"What are you two doing?" Elden stood at the foot of the stairs.

Evazee rolled herself out from under the bubble. "I can't close it. Bree isn't coping."

Elden dropped to the floor on his belly and inched like a worm. He reached out and shut the pendant. The moment the vision vanished, he was on his feet in a steaming fury. "What are you girls doing? Evazee, you should know better than this! After what we'd just been through."

Bree sat up and leaned her forehead on his leg. She shook like a leaf. "Stop yelling. It was my idea." A shudder passed through her, and she clung to her brother's leg. "It's so cold."

Elden glared down at her, but softened. He took off his hoodie and draped it around her shoulders. "I thought you, at least, would know better."

Avoiding Elden, Evazee sat on the floor opposite Bree and crossed her legs. "Did you see anything useful?"

"I saw a bridge out of the window that I recognized. It's a building across town."

Elden extricated his leg from her grip and sank to the floor. "Wait a moment. What are you girls up to?"

Evazee caught Bree's eye, and she shrugged. Evazee took the pendant from Bree's hands. Careful not to touch the cold metal, she slipped it into her pocket.

Elden shifted on his rear. "You two are clearly planning something. You have to tell me."

Bree pulled his hoodie close and eyed him frankly. "But if we told you, you'd try stop us. I know you."

Elden's head hung. "I knew it. Not only are you up to something, but it's something dangerous. What am I going to do with you two?"

Words fought in Evazee's head. She had stopped expecting any of them to glow golden and this time was no different. She sighed. "If we tell you, you have to promise not to interfere. We are going to do this whether you like it or not."

Elden's hands shot up in mock surrender. "Fine. Lay it on me."

Bree tucked herself under his arm. "We're going to find Dad."

"So you are you going to trust the vision from a pendant that may or may not be accurate. Have you considered that it could be a plant to deceive you?"

Evazee clucked her tongue, "Obviously. What ideas have you got for finding your father?"

Elden stared from one girl to the other. "Maybe I don't want to find him all that much. I remember more of him than you do, Bree."

"Thanks for reminding me. It's not like I had a choice—"

"Hold it, you two." Evazee inserted herself between them. "Elden, you said you wanted to find him. Don't deny it now. Guys, this isn't a big deal. Bree, you said that the lab in the vision could be quite close?"

"Just across town."

"So why don't we go check it out. Elden can come with. It won't take long. Then we'll know if the pendant is to be trusted or not."

"It might work. As long as Elden agrees not to go all *mother bear* on me."

Evazee put her hand on Elden's mouth before he could bite back. "Bigger problem: how will we get all the way across town?"

Elden took her hand off his face and held it. "That's not a big problem. There's an OS bus in the basement, and I know where they keep the keys." He hung onto Evazee's hand as she tried to pull it away and scowled at Bree. "What do you mean, *mother bear*?"

Evazee sighed. Being a referee in this boxing match was getting old. "Elden, you go get keys. Bree, come with me."

Elden went off muttering to himself about bears and sisters.

Evazee pulled Bree up off the floor and steadied her as they climbed the stairs.

6

Kai stepped onto the roof into the sunshine. It warmed him through to his bones. He led his small troupe to the middle of the rooftop, and they settled against the sunny side of a square, brick structure jutting up from the floor. Kai could only think it was part of the ventilation system. Right now, it formed a wind break, and that served his purpose.

The five were subdued. Where to begin? "Hey guys, I'm Kai."

The shortest girl blurted, "We know who you are. You turned the green tubes amber." A shy smile broke through on her pimply face. "I liked the amber much better." She probably wasn't much older than thirteen, swimming in the middle of puberty-induced hormone soup.

One of the two guys in the group slouched against the bricks as if his spine had melted. His black hair ran amok on his head, and his eyes were dark enough to be mistaken for black in the wrong light. He stared down Kai with his hands tucked into his armpits. "Yeah, we know you. You wrecked our training."

Kai blinked, taken aback. He'd known that some of them may not be happy about being rescued, but staring it in the grumpy face was different. He carefully levelled his voice. "That's true. What did you like most about getting trained?"

"Power."

"Do you know what your gift is?"

The black-eyed boy squirmed as if sitting on an ant nest. Kai thought he might be torn between the desire to talk about his gift and the desire to remain the mysterious enigmatic figure that he obviously worked hard to be.

"They identified a few things." He shrugged and sat quiet.

Kai chose not to play his bluff. "Anyone else?"

The other guy of the group hid behind his mousy brown fringe. He flicked it to the side and Kai saw both his eyes for the first time. "They told me I'm a Breaker, but I was never much good at it. I kept trying to put things back together after I'd broken them. They said that my gifting was flawed, and I had to work on resisting temptation to undo the work I'd completed. I don't think I'm very gifted. In fact, I think my gift is broken."

A sharp zing of Affinity sped through Kai, and the guy behind the fringe suddenly flashed a green light that pulsed. He'd been lied to many times, and he'd believed every one. "Wait a moment, you aren't broken and you aren't weak. Your gift is like mine. Do things glow green for you when they're broken?"

Brown-hair nodded, a frown creasing his forehead. "How do you know?"

"It's the same for me." He grinned at the guy and left him to process what that meant as he turned to a girl in the middle. Her golden hair was cut short into a tousled cap of messy curls. "How about you?"

She pointed at his guitar. "I like playing. I wasn't allowed to do that though. They were teaching me to pick pockets instead."

The black-eyed boy snorted an acid laugh. "They taught us all how to do that. How else would they fund this whole op?"

The golden-haired girl rolled her eyes and shifted her attention back to Kai. "They told me that I would get my guitar back when I was proficient. They even gave me a target that I had to reach. Five-hundred dollars would get me my guitar back."

Kai reached for his guitar and then held it out. "Do you want to play something?"

She blinked like an owl, not comprehending what he was saying.

"Take it! Play something for us."

The girl didn't move.

"What's the matter? I want you to play." He smiled as he offered her the guitar again.

She shook her head. "No, I know this trick. I've fallen for it before."

Kai laid the guitar at her feet and backed away with his hands up. "No tricks."

The girl looked sad as she tucked her hands into her armpits. He thought he saw moisture glisten in the corner of her eye. She wouldn't budge. *Tau, what do I do?* A wave of compassion washed through him, so strong it took his breath away.

~*~

"The bridge is about an hour away." Elden checked his watch as he climbed in behind the wheel. The van was a beaten-up, old brown thing, with spots of rust growing at the corners of the windows.

The door rattled as Evazee pulled it shut, and she moved to the opposite side of the seat in case it decided to fall off half-way to the bridge.

Bree rode shotgun, sitting cross-legged on the front seat and peering out the window as buildings and trees whizzed past.

As they pulled out of sight from the OS, Evazee's belly flipped. She didn't like going against the rules at the best of times, to be blatantly leaving without telling Kai sat wrong between her shoulders. But then she didn't particularly want to be at the OS either. She also wasn't used to feeling this confused. It was all thoroughly exhausting.

Elden drove fast, weaving in and around the slower cars. The rhythm of it lulled Evazee, and she propped her head up between the safety belt and the headrest, her thoughts slowly grew fuzzy and blurred.

"Wake up, Sleeping Beauty. We're here." Elden prodded her knee and she shoved his hand, wanting the sweet oblivion back, but he just kept on poking her.

"Go away. I'm up." She slid from the van and hung on to the side of it to stop herself swaying. A cold breeze blew off the river and smacked into her. In an instant, she was properly awake. "Where are we?"

Elden shut her door and locked the van, pocketing the keys. "Not the safest part of town. I have a feeling I know where the lab is. Our old school is just around the corner. The view of the bridge would line up with what Bree saw out the window."

Bree had her hood pulled up over her mop of hair. The tip of her nose that stuck out was red from cold. "I don't remember much about a school, Elden. Did we go there?"

Elden had his hands shoved deep into his pockets. "Maybe seeing it will remind you. Come on, let's go." He positioned himself between the two girls and slid an arm around each of them as if to protect them.

Evazee felt the heat from his fingertips and shivered. The pavement they walked on was chipped and broken. They picked their way forward carefully, stepped gingerly in between sharp bits of glass bottles. They made their way past a wall covered in crude graffiti. The school gate hung on one hinge, the other had rusted through. The school itself was a burnt-out shell of what was left standing after a raging fire had torn through the place. A sign on the outside wall declared that the school was in the process of being rebuilt, but judging from the rusted sign, it was a project that had been long abandoned.

"I guess this isn't it." Evazee felt silly for stating the obvious.

"Either that, or the pendant wasn't accurate." A crease marked Elden's forehead. "Remind me again why we thought that thing would show us something real?"

Bree focussed on the tuft of grass beneath her sneakers. She kicked at it repeatedly, looking small and alone.

Evazee studied her for a moment, wishing for some glowing words. *C'mon, Jesus. Anything.*

Nothing.

She slipped her arm around Bree's shoulders. "Should we go look around anyway? Maybe we'll find a clue or something."

Bree sniffed and rubbed her sleeve across her nose. "Yeah."

Elden hung back for a moment as if waiting for someone to ask his opinion.

Evazee waved to him to join them. "We came all this way. We might as well have a quick look."

"I don't know if it's a good idea." Elden's forehead was creased.

"It's your old school. I know it will feel weird, but aren't you curious? I want to know what caused this fire." Contrary to what was coming out of her mouth, Evazee had no real desire to go near the charred structure. It was an all-too-real reminder of just how harsh life could be. But her heart ached for Bree, and it was enough to make her pump some enthusiasm into her voice and to steer her feet towards the building.

Elden held the gate for the girls to pass through and followed after. He whistled low. "Look at the gardens."

"What gardens?" asked Evazee.

"Exactly." Elden waved to a tangled, overgrown mess. "This here. It used to be a riot of colour, and now it's all weeds. I don't even think weeds are thriving. Nobody has been here in a long time."

Bree sniffed, "I disagree. There's a smouldering cigarette butt."

Evazee stared at the smoking object and her belly twisted as her pulse quickened. "What if they're still here?"

Elden held his finger to his lips and slipped into stealth mode. He melted into the shadows with his back against the wall, tiptoeing sideways, making no sound even on the dry grass.

Evazee caught Bree's eye and they both stifled giggles. Elden glared at them, motioning for them to join him. Evazee felt like a prize twit as she sidled into the shadows next to him. Bree rolled her eyes and shuffled in next to Evazee.

No sooner were they hidden, when two men strode out of the passageway to the school entrance.

Evazee bit her lip to keep from gasping. The men wore white lab coats and spoke in low, urgent voices. One held a device between them that they studied as they walked.

Evazee's heart pounded so loudly in her ears, she could hardly hear over the thump. She forced herself to breathe slower and tried to shut her eyes. The feeling of imminent discovery overwhelmed her. She had to see where the men were, and if they were coming closer. Sweet aftershave drifted on the breeze, and Evazee blocked her nose to stop from sneezing.

The men were so engrossed in their discussion that they passed by the three without spotting them.

Once they were safely out of earshot, Evazee grabbed Elden's and Bree's arms and whispered, "Was that your dad?"

Elden looked at her as if she'd crawled out from under a rock. "Do you need glasses? Those guys were our age."

"I was too scared to look that closely in case they *felt* me looking and saw us. I focussed on the thing they were staring at." Evazee sniffed.

"Girls make no sense. Honestly." Elden pulled away from her hand and froze.

"Elden? Is that you?" The voice was deep and male. One of the lab coat guys was back. Tension radiated off him in tangible waves. "Where have you been? We thought you'd been taken to the Crux."

Elden cleared his throat, "Girls, give me a moment. Stay right here, I just need to have a word with this guy." Elden and the lab coat took themselves around the corner, out of sight and earshot.

"Well that's not half suspicious." Evazee tried to read the expression on Bree's face. It was a curious combination of relief and disgust.

Bree shrugged, her mouth in a tight line. She peeped around the corner. "They aren't close by. I think we grab the gap and go look around inside."

"I don't know, Bree. What if there are more of them?"

"Then we hide or run. Simple."

~*~

Kai shut the door to Torn's office and set his guitar down on the stand in the corner. He'd have to stop thinking about it as Torn's office, but for now the name stuck. He'd been so sure he could help these kids, but he was hitting blank walls trying to get through to them.

Runt's necklace—now there was an interesting artefact. Perhaps if he could fix it, it might be able to show them something useful. He reached into his pocket to pull it out, but his pocket was empty. Odd. He patted the other side and dug in deep. Also empty. There were no holes, it couldn't have slipped out the bottom and the pockets were too deep for anything to have fallen out easily. Maybe he'd lost it when he tossed his jacket to help the cleaning girl.

He traced his steps back to the stairs and was bent over double, searching the floor behind the staircase when Zap and Ruaan found him.

Zap tapped Kai on the shoulder and as he stood up, slapped a hand on his forehead. "Are you sick or something? You're being weird."

Zap bounced from one foot to the other in the way he did when he was nervous, but it was Ruaan who spoke. "We have to talk to you." Ruaan's face was a few degrees more serious than before a meal.

Should he lie about what he was looking for? His mind spun through options.

Zap paled a fraction. "You lost the thing."

Kai sighed. Apparently, his friend's ability to hear thoughts was working just fine.

Ruaan blinked like an owl. "What thing? What are you both talking about?"

Kai looked for a distraction. "You wanted to ask me something?"

Zap rubbed his chin and stared upwards as if the words were written on ceiling. "Not ask. Tell. This teaching thing you want us to do. I don't know how to put this..."

Ruaan shoved his shoulder and blurted, "It's not working. It's just not. I don't know what you were expecting, but we wasted a few hours today and left with nothing to show for it but some irritated kids. It was a dumb idea."

Kai dismissed his statement with a wave. "It's still early days." He saw a muscle twitch in Zap's jaw and knew Zap was about to talk. Kai scrambled for something to ask before Zap could get back on the subject of the pendant. "Have either of you seen Evazee? I haven't seen her since early this morning."

Ruaan scratched his head, "But you sent her on a mission, didn't you? Evazee, Bree, and Elden were getting into the OS bus as I came back with my group. I asked where they were going, and Evazee said they were going to check something out. She told me you'd asked them to go."

Kai's forehead crumpled, and he searched his memory for anything he'd said that could have given such a wrong impression. "I'm drawing blanks here. I didn't even know the OS had a van. Where could the three of them have gone?"

Ruaan leaned forward, whispering in such a loud hiss that it probably could be heard across the building. "I think they are trying to find the place they saw in the pendant vision."

Kai paled. Maybe his empty pockets weren't empty by accident. "But that's daft. It is damaged. Obviously, whatever it shows isn't accurate. Even I know that."

"How do you know it's damaged?" Zap had a hand on his hip in his best challenge-authority pose.

"You're forgetting what I do."

Zap's eyes widened, "Of course. This is the microwave all over again. I didn't doubt your skills for a moment. Why don't we have a look? Maybe with the right clue, we can find them."

Kai smacked his forehead. "They took it." Kai flinched as the memory of the awkward conversation came back to him.

"What? The pendant?" Ruaan's eyebrow lifted, pulling his face askew.

Zap spoke at the same time. "Bree and Evazee?"

"Bree and Evazee. I thought it was odd. They've never been friends, but they came to me together and chatted about nothing, then left." Kai grimaced. "It was at the exact time I'd taken my jacket off. One of them kept me so busy, I didn't keep an eye on the other. And now they've drawn Elden in too. We've got enough on our hands with this lot." He waved vaguely, motioning towards all the kids upstairs. "And now to have to babysit our own? That's a bit much."

7

"We should go back. There's nothing here." Evazee peered back down the tunnel to see if Elden was back.

Bree bent over, searching the ground for any sign of anything other than the charred remains of the school. "I think I see something. Come on." Bree scuttled down a hallway through patches of sunlight and shade caused by missing portions of the roof that had been destroyed. She ran like a nimble rock rabbit. Or a bloodhound on a scent.

Evazee cast a wistful glance where they'd come from, shook her head, and followed Bree. Her belly twisted as she moved past burnt classrooms, hollowed shells peppered with the debris of all it took to massage knowledge into the heads of children. A sick thought, were the children still in school when the fire hit? Evazee swallowed hard and hurried after Bree.

Evazee found her down the passage, on the other side of a hall big enough to seat the entire school for assembly. The walls were sooty, but mostly intact, though the ceiling was broken in patches. Bree grinned smugly, her hands on her hips.

"I told you. There's more."

Evazee scuttled across the wide-open space, running on her tiptoes, hunched over as if she could make herself smaller and lighter. She hissed at Bree,

"All the more reason to get out of here."

Bree waved her over. "Look." She turned and disappeared down a few steps.

Evazee followed, hoping her compliance would be enough to persuade the redhead to leave. Surely Elden would be back by now. Hopefully Kai was so busy at the OS that he wouldn't have noticed their absence.

The stairs that led under the stage were standard for those that led to an orchestra pit. The door at the end of them, however, was most unusual. Surrounded by scorched wood and bricks, the shiny stainless-steel surface reflected the damage without being touched by it. A small panel glowed softly in the centre of a door without a handle.

"You can't tell me this is a regular under-a-school-stage type of door. There are some secret things happening behind here." Bree's eyes were sparkling.

Evazee longed for golden words that carried enough urgency to convince this girl it was time to leave. None appeared, so she put on her best furious face, even flaring her nostrils a little. "We have to go. Now."

Bree frowned at her, focussed on her nostrils and backed off. "What is up with your nose?"

"Now."

"Fine. I just want to see if—" She reached for the glowing panel.

"Don't touch that! What if you set off an alarm or something?"

"She's right. Don't touch that." The voice was male and not Elden's. "It's fingerprint coded. You would have got a nasty surprise."

Cold shot through Evazee. A man came down the stairs two at a time and pulled Bree away from the door. He was one of the two who had recognised Elden. Under his lab coat he wore a heavy metal T-shirt and jeans. Without hesitation, he reached for the glowing panel and pressed his thumb against the smooth surface. A trail of lights circled the button, and the door swung open with a slow hiss.

Elden and the other one joined them.

Evazee tried to read his face, but she got nothing. His jaw was clenched hard enough to make the muscles in his cheek twitch.

They stepped through the doorway and left the burnt devastation behind. Stainless steel gleamed from the walls, floor, and ceiling. Brightly lit passages led off in three directions, and there were no windows that Evazee could see. The whole set up was underground.

"Take the girls to Marking. Elden, come with me. They're waiting for you in the boardroom."

Heavy metal T-shirt grinned. "Sure. I'd far rather spend time with these two pretties anyway." He shuffled in between the two of them and hooked their arms to lead them down the passage to the left.

Evazee panicked. "Elden!"

Elden mouthed a few quick words to his captor and jogged back to Evazee. He leaned in close and whispered, "Just go with it. They know you're with me. You won't come to any harm."

"Elden, we can't keep them waiting." Lab coat's foot tapped the floor.

"I will find you."

There was an edge to Elden's voice that raised the hair down Evazee's arms.

~*~

Fresh air washed over Kai as he stepped out onto

the roof. He took a moment to breathe. Moonlight had a way of softening reality that he needed, and he drank it in. The harsh lines blended and glowed in a soothing shade of blue. He made his way to the centre of the roof and stretched out on his back with his guitar across his chest.

"Tau, I need you. None of this works without you. I'm not moving from here until you show up." Cold seeped into his back through his sweater, but he welcomed the sensation. His fingers found strings, and he plucked out a gentle tune. He shut his eyes and let the music take him. Soaring riffs, tingling harmonics danced from the union of fingers and strings, blowing helium and lifting the weight he'd been living under. He laughed.

Tau.

His skin felt it first. The warm glow more intimate than sun rays. His fingers slowed, but he kept playing, scared to do anything that would chase this moment. His awareness deepened. Blood rushed through his veins, through his heart, tingled down his back, and flooded warmth where there'd been ice.

And then a shift. Tau was on the roof. Kai knew it even though his eyes were tightly shut. His self-consciousness, his failings, short-comings and grief rose up as a wall between him and Tau, but Tau slipped right through.

"You can open your eyes. I'm not going anywhere."

Kai peeped and sat up in shock. His friend sat on the rooftop, grinning at him. Tau was here, and he'd brought daylight. The rooftop beneath Kai's fingers was silky smooth, no longer cement, but obsidian. Lava Rock. The first time he'd seen the OS in the spiritual, it had been an oppressive, dark square that brooded over the area. Now, the obsidian seemed lit from inside and glowed in colours that took Kai's breath away.

"Is this the same place as before?"

Tau tipped his head to the side, "What do you think?"

"It is the same, yet completely different. I can hardly breathe."

Tau stood up and stretched as if he'd been sitting next to Kai for a long time. "You haven't seen the best part yet. Come check this out." Tau took Kai to the edge of the building. Kai steeled himself, expecting the slums.

Tau sat down on the edge with his legs swinging. He leaned back and breathed deeply. "What do you think?"

Kai crept towards the edge and gingerly swung his legs over. An expanse rolled out before them, not shacks and squalor, but sparkling lawn in an exquisite shade of turquoise dotted with patches of deep colour. The light from the OS cast a warm glow on the area, no longer brooding over it in malevolence, but rather transforming.

Kai laughed, though it was tinged with sadness. "This is not real. This is just because you're here. When you go, it's all as dark and messed up as it was before. I haven't been able to fix anyone. I don't understand it." He shot a sideways glance at Tau, who leaned back on his arms next to Kai with his eyes closed. "Are you even listening to me?"

"You are trying to vacuum the floor without plugging in the vacuum cleaner. How's that working out for you?"

"What are you talking about?"

A smile lit up Tau's face. It was nearly enough to shift Kai's frown. He heard movement behind. It was the little Chinese girl with paintbrush ponytails.

"What *is* this place? I'm dreaming, right?"

Tau swung his legs back onto the roof, turned to face the girl, and crossed them, contemplating her without saying a word. Love rolled off him.

It hit Kai as a delicious heat wave.

Paintbrush girl skipped to Tau and sat close enough that her knees touched his. She examined him through narrowed eyes. "Do I know you?"

The green pulsed around her heart. It seemed to pull tighter with each breath she took. Kai felt his own heart constrict in sympathy. *Help her, Tau.*

"Not yet. Would you like to?" Tau wasn't smiling, yet it didn't seem to bother Paintbrush.

"Do you know me?"

"I know you like three sugars in your tea, but you only take one because three feels wasteful. You don't want a puppy or a kitten, but you do want a chameleon. You'd like to learn how to paint the sea, but you feel you can't because you've never seen it for yourself. When you're sleeping you either dream of drowning in waves bigger than buildings, or you dream that you're flying over the top of the waves. You don't want to wake up when you have the flying dreams because you feel free."

Paintbrush's eyes stretched so wide, Kai thought she might faint.

Tau held out his hand, and Paintbrush slipped hers into his without hesitation. Her eyes locked on his.

Kai held his breath and wondered if he should be sitting in on this moment, but to move away would be more disruptive, so he stayed put.

A slow smile tugged at Tau's mouth. Paintbrush grinned back, and Kai watched the green lines criss-crossing her heart snap back a strand at a time. Paintbrush shuffled across, crawled onto Tau's lap, took his arms, and wrapped them around her. She snuggled into his chest with her head tucked under his chin.

For a split second, Kai saw her hollow. He watched as light trickled in, absorbing the darkness, dispelling it until the small girl pulsed with a radiant glow. He blinked, and she was normal again. With a deep, contented sigh, she fell asleep.

"I've never seen that before. She is whole. How?"

"She believes. In me, in everything that I've done for her. Here, take her."

Before Kai could protest, Tau bundled the little glowing, sleeping girl onto his lap. "Right, I'm done here. Remember, what you see in the real world is not always accurate. Yes?"

"But what about the others? I can't do what you just did."

Tau laughed. "Think about the vacuum cleaner. You'll do just fine."

"But..."

Tau breathed on him and leaned in close. Kai prepared himself for a download of wisdom and direction.

All Tau said was, "Think vacuum cleaner." With a wink, he was gone.

~*~

"Have a seat, girls. I'll be back in a moment."

Evazee and Bree huddled together on the couch

he'd shown them to.

Bree spoke through clenched teeth as a ventriloquist would. "I say we make a run for it."

Their escort stuck his head around the corner. "And don't think of leaving. We lock the doors in case people get cold feet. We help them to stay strong." He flashed a thumbs-up and left with a distinct click of a door lock sliding into place.

Evazee waited until she couldn't hear footsteps in the passage. "You know the storage room we walked past? What do you think was in the canisters?"

Bree rubbed her arms against the chill in the room. "More like a warehouse than a room, really. I know those canisters. I would bet my good arm that those are full of serum."

"Affinity serum? That much? They were stacked floor to ceiling. That room must be five times the size of a normal school hall. Why so much?"

"They must have big plans."

"That makes me feel a bit sick." Evazee hung forward with her head between her hands. She studied the room they were in, looking for anything that could help them.

Bree sat next to her, muttering under her breath.

"I don't want to be marked. Do you?" Evazee focussed on slowing her thoughts, slowing her lungs.

Bree shook her head. "I don't even know what that means."

"The gurneys have restraints. Arms and legs. I don't like the look of that either. There's also a gas bottle on the floor between them. Entonox."

Bree was on her feet, pacing along the edges of the room, scanning for a way out. The room was sealed shut, a box with no windows and only one locked door. "Gas? What the heck? Are they going to poison us?"

"It's not poisonous. It's for pain relief." Pain. It was only a small gas bottle, but Evazee paled as the blood left her face and her nose and feet grew cold. First her imprint removed and now this...*marking?* She wanted to pray but no words came. She was so out of touch, Jesus probably wouldn't listen anyway. She stayed in the chair as hope drained out of her.

Bree checked to make sure the gas was turned off, picked up the bottle, unhooked the tubes and lugged it over to the side of the door. "Pain? I'll show them pain." She hoisted the bottle up and propped it up between the wall and her shoulder.

"Bree, no!"

The lock clicked again, and the door swung open. Bree launched the bottle with as much force as she could. Too heavy to go over the top, it swung sideways and rammed into a stomach. Elden's stomach. With a deep *oomph*, he doubled over. Bree dropped the gas bottle and fell to her knees next to him.

Evazee leapt up, squeezed her hands, and sat down again.

"Don't panic, I'll live." Elden eased onto his rear, grunting with effort.

Bree glared at him, "You twit! How can you just waltz in here without warning? I could have hurt you."

Elden bit out words through clenched teeth, "I came to get you girls out."

The two lab coats stepped into the room, and one whistled. "Quite a wildcat we have here." He grinned at Elden on the floor. "Glad to see you've got them under control. We'll take it from here." He shook his head as he crossed the floor to retrieve the gas bottle and set it back in place between the two gurneys. "There isn't time to hook up the gas now. We'll just have to go on without it."

The other grunted, which seemed to mean that he agreed. He took Evazee's arm and led her to the closest gurney. Each had a padded hole at one end for breathing. A red mark on an arm restraint caught Evazee's eye. Dried blood. Her chest squeezed tight. Adrenalin pumped through her veins, and she dug in her heels.

There were more muscles to her captor than what the lab coat showed. He kicked behind her knees and caught her as she fell. A hard thwack to the back of her head and stars spun across her vision. Pins and needles claimed her arms and the fight left her. Face-down on the gurney, cold radiated through her as the cuffs clamped down on her arms and ankles.

She fought rising panic that crawled under her skin like spiders. Her hair was caught up on top of her head, her pony tail swung over the end of the gurney.

"This one is already marked." The voice came from across the room where Bree struggled against her restraints, muttering under her breath.

Evazee's lab coat grunted in response. His fingers felt like cold snakes on her skin, and she ground her teeth not to scream.

"This one isn't. Wheel the machine this way." A thin whine filled the air, which nearly drowned out the rattle of wheels on the tiled floors. "Get the lights."

A sharp click plunged the room into darkness. Before Evazee could think of screaming, burning hot pain seared the base of her skull. Her mind turned somersaults. A swoosh of icy cold washed over the back of her head and gave her an instant headache. At least the fire in her head had been damped.

"That's a bit skew, don't you think? Honestly. You need to practice."

"Oh, please. Nobody cares. Anyway, if the general has his way, I'll be getting more than enough practice soon enough."

"True. True. Let's get these two to recovery."

"Not that yours has anything to recover from." The two chuckled as if they'd made the funniest joke ever, and Evazee wanted to scream.

Her brain swam, and she fought to stay conscious. How could Elden have let this happen?

8

Kai tucked Paintbrush into bed and pulled the blankets over her. Peta sat on the mattress opposite, watching. Kai tucked the blanket under Paintbrush's chin the way he liked them to be, and straightened up to stretch out a knot in his back.

Peta quietly padded over to him. Her silvery hair was tucked behind her ears, and she had dark rings under her eyes that made her seem more porcelain-fragile than usual. She tugged on his shirt. "Where's Evazee?"

I would love to know that myself. "She'll be back soon, I'm sure. How are you?" He hadn't seen much of the girl since they'd come home through the mist.

Peta ignored his question. She balanced on one foot and drew circles on the floor with the other. Her whole attention was on Paintbrush. "Why is she all glowy?"

"You can see that?"

"Is it catching?" Peta backed up a few steps, holding her hands up.

"No, not like chicken pox. Do you like it?"

Peta wrinkled her forehead and as she was about to answer, a commotion broke out outside the room. Kai ran to go see.

Evazee flew down the passage, red blotches riding high on her cheeks and trailing down her neck.

Elden half-ran, half-walked to catch up.

"Evazee, please just listen."

"I don't want to hear anything more from you. Back off." She brushed past Kai, misjudged the space, and slammed him against the wall.

One look at her face took the words off his tongue. He caught Elden's eye, but Elden looked away.

Kai stopped him with a hand on his chest. "What's going on?"

Elden waved at Evazee's departing back, ran a hand through his hair, and shrugged. "Women. I don't get them."

"She's steaming. You must have done something."

Bree pushed past Elden. "More like what he *didn't* do." She smacked her brother on the back of his head. "For the record, I would also be mad at you. Just saying."

"But I'm trying to explain myself, and she's just not hearing me."

Peta poked Elden in the belly, waited for him to look at her, and then graced him with the fiercest glare she could muster. She turned on her heel and stormed off after Evazee.

Elden followed them with his shoulders bunched and his hands in his pockets.

Bree patted Kai's arm. "We are in deep—" She glanced around, and her voice dropped to a whisper. "Is there somewhere more private than this passage?"

Kai took her arm and led the way to Torn's office. The door shut behind them with a loud click that made Bree jump.

"You stole the necklace." The statement popped from Kai's mouth as a hard accusation.

Bree rolled her eyes. "Never mind that. You need

to know what I saw. Kai, this is beyond anything I've seen. It's an onslaught."

Kai perched on the edge of the desk and held out a hand. "Necklace."

"Are you serious? You won't listen to me until I give it back? Plot twist. I don't even have it. Evazee made sure she took it the moment it closed. Which I think is pretty dumb because my imprint is on it, not hers."

"Your paintbrush imprint was on the necklace?"

Bree sighed as if he'd managed to drain her last splodge of energy. "Identical."

"Anyway, we borrowed it. We didn't steal it. We were going to give it back as soon as we could. Now, can we please get back to the onslaught?"

Kai made a mental note to get the necklace from Evazee. Though he should probably wait for her to calm down first. Bree was making no sense, and today had been too long. Once she'd gotten this off her chest, maybe he could convince her to make coffee.

Bree poked him in the chest. "You're not listening to me. I can see it in your face."

"You're not saying anything that makes sense. Beyond thievery and general doom and gloom, I'm not hearing much to be concerned about."

"Fine. I'll just say it. A building full of dark Affinity serum. If you think what happened here at the OS was bad, this was nothing. A gnat in the Amazon. This setup is not some haphazard thing to mess with some school kids. This is a carefully planned operation with a calculated mind behind it that is terrifying."

Kai shook his head. "Are we talking about reality, or something you saw on the internet?"

"We walked through the rooms. I could have run

my fingers along the glass bottles if I'd wanted to."
Bree shuddered.

Her words sank in, and Kai's stomach twisted. "If what you're saying is real, I don't know how one would ever reverse the effects of that much serum. Right now, I'm having a tough time undoing the damage done to this building full of kids. I'm not getting it right." He blinked and shook his head. "Somebody needs to sort this out."

Bree paced. Her red hair bobbed as she walked. "Yes, you. You are here to fix this. There is more to this than the lives in this building."

"I don't buy that. You make me sound like some sort of chosen one."

Bree stopped pacing. "You think you're involved in this because of some freak accident."

"I'm the only person I know to get knocked over by a bus, so yeah, that fits."

"Don't be cheeky." She waved a finger in his face, one eyebrow riding dangerously high. "You know what? I don't care if you are here by accident, or by some divine choosing. The fact is—you're here. You can do something. I've seen you cringe as you walk amongst this bunch. If that serum is released, I can't begin to imagine how far the damage will spread. You can't ignore this."

"I could say the same of you. You are also here. Same with Zap, Evazee...even your brother."

"You're right. I will do whatever you tell me to. But like it or not, you are the catalyst."

Nothing Kai thought of seemed an appropriate response to that. The best he could do was to not laugh out loud. "Your opinion has been noted, I still say we've each got a job to do. Now tell me where you were."

"We tracked down the pendant vision. I was hoping it would take me to my father. You know how you keep saying he's alive?" Bree scuffed the carpet with one foot, avoiding his eyes. "There's a part of me that really wants to believe you. Anyway, what we saw through the window looked familiar. The vision led us to my old school. It was horrible. It's all burnt down, a charred skeleton of a building. But it turns out that the school is just a cover. Below the school is a massive storage depot. Somewhere they are pumping out and bottling the stuff faster than we can pat ourselves on the back for making it back home through the mist. There's a lab onsite. I don't know what for, maybe quality control? There must be some rich sponsors backing the whole operation. I didn't get a chance to see it all properly. We were dragged through so fast."

"Wait, are you saying that those people knew you were there?"

Bree went back to pacing, squeezing her fingers. "This is where it gets a little complicated. You know Elden was involved in the whole OS thing? Well, we ran into two guys who knew him. They thought he had sought them out on purpose, they didn't seem to realize he is with us now. While they were talking to him, Evazee and I had a look around."

"You went snooping? Are you nuts?"

"We didn't think it through, but it seemed like a good idea at the time. The guys who know Elden work in the labs, and they came and found us."

"And they took you on a tour and happily let you waltz out of there to come back here? I'm not buying it." He grabbed a paper from the desk drawer, wrote on it, and held it up. *What if you're bugged?*

Bree snatched the paper, crumpled it up and threw it at his chest. "We weren't bugged, that's such a dumb idea. Good grief."

Kai threw the paper ball back at her, and it hit her on her nose. "You don't know that. Why is Evazee so angry?"

Bree squirmed. She shut her eyes tight and blurted, "They took us for marking. I got off lightly, but they did her. Elden stood by and watched. He didn't stop them or say anything. She's a bit cross."

"I don't get it. Is Elden still working with them, or is he with us? And what does it mean, they *did* her?"

Bree shrugged and looked lost. "Evazee was marked. Elden? I don't know."

"You said you got off lightly. What does that mean?"

"I'm marked already, Kai. But you know that."

"Your marking got us safely through the Spirit Cuttings. I remember." Kai rubbed his neck. A few more knots had developed while he'd been talking to Bree. "This is a lot to take in. I don't know what to do."

"You're always speaking of Tau. Why don't you ask him?"

"I do ask him about things."

"Then surely he should show up and tell you what to do."

Kai snorted, "It doesn't work like that. I can't just rub a magic lamp and suddenly *poof*, there he is."

"So how does it work, then?"

"I'm still figuring it out. A lot of it is joining the dots, and believing what he says."

"That makes no sense. But all that aside, listen to me carefully. If that serum gets released, you would never be able to undo the damage. The way I see it, you don't have a choice. You have to stop it before. And to do that, you're going to need an army."

~*~

Evazee stalked through the OS with her fury as a barrier. She made it to the lounge of stolen fruit without anyone speaking to her and shut herself in. The moment the lock clicked, hot tears ran. She felt her way to the couch and threw herself into its softness, fury blazing through her. None of this was fair. None of it made sense. To have her gift stolen was bad enough. Being marked as one of *them*? That disqualified her utterly and completely.

Elden. The biggest sting, the pimple on the abscess. She couldn't deny that he'd slipped through her defences, got under her skin. From the moment he'd taken over her training, she'd seen the tender side of the man. Feeding her on the roof, protecting her. But today? Today had been the ultimate betrayal. He'd stood by silent and allowed her to be marked, *branded!* as one of the enemy. There were a hundred ways he could have stopped it, but he didn't. The memories blurred and bled together, but she remembered screaming. Screaming his name.

Nothing.

How could she have been such a fool to think he cared for her at all? *Jesus, I don't want this. I don't want any of this. Help me.*

Nothing.

No warm glow, no quiet peace inside. Cold, hard nothing.

Her tears dried up, and she stayed on the couch, a small, curled bundle of heartache, shivering in the dark.

The click of the door catch woke her. Another click and light flooded the room. It was Kai. He crouched down to her level. She could hear him speaking, but the sounds were like underwater bubbles. A familiar scent drifted through the air. Tea.

"Evazee, wake up."

"What do you want?"

"I made tea, you have to drink it. I don't make tea for anyone."

She may be disqualified and outcast, but she couldn't find it in herself to be mean, so she pushed herself upright and squinted at Kai through crusty eyelashes. He grinned and placed a hot mug in her hands. It stung her fingers, but it was good to feel again. She sipped and swallowed and felt warmth curling through her insides. She made it half-way through the cup before she was ready for talking. "I'm drinking your tea. What do you want?"

Kai bottomed down on the carpet and ran fingers through his spiky hair. "We have a problem, and I need your help."

Evazee kept sipping, not trusting any words that might come out of her mouth.

"Bree told me about your field trip."

Did he know about the marking? Surely not, or he wouldn't be asking for help. Tainted help.

"Bree thinks I need to raise an army to stop the serum from being distributed. What do you think?"

"I don't know if an army will be enough. This is a full-on onslaught."

"There's that word again. Onslaught. Did you and Bree rehearse your speeches?"

Evazee drained the last drop and set the mug on

the table next to a lamp that sat off-centre on the round top. "Don't be daft. We're just calling it as we see it." Who would deliberately put a lamp off-centre?

"As I see it, all we need to do is shut down the serum factory and the distribution centre. Trying to use this bunch of kids? It would never work. They'd need to be effective in the natural and the spiritual realm, and immune to the negative serum. Right now, they're just a lost bunch of broken souls. We don't have time to fix that. There has to be a better way."

"I agree. They will never be the army you need. If you're not getting anywhere, why do you keep working with them?"

"How can I send them away from here, broken? What kind of life would they have? Forget training these kids to fight. I just want them whole. Here's the thing, Zee, you saved me from dying. I would have kept walking through those black gates. But I didn't because you showed up. That's one example of many. How do you do it, and why won't you train others?"

Evazee pushed the lamp to the centre of the table. Much better. Her hand brushed the switch, and the darkness flooded in. She felt for the switch again and light returned.

Kai sat frowning at the lamp as if it were a two-headed alien. His face lit up, and he grinned at her. "Evazee, you are a genius. Thank you!" He jumped to his feet, kissed her on the head, and ran out.

Evazee sat, blinking. Maybe her friend had finally cracked under the pressure.

~*~

Kai found Zap and Ruaan raiding the fridge in the kitchen. Runt sat cross-legged on the counter-top, humming to herself with a kitten on her lap.

"I want my necklace back."

Kai ruffled her hair and stroked the kitten. "We've been through this. I'm not budging. As soon as it's fixed, I will give it back to you."

Runt huffed, but went right back to humming without missing a beat.

Kai tapped his friend on the shoulder. "Zap, you're a bit of a lab rat, right?"

"Excuse me? I believe lab *technician* is the term you're looking for."

Kai waved off his correction. "Same thing. I need you two to start developing an antidote to the negative Affinity serum."

"There is a formula under development that they use for the Recruiters. I don't know where it's kept though." Zap paused and his nose wrinkled. "I might be able to recreate it from memory. But I must warn you, it has some nasty side effects."

"As long as it doesn't stop us from using our Affinity. We can deal with side-effects. Runt here, she seems to be immune. Maybe she can help."

Runt's eyebrows lifted, but she kept humming and stroking the kitten that stretched, purred, and curled up into a tighter ball.

Zap was tapping on the palm of his hand as if making a shopping list. "I think we've got all the chemicals I need. Come on Ru. I need you."

Ruaan gave one last longing glance at the contents of the fridge, but Kai pushed him back and shut the door. "We need this yesterday, guys. Go, go, go." Kai shooed them both out the kitchen.

Ruaan was still staring at the fridge as the kitchen door closed behind them.

Kai turned in a slow circle. "So Runt, I have a question for you. The fridge, urn, toaster, oven...what do they all have in common?"

"Obvious. Food."

"Bad examples. Let me add a lamp, computer, and a heater. Now what would you say?"

"Is this some kind of test?" Runt tilted her head at him as if he were nuts.

"More like an epiphany."

"An epipha-*whaty*?"

"None of these things work unless they are plugged into a power source. Once they're plugged in, they automatically do what they were built to do." Kai flourished his hands like a magician revealing the bunny in the hat.

"That's a very obvious epipha-thingy."

"But you see, I've been trying to get this building full of people to operate in Affinity without first connecting them to the *source* of their Affinity. For some of them, it sort of works. You can sweep a floor with a vacuum cleaner brush if you try really hard. But it's far better to plug it in before trying."

"So what are you gonna do?"

"Introduce them to the Source."

"How are you gonna do that?" The kitten woke up and tried to jump off Runt's lap, but she tucked it close to her chest and held on.

"The only way I know how."

9

Kai found a group of seven people playing cards in the hall. He didn't know any of them, but their insides were a hot green mess, and he had to start somewhere. "Training time. Follow me."

The group sat blinking like owls at him and his guitar.

"Now. Get moving." Kai didn't wait for them but walked off towards the stairway that took them to the rooftop. He climbed the last step with all seven in tow.

"What are we here for?" It was a redheaded girl, about his age. Her face was familiar. It was the girl who'd been sweeping with the vacuum cleaner. How appropriate.

"Do you remember trying to sweep with the vacuum cleaner?"

Giggles rippled through the other six.

A dark-eyed girl piped up. "Please tell me you didn't."

The guilty girl's shoulders drooped. "Like I said, I thought it was broken."

Kai pulled her next to him. "Oh, I'm not teasing you. That was an important moment for me."

More laughter, this time at Kai.

A tall, lanky fellow shoved his hands deep in his pockets. "This is rubbish. I'm going back to our cards."

Kai wavered. "Go if you want. The rest of you,

hear me out. You came to this school because you wanted to learn to use your Affinity, right? Your gifting. Instead you got pumped full of serum that turned a good thing dark and ugly. I would like to change that by introducing you to the True Source of your ability. All I ask is that you leave now if you're not interested." He stood silent for a minute. Nobody shifted, but movement caught his eye on the far side of the roof—a quick flurry of a dark shape that swished from one shadow to the next.

Kai frowned at the patch but decided his current mission was not one he'd allow himself to be distracted from. "Let's get started." Kai led them to the centre of the roof where they sat in a circle around him and his guitar. "I want you to relax. Close your eyes if it helps you." He ran through a quick series of riffs to check the tuning, twiddled a few knobs. *Tau, you are welcome here.* His mind filled with memories of Tau. Snatches of conversation, the love that beamed from the man's face...warmth flooded through Kai's belly and his fingers danced across the strings. He played on. Three separate pieces from three different memories. Building, soaring, landing as gently as a butterfly on a dandelion.

He opened his eyes, expecting light, warmth and Tau himself. But they were in the dark, on the rooftop with no Tau in sight. Kai's chest pinched tight. This wasn't working.

~*~

Evazee went looking for Kai. Over the last few days, he'd got into a strange pattern of smuggling small groups of people up onto the roof with his guitar in hand. They came down an hour or so later, and each time Kai's face grew stonier. If she trusted her words at all, she would have stopped and asked him what was going on.

A batch of them came through the door, Kai trailing behind. His skin was ashen and matched the shadows under his eyes. He stopped when he saw her and leaned on his guitar.

Evazee waited until the others had left. "You look exhausted. What are you doing?"

"I'm attempting to plug this lot into their power source." He knuckled his back and stretched.

"How's that working out for you?"

"Time will tell."

"Seven at a time and you're not even sure it's working?"

Kai shrugged. "And the problem is?"

"But it will take forever, and you're working yourself to death."

"But it might be working. In case it is, I have to keep at it." Kai stepped sideways as if arguing with her was taking the last of his energy.

"I'm sorry, Kai. I don't mean to drain you. It's just that you asked me what I thought about raising an army, but you didn't hang around long enough for an answer."

Kai transferred his weight to lean on the wall, his face deadpan. Concern rushed through Evazee with a force she hadn't felt since he was dying in hospital. Evazee blinked and tried to line up her words.

"The organisation scares me. This is way beyond a little backyard operation for laughs. This a cold, calculated —"

"Let me guess. Onslaught."

Evazee frowned at him, "I was going to say plot,

but onslaught works too. You'll need at least an army to move against this. It will have to be an infinitely, carefully planned and executed strike to make any dent in their supply."

"So we don't have a choice, then. An army, it is?"

Evazee's arms were suddenly cold, and she rubbed them. "I don't like the word army, but basically, yes. I don't see any other way."

"That's not going to happen."

~*~

Fixing the OS intercom system took Kai and Ruaan most of the day, but with some rewiring and a lot of fiddling, it all seemed to be working by the time supper was dished up.

Runt and the kittens hung around them as they worked. Runt hummed to herself and taunted the kittens with a piece of string that they could never quite catch. In between, she stared at the boys with a slight frown that either meant she didn't understand or didn't approve of what they were doing.

Kai sat in front of the microphone, finger poised over the button. In the history of weird ideas, this one was probably way up there, but he was going to do it anyway.

He pressed the button and spoke. "Hey, guys. Some of you have been up to the roof with me and some of you haven't. From tonight, the rooftop meeting is no longer by invitation only. I'm opening it to anybody who is keen. This place is called Open Sessions, and I think we should stick to that." He took his finger off the button to cough, then pressed it again. "Also, supper is ready. See you in the dining room."

Ruaan poked his head around the door.

"Nothing."

"What do you mean by *nothing*?"

Ruaan tapped his ear, then pointed at the microphone. "We failed. It's not working."

"My whole speech didn't go anywhere?"

Ruaan shrugged. "Sorry about that. You'll just have to tell them at supper. C'mon Runt, it's your turn to do the food call."

Runt huffed but got up without being asked twice. "Which version, new or old?"

"You choose. I really don't care that much."

Runt shut her eyes for a moment and waggled one finger back and forth, apparently in time to a tune in her head. Her eyes popped open. "New it is, then." She stood just outside the door, took a moment to compose herself, and then launched down the passage, jogging in a rhythm that struck Kai as something straight from the military. She belted out a line in the sing-song way soldiers do on training runs.

"Can you smell it in the air?"

Words drifted back in an echoed response from different rooms in the building.

"Let your belly take you there."

More echoes, louder this time.

"Beans or rice or caviar..."

Footsteps running in rhythm, bouncing words. A swell of people drawn out by the song, picked up the tune and made their way towards the dining hall.

"Our cooking will take you far."

"Sound of...rumbling...sound of chewing..."

The song grew faint as Runt and her followers moved out of earshot.

Ruaan frowned as his belly gurgled. "Big voice for such a small girl."

Kai shoved the failed microphone to one side as he stood up. He patted Ruaan's stomach. "Big voice for such a small organ." He dodged Ruaan's punch just in time.

~*~

The older group had divided the job of cooking for everyone amongst themselves, but some definitely had more experience than others. Tonight seemed to be a less-experienced team's turn as they'd managed to grill some sausages for hotdogs.

Kai had found a stash of money in Torn's office, enough to keep them in groceries for a while at least. Feeding them all was expensive. He could understand why the previous regime had focussed on training pickpockets. They needed to be healed and sent home before the money ran out. He sniffed hotdogs on the air and decided not to hang around long enough to eat. He took his guitar straight upstairs and found a spot in a puddle of light.

He shut his eyes, leaned back on the bricks, and played, starting with old favourites to warm up. Once Kai's fingers were limber, he set his mind on Tau and improvised. New tunes flew from his strings. He felt words come and he sang them, and they fitted the tunes he played as if he'd planned it.

Joy bubbled through him, and he laughed. A few lines rang through his head so he sang them, repeating them over and over, soaring and dipping with the tune. The sound of other voices singing filtered through to his consciousness as gently as a falling feather.

He had to see what was going on. Peeping though his eyelashes, he counted a group of about twenty.

Many of them had been up to the roof with him before and seemed keen for more. Some lay flat on their backs, while others sang with their eyes closed. They'd picked up his words and were singing them to Tau. A few others hung around on the edges, watching everything that was happening but not quite willing to step in just yet.

Maybe this time would work.

Kai kept playing, the words came easily. *Tau, you are welcome here.* The voices from the crowd grew louder. Kai watched those on the outskirts. They focussed on a patch of nothing but fresh air, chatting and listening in turn.

How odd and yet he knew Tau well enough to know that He was probably right there. When the time came to call it a night, half of those on the edges had sneaked closer to the main group. They'd sang to Tau, Kai had felt the glow, and yet he wasn't seeing any change in the green.

~*~

Evazee sat on the outskirts watching, fiddling with the scarf around her neck. It was the third night that Kai had run an open session on the roof, but the first time Evazee had found the courage to come along. The numbers increased every time. Evazee tried a head count, but gave up at eighty-something.

Those closest to Kai sang with an abandon that made Evazee's heart ache. She remembered feeling free, loved. She remembered a flow of golden words, so clear she knew that speaking them would bring life to those who listened. Her finger slipped from the fabric to the skin between her collar bones. The sting of loss overwhelmed her. No imprint. No gifting. She'd never felt so useless in her life.

Threads of guitar music drifted over her. She wanted to run. Get away from this whole scene. For a moment she considered sliding into the thick of what was going on, but then she saw Elden on the other side of the group, lurking in the shadows. Their eyes met for a second and he tilted his chin, tipped an imaginary hat. Heat flooded her cheeks. Apparently, she was still angry at him. He got her into this mess, so maybe he could fix it. An idea blossomed on the edges of her mind.

Bree sat down next to her, breaking her line of thought. She'd French-plaited her bushy red hair, and it hung in a long strip down her back. She waved a hand over the rooftop party. "What is all this?"

"Army training."

"What? I don't get it."

"I'm kidding. He should be recruiting an army. Instead? He's up here with this bunch doing this." She waved a hand over the group. "He's planning to send them all home when they're no longer messed up. I must say, looking at them all? I agree with him. Home is the only place they should be going."

"A lot of these kids don't have homes, though. Besides, I don't see how singing would fix anything."

"Yeah. It's weird. I think he's going about it all wrong. But that's just my opinion. I just keep thinking that I could have helped them before..." Evazee shut her mouth. Putting her loss into words was not something she relished.

"Before what?"

"Nothing really." She patted Bree on the arm, "I need to have a word with that brother of yours."

"Good luck." Bree stayed on the floor with her

knees drawn up.

~*~

Elden pushed himself off the wall he was leaning against as Evazee got close. She breathed deeply against the brewing rage. She had to lean close to make herself heard above the noise of the singing. "You owe me."

Elden pulled back with a frown. "Excuse me?"

"Downstairs. We need to talk."

"Why do I feel like I'm in trouble?"

Evazee aimed herself at the door and walked. He'd better follow or she'd be truly mad. As they got down the stairs, Evazee checked to make sure they were alone before rounding on him. "You got me into this mess, you're going to help me fix it."

"I'm not following."

"I want my imprint back. I want this mark gone. You are going to help me."

"But—"

"No! Don't argue."

"There is no way—"

"You have to help me. You're the only one who can."

He caught her hands in one hand and held her chin to stop her moving. "I don't know how to do that. That's what I've been trying to tell you. I'd help you if I could, but I don't know how."

"What about a testing arch? Don't they have one here?"

"Are you seriously asking me to put you back in one of those? They are built to remove those things, not put them back."

"But maybe I could fix it somehow. Maybe find

whatever I lost. I don't know." Lost. She felt lost.

Elden reached for her hair and trailed his fingers through it. "I don't want to put you through that again. Last time..." His voice grew gruff and he coughed.

Images from last time flooded through Evazee's brain. She'd stepped into the arch expecting horror. Instead she'd found breathtaking beauty, a waterfall pool, and Elden. The feel of his skin on hers. Heat flashed through her. It may have been beautiful, but the experience had robbed her of her imprint, the symbol of her gifting, and taken her ability with it. "How do you know what happened the last time I went through the arch?"

Elden shrugged. His eyes were fixed on something over her left shoulder. Evazee resisted the urge to turn around and see what it was.

"Let's just say that they are not designed to fix things. The only thing they can do is corrupt or remove."

"But that's perfect. It can remove this thing on the back of my neck. You owe me, you know you do. So, you're saying that there is one here at the OS?"

The poor boy was shifting from one foot to the other as if dancing on hot coals. Evazee wanted to jump up and down and scream in his face, but she forced herself to stay still and glare at him.

"I didn't say that."

"But you didn't deny it either."

"OK, fine. I'll take you. But I need to do something else first." Elden held a finger to her lips as she was about to object. He shook his head with a smile that made her tummy flip and that got her irritated. With that, he extricated himself and aimed at the stairs.

"I will find you. You can't avoid me forever!"

Yelling at Elden's back as he disappeared up the stairs to the roof was not satisfying at all.

10

Kai looked out across the group in front of him. They sat in the afterglow of their time of singing, some chatted quietly, others lay stretched out with their feet crossed, staring up at the stars, nobody in a hurry to leave. Kai's Affinity pulsed through his veins, and in a flash he saw a deep sea of green lodged over each and every one. How was it possible that nothing had changed?

"This is the dumbest army training I've ever seen." Zap picked his way through the rooftop full of blinking kids.

"Yeah! We wanna fight." Paintbrush sat at Kai's feet, as close to him as she could get without being bopped on the head by his guitar. She jumped to her feet and boxed the air in a flurry of fists that made her paintbrush ponytails bounce alarmingly.

Kai tucked both her fists into one hand and lowered them. He frowned at Zap. "How did you get on in the lab?"

"Yeah, about that. I came to tell you that we might have found a way to un-taint the serum."

"Might?"

"I'm still running tests, but it looks promising."

"Promising isn't enough. We have to figure out how to destroy or neutralize room-full's of the stuff. *Might* and *promising* don't cut it."

"When did you become such a pain in the rear? I know all that. I've been in that lab now for days. Barely slept."

"Bree's dad—"

"I know that too. He's running out of time. Why is he so important anyway? It's not like any of us have ever really had a dad, and we're all OK. Right?"

Elden stepped out from the edge of the group. "A word with you? Away from here."

Kai's belly twisted in the usual contradiction of whether to trust the man or not. Elden's face gave no clues. "Sure."

They moved away from the crowd, closer to the edge of the rooftop.

Night lay thick, but the black canopy was peppered with stars and the air was fresh and cool, laced with the smoky aroma of barbequed sausage from a street vendor. This darkness was wholesome, natural, lit slightly by the lone streetlight below. Nothing like they'd been trapped in before.

"What's up?"

"You know I've been involved in recruitment and training on the other side." Elden coughed, looking like a lizard on a hotplate.

Was it guilt, or was he hiding something? "I know that."

"There's something else you need to know. I've watched you work with these kids to reverse the training they've been through. Tell me if I'm wrong, but you don't seem to be getting anywhere."

"If you're here to gloat, I can save you the trouble. I know. I'm just out of options."

"I'm not trying to rub it in. I just know something that might help you." Elden fidgeted, flicking his thumb off his forefinger. His gaze darted.

Kai watched the pulse in Elden's neck beat faster. Kai rested on the edge of the rooftop wall, leaning casually, but his mind zoomed, trying to suss out what Elden was attempting to achieve and whether he could be trusted. What kind of man allows his friend to be marked and does nothing to stop it?

Elden rubbed his chin. "Let me get this straight. You want to reverse the effects of the training so that you can send these kids home, right?"

"I want them untwisted. Free."

"You're not going to achieve that with what you're doing now."

"But it worked on Paintbrush."

Elden's nose crinkled up.

Kai realised he'd need to spell it out. "The little Chinese girl. She's free."

"Oh, you mean Ziqi? The one with ponytails that stick out like this." Elden waggled his fingers next to his head.

"Like paintbrushes. Yes." Ziqi. Now she had a name. Kai wished he hadn't found out. Some things are better not to know. As much as he hated to admit it, Elden was right, Ziqi was the only one he'd seen a change in. "What do you suggest I do?"

Elden took a deep breath, and hunched towards Kai as if he were scared of being overheard. "The process they go through in training is brutal. They get pumped full of dark Affinity Enhancer and then they get put into simulations that are designed to annihilate trust and belief. Let me put it this way, you can't free something in the natural that is locked up in the spiritual world."

"It was the opposite with Runt."

"Exactly. While her body was locked up in a dingy room, nearly starving to death, her spirit was free and full of life."

"So I need to go back? Where, though? This building is ours now. Nobody is trapped here in either realm."

Elden shook his head. "I don't mean it like that. During their training, certain things can get," he struggled for the right word, "*siphoned* out of them and stored. At headquarters, the Crux, there's a vault—"

A drawn-out screech of tires skidding on tar screamed from the road three stories below. The crash shook the building. An explosion of shattered glass rocked the air. Streetlight dipped, replaced by a dirty orange glow that flickered.

Ruaan ran towards the edge of the roof but stopped before looking over. His eyes glowed grey in the dark. "The building is on fire."

11

Dusty haze billowed up from the chaos on the road below. A bus parked diagonally across the road. Two or three cars had collided, it was hard to tell. One had been catapulted straight into the side of the OS, taking a sausage vendor's barbeque fire with him. Liquid ran in puddles on the road. Gas. They had to get the people out before the fire sent the whole lot up in smoke.

Kai took off down the stairs.

Elden's voice rang out across the rooftop, calmly directing the crowd off the roof safely. He had them covered. Kai ran.

Bree kept pace with him. They hit the ground floor running. The bus was closest to the blaze. The door had jerked open in the collision.

Alarm slammed through Kai. Screams, smoke. Kai climbed the bus steps two at a time and found an African driver draped over the wheel. Kai undid his safety belt and hauled him out of reach of the fire. He seemed familiar, but Kai didn't waste time studying the man. Back on the bus. It was full of dark-skinned guys, some conscious, some not.

Bree flew up the stairs and started guiding the able-bodied ones off the bus and out of reach of the fire.

Sweat ran down Kai's spine as he carried another

unconscious one to safety. The fire was closing them in. There were still too many on the bus. Panic ran hot through Kai.

Something crashed. The burning door had come off the twisted hinges and fallen across the opening. They were trapped. Sweat blurred Kai's vision and he blinked hard, looking for a way out. Time melted, blurred. Kai took it all in. The building flames, the blocked doorway. Through the window someone stood watching from the shadows, casually leaning on the wall. Kai blinked, and then there was no one.

A hissing sizzle filled his ears, louder than the crackle of flames. White foam smacked into the windows with force. A jet of foam carved through the solid wall of flames and somebody screeched like a banshee. Sweat poured off Kai. He stood paralyzed, but his mind darted frantically as he tried to find a way out. He needed something to smash a window. He staggered through the bus to the driver's seat and found a canister of CO2 latched underneath. He unhooked it and struggled to break the seal with sweat-slicked fingers.

It wasn't working. He lugged it through the bus, aimed at one of the windows covered in foam and flung hard. The canister smashed into the glass and shattered it. White foam poured in through the gaping hole, sizzling on the seat that had caught alight, turning melted plastic to hard, brittle and charred.

Evazee stood on the street with her feet planted wide, holding the fire hose as if it were a loaded semi-automatic. Sweat ran in rivulets through the dust on her face, and her chest heaved. With a last defiant whoosh, the flames flared and imploded in on themselves. The fire was out.

Kai ran to the mangled door and kicked hard. The damaged hinges gave way. He jumped down the steps of the bus and rushed towards Evazee. He tried to hug her, but she was frozen stiff. He coaxed the hose out of her hands, shut off the stream.

Evazee snapped back to reality with a jolt that brought tears to her eyes.

"Are you with us, Zee?"

"Did it work?"

"You put the fire out. It did!"

"I can't believe that worked." Her face was a mess of sweat and tears.

"I never thought I'd see you armed with a fire hose. It's a good look for you."

"We should help." She stood up and moved away from him, but for a moment stopped dead still.

Kai expected to see her in full swing, moving, stopping blood flow, running triage. Instead, she stood and stared at the bus driver.

"It's Zulu. Look!"

Kai stepped carefully between the injured. So much blood, pain.

Sure enough, there was Zulu. Stretched out on his back with a bleeding head wound. Blood trailed down the side of his face.

Kai knelt and ripped off a wide strip of Zulu's own shirt to press against the wound. "Evazee, help me."

The entrance to the OS was charred and smoking.

Elden and some of the older kids picked their way through the damaged doorway. He came across to where Kai and Evazee were struggling to lift the deadweight of Zulu. Without asking, Elden moved Evazee out of the way and lifted Zulu's feet.

Kai sweated under the weight of the African. His fingers were buried deeply into Zulu's armpits. "Let's take him to my office."

Evazee hovered around Zulu like a fly. "*Your* office?"

"Torn's office. Make yourself useful and clear a path for us." Blood rushed to his cheeks.

"Are you blushing?"

"Oh, please. This is from lugging this hunk of muscle around."

~*~

Evazee sat opposite her enormous dark friend with her feet drawn up onto the couch. Zulu's head was wrapped in bandages, and he looked like a zombie in the semi-light. She'd only ever seen him in the spiritual realm before where he towered and presented a commanding presence. In real life, he was no less impressive, though rougher around the edges. The scar that chiselled across his face seemed harsher, deeper, and less romantic. A romantic scar? *Evazee, what are you thinking?*

She shut off her thoughts and tried to focus on the words coming out of his mouth. His voice rumbled from his chest with the same deep vibration that she remembered.

"Are you hearing me? Friend-Evazee?"

"I'm sorry, what?" She shook her head to bring her focus back to the here and now. "What are you doing here?"

"I came looking for you and Kai. Things in my village are not good. It is time for change, but I cannot make this change. I need help."

"I don't understand what you mean by *not good*.

Why did you bring all these people with you?"

"They were planning another ceremony. A turning ceremony." Zulu's dark eyes bored into hers. "You remember the boy?"

A chill tingled down Evazee's spine. "The boy who drank and died. That boy?" The image of his lifeless body being shoved off the wooden deck into the river was forever stuck in Evazee's mind.

"Yebo. All these were to drink tonight. I brought them to escape. To show them the better way. I asked your Tau to show me where to go. He brought me here."

"With an accident that nearly killed you all?"

"The accident was not His idea. The accident was because of a drunk man. But this way, or that, we are here now."

"I don't know how to help you."

With a knock on the door, Kai came in, followed by Ruaan and Zap.

"Zulu, welcome. Your friends are being cared for downstairs. I didn't expect to see you here."

Evazee knew she should let Zulu speak for himself, but the words popped out. "He's asking for our help. They do this ceremony thing in his village. It would put all of those who are with him at risk. They could all die. Kai, there must be something we can do." She frowned at Zulu, "You didn't want to go back to your village. What made you go back now?"

"The smallest one is my brother. He sent me a message, he was scared of ceremony. I couldn't leave him."

"But they wanted to make you a priest. What about that?"

"Tonight, I would wear my Priest-clothes. Tonight,

I would make them drink."

A chill skittered across the back of Evazee's neck. "You would have to make them drink. I can understand why you left."

Kai rubbed circles on his temples. "So how would we help you? Do you want somewhere to hide?"

Zulu shook his head. "They would find us. It might take time, but they would come."

"What, then?" Kai plonked himself in a chair opposite with his feet propped up on the coffee table as if he were completely relaxed. Evazee knew him well enough to recognize the clench in his jaw, the white spots on his knuckles as he clenched and unclenched his hands.

Zulu's gaze flicked over the room, taking in all the minute details before levelling with Kai's. He breathed deeply before answering.

"Come to Benan. Come show my people this Tau that you speak of. They will listen to you."

"But what if they don't? What, then? They don't sound like the kind of people who will wave farewell and let us leave with their blessing if they don't agree with what I would say about Tau. Especially not as you lot ran away and trashed the family bus all in one afternoon."

"No, no. Not family bus. Bus came from bus stop."

Evazee sat upright and turned towards him, hoping against hope that she'd heard wrong. "This is funny. I could have sworn I heard you saying that the bus came from a bus stop. As in you'd stolen it from a bus stop."

"Not stolen, borrowed. Like Beaver and Shrimp's boat. Yes?"

"I can't believe you're bringing that up." Evazee

reddened.

"Borrowed and broken. But no life lost. All good."

Kai's elbows were propped up on the armrests, fingers tented in front of his mouth. It was hard to read his thoughts. His face gave away nothing. He shut his eyes, and Evazee watched his lips move wordlessly.

Evazee was about ready to throw a cushion to wake him up when his eyes shot open.

"I'm sorry Zulu. We can't help you. There is some horrific stuff going down here that we have to prevent. This lot need me here."

~*~

Kai shifted a box out of the way with his foot. It sent a cloud of dust up his nostrils, and he sneezed. Meeting in the basement was not his first choice, but he didn't want eavesdroppers or anyone walking in on them unexpectedly.

Zap was rubbing his arms as if being here made him itchy.

Ruaan studied them both with cool eyes.

"So you guys agree that our attempts to reverse the OS training haven't worked?"

Zap huffed. "We've been telling you this for days now. Are you only just figuring it out?"

Kai waved off his sarcasm. "And you agree we need another plan for these kids?"

"Where are you going with this?" Ruaan brushed dust off his hands from the box he'd been leaning against.

"Elden told me about a vault in a place called the Crux. If I can get into the vault, I can free these kids."

"And we can get our lives back." If Ruaan was excited at the thought, he didn't show it.

Zap snapped out of his thoughts. "Do you trust Elden?"

"That's where you guys come in. I want you to come with me to help keep an eye on him."

"Where is this place again?" Zap wasn't falling over himself with enthusiasm.

Ruaan snorted a laugh. "So we either babysit a bunch of kids, or we babysit an ex-OS trainer. What a choice."

"Guys, come on. When I say I've got to go on a quest and face unknown danger for the good of all mankind, you're supposed to say that you couldn't possibly let me go alone, and that you'd follow me to the ends of the earth. That's how it's supposed to work."

Zap and Ruaan frowned at each other.

Zap stuck a hand in the air as if asking for permission to speak, but blurted out, "It's that bit about unknown danger that makes me twitchy."

"Fine. Stay here with this bunch. Wipe their noses. I'll be back soon. Hopefully."

"No! Wait! We'll come. Won't we, Ruaan?"

Ruaan sighed as if he was about to give away his last block of chocolate. "Whatever."

Kai nodded, satisfied. "I'll go work on Elden."

"The things we do for you." Zap waggled a finger at a Kai, but Kai just grinned at him from halfway up the stairs.

12

Kai stuck his head into the sleeping hall.

Paintbrush had finally fallen asleep. She had tossed, turned, and hummed to herself long after the others had nodded off.

Kai tiptoed across the room to where Evazee lay sleeping with Peta in her arms. He stuck a note on her pillow. Runt's bed was next to them, and she lay on her side, pegged in by the two kittens.

Evazee would look after her. Before his resolve could soften, he walked out the room without looking back.

Ruaan and Zap were waiting inside the charred hole in the wall. Ruaan ate a sandwich that could have been peanut butter based on the smell. They should have done something about that hole before leaving, but it was too late now.

Elden stood up out of the shadows as Kai got to the other two. He wore his cap pulled low over his eyes and carried four syringes in his hand that glowed green in the dark.

"What are those?" Kai wished he could see the guy's face.

"Cotton candy. What do you think they are? Our ticket to the spiritual realm."

Zap backed away with his hands up. "That's dark Affinity Enhancer. I didn't sign up for more of that. No ways. I won't do it."

Elden checked the caps on the syringes and tucked them into his bag. "Just kidding. Let's call these Plan B." He shouldered his bag and shifted it onto his back. "Right. Let's go. Follow me, gentleman. The van is this way."

Ruaan's face was thunderous. "It's not like we have any choice in the matter, now is there?"

Elden pushed back his cap and his eyes gleamed in the moonlight. "You always have a choice. Always."

~*~

Kai lost count of how many hours they'd been driving. They'd cleared the city, leaving behind the broken brick buildings. On the outskirts of the city, the landscape changed to a less formal dotting of houses. Moonlight softened the scene, but the brief flash of broken fences and overgrown gardens hinted at neglect, poverty. The road had taken them past suburbia, into an industrial section with tall, blackened buildings belching smoke continuously into the air. Noxious gasses made it hard to breathe without gagging.

Beyond stretched a great expanse of nothingness, unlike anything Kai had seen before. It rolled on for miles, greenery yielding to desert sand that formed soft deceptive curves. The road cut straight through it.

Ruaan and Zap had fallen asleep, Ruaan—a tightly contained ball propped up by his knee, Zap, a sprawling, snoring thing.

Kai thought sleep would be a good idea, but his jumpy insides wouldn't hear of it. "How far is this place?" Kai checked the time on the dashboard. It was past 3:00 AM.

Elden squinted at the dash, his brow furrowed as he calculated. "Another half-hour or so."

"What are we walking into? Will we have to sneak in?"

Elden shrugged. "Just take your cues from me. I'll talk you through when we're there."

"Tell me something about the place. I prefer knowing what I'm in for." Getting information out of Elden was proving to be quite impossible. It did nothing for Kai's levels of trust.

"The Crux is headquarters for a global operation. Some say it's impressive. High tech." Elden faltered. "Probably easier for you to wait and see."

"If some say it's impressive, what do you think?"

"It's big and organised. Unstoppable."

The word fell between them like a dead whale, and their stilted conversation died.

Kai stared out the window at the rolling, moonlit hills. There was something hypnotic that soothed his insides, and he found himself nodding off.

"Guys, we're here."

Elden's words hit him like ice water dunked over his head, and he was instantly awake. The two in the back groaned and stretched as they pulled up to a gate in an electric fence as tall as a triple-story house. As far as Kai could see, nothing but more desert sand stretched away beyond the fence. How odd.

To the right of the gate, stood a guardhouse.

Through the tinted glass, Kai thought he could see people moving. Pins and needles prickled all down his back. For such a harmless-looking place, it had rattled him.

Elden unbuckled his safety belt and eased out of the van. "Sit tight. I'll be back, now."

Kai watched the man stroll up the guardhouse and walk straight in as if it were his family's home. What had they gotten themselves into?

~*~

Evazee's arm had gone to sleep underneath Peta. It was hard to believe that such a tiny girl could be such a dead weight when she slept. Early morning sunlight shone through the gap in the curtain. Loathe to wake Peta, Evazee inched herself upright, gently extracting her numb limb. Something fluttered off her pillow. A note.

She fumbled it open using one hand and her teeth instead of her useless arm. Squinting through sleep-crusty eyelids, Evazee had to reread it three times before the words sank in.

Zee,

We've gone with Elden to untie what is holding the OS kids back from being free. I can't tell you more. We'll be back soon. Look after them all.

Kai

Evazee's belly flipped. He was trusting Elden. The same Elden who'd let her be marked and had done nothing to stop it. Not only that, Kai had taken Elden away before he could take her through the arch. This was not good. She crept from the room on quiet feet.

Zulu crouched next to her door. Her heart jumped as she saw him.

He stood up, towering over her. "Friend-Evazee, where is Kai? I need to speak to him."

"You gave me such a fright. Walk with me. He's not here. He's gone with Elden on some secret mission." Her neck grew hot. She was annoyed. Annoyed and angry. How could he just leave like that?

Zulu's face crumpled. "That is not good news."

"How are your boys? The injured ones?" She aimed towards the lounge where they'd settled them.

"I've watched them through the night. They are resting. More than that, I cannot say."

"Let's have a look." She pushed the door open, unsure of what waited for her on the other side. The couch was empty, as were all the makeshift beds they'd set up on the floor. The boys themselves were nowhere.

Zulu's dark skin paled, and he blinked rapidly. The sound of faint singing drifted through the open door.

"Do you think they're on the roof?" Evazee had helped them get settled the night before. She knew without a doubt that some of them would have been unable to leave this room on their own legs.

Zulu's eyes were so wide, Evazee worried they might pop right out. "How do we get there?"

"Follow me." Evazee strained to hear who was singing. She couldn't hear the words, but the song tugged at her insides. They climbed the staircase, and the song washed over her as she pulled the door open. Their voices were pure, and they sang words in a language that Evazee couldn't understand but raised gooseflesh all down her arms.

Zulu spotted them first. The boys were standing in a circle in the centre of the roof, all of them on their feet.

"This is not possible." Evazee's pulse raced.

As Zulu came close, the circle opened to a straight line, and the boys stooped from the waist.

"Be content." Zulu held up a hand to dismiss them, and the boys relaxed. "How is it possible that you are here? What about your burns? Boety?" The boy he addressed was clearly his brother. They had the same nose and jaw line. Boety's eyes were different though—pale icy blue.

"We found water to drink." He shrugged his skinny shoulders as if the rest should have been obvious.

"And then?"

Boety laughed. His white teeth gleamed against his dark skin. "We sleep, woke up better."

Zulu checked them one at a time. Evazee peered over his shoulder, curiosity getting the better of her hesitance. Second degree burns had healed to first degree. First degree burns had healed completely. Bruises which should have been dark had lightened, and some were gone completely. She'd seen these boys come off the bus. She'd known that they were in for a long recovery, and yet here they were. There was no natural way they should have healed this fast. Evazee tugged on Zulu's arm. "Do you think they drank water from the Healing Stream?"

"Blue water? Like your Peta-child?"

"Yes! It's the only thing I can think of."

She turned to Boety and held out a hand to shake his. "I'm Evazee. I'm Zulu's friend."

He eyed her shyly, but at a nod from Zulu, he shook her hand and smiled.

"Where did you find the water? Is there more?"

"One bottle in the room, is all." He held his hands apart, palms up—he didn't know about any more. "Very thirsty." He grinned and pointed to all the boys in the circle.

Evazee leaned close to Zulu, "They'll probably be hungry too. You should send them downstairs. I'll make them something."

Zulu squinted at the sky. "One, Three, Five, Seven, and Nine, stand watch from the roof. Eleven and twelve, watch the wall-hole downstairs. Two, Four, Six, Eight and Ten follow me."

Boety's shoulders slumped. "But my stomach growls."

"You forget your rank, Number One." Zulu said nothing more, but his brother turned to the others and directed them to different sections of the roof.

Evazee tackled him on the way downstairs. "That was harsh. Why don't you call them by their names? Your brother went from being Boety to Number One. What's up with that? And surely they can all eat and then split up for guard duty?"

Zulu's mouth stayed shut, a tight line between his clenched jaw muscles. Only when they were alone in the kitchen did he answer.

"My people will come. They will come with the fire of their anger as hot as the sun. We have to be ready."

Evazee had her hands on her hips in spite of a sliver of fear down her spine. "What about their names? It's rude."

"No names until they pass their tests. Calling Number One by his name was a mistake."

"Maybe I'm wrong, but surely that is the system you brought them here to be free from. Can't you see that?"

Zulu's eyes narrowed and Evazee swallowed hard. This was not a man to be messed with. Still. What he was doing was wrong.

He passed a hand over his face with a shudder. "I'm sorry Friend-Evazee. I took the boys without thinking. Right and wrong? I don't know those yet. I'm only learning now."

She patted his arm, rock hard muscle under his skin. "We'll figure it out. But first, food."

13

Elden jogged back to the van with three badges that said *Maintenance* in bold red letters. "Here, take these. For now, you three are on my maintenance crew. Shut your mouths and we'll get to do what we came here for."

It took another five minutes of driving through empty desert before they arrived. The sun broke the horizon as they crested a hill. In a dip on the other side stood a glass and aluminium structure unlike anything Kai had ever seen before. Rising out of the sand, the multi-storied building angled off in two directions with a tall glass tower rising up where the two corners met. Two more sections rose up tall, but neither of them rivalled the central tower. One could get lost for days wandering around in a building this size.

Elden pulled in to a parking bay. He opened up the cubbyhole and took out a laptop. It booted within seconds and he opened up a program that was unfamiliar to Kai and tapped away through a number of changing screens. "Just give me one more minute." Elden pressed enter and folded his arms to wait.

"What are you doing?" Zap asked what Kai was thinking.

"Creating a reason for us to go where we need to go. Here we go, in three, two, one. Done." The screen winked out, and Elden's mobile rang.

"Maintenance." The man on the other end sounded like a tiny angry gnat. Elden pitched his voice low, deep, and soothing, "Sure, right away. What is the reference?" He listened with his eyes shut and his lips moving before ending the call and turned to the others. "Our time starts now. Follow me and hush up."

At the top of a flight of polished marble stairs, Elden aimed his thumb at the fingerprint reader mounted on the side of the glass door. It scanned his thumb with a green light, and the door popped open with a hiss. The security man at the front desk called him over and stood as they approached.

"We're responding to a call for Maintenance. Reference ZE459."

The guy behind the desk scrolled on his monitor and tapped the screen. "You're cleared for sections S through Z." He gave Elden a device that looked like a wristwatch. "You've used one of these before? I've set it to take you to S."

Elden clipped it to his arm and studied the buttons along the edges. "I've used an older one. I can figure it out. Don't I need a passkey?"

"Nah, I've updated the fingerprint logins for those sections. New tech. Just don't go where you aren't allowed."

"Sure. Thanks." Elden's mouth was set in a thin, unimpressed line.

In the shiny silver lift, Kai asked, "What is that thing?"

"It's a navigation device—a Naviband. This place is so big, even those who work here get lost."

Zap took it all in with owl eyes. "What? You're kidding, right?"

Ruaan elbowed Zap in the ribs. "He never kids.

Never."

Kai watched Elden closely. He was not happy at all. "What's the matter? Are we in trouble?"

Elden checked the Naviband and ran his fingers through his hair. "They used to issue passkeys. I know how to tweak those. The room we need to get into is just next to the sections that he's given us access to. With the new fingerprint thing? I'm not sure we can get in there."

~*~

Bree was sleeping in a corner away from the others with her knees pulled up to her tummy and her bare feet sticking out from under the blanket.

Evazee didn't know how to wake her. She prodded her shoulder and dodged as Bree swung around, hands swatting. "Stop that! Wake up. I need you."

Bree's red curls fanned the pillow, surrounding her head like a messy halo of simmering flames. Her eyelids fluttered but stayed glued in a tight line of lashes. "Need sleep. Go away."

"Your brother has left." There wasn't time to ease Bree out of sleep. The girl had to wake up, and she had to wake up now.

"What?" Bree pushed to a sit and rubbed her eyes. "What do you mean?"

"Elden, Kai, and the other two have gone off on some half-baked quest to release something that will apparently free all these kids."

"Well, that makes no sense." Bree scraped her hair off her face and tied it around itself to make a bun. "What are we supposed to do with them all in the meantime?"

Evazee slid down to the floor with her back to the wall next to Bree, her arms looped around her knees. "Exactly. To make it all more fun, Zulu's enraged family are on their way over and, according to him, they don't want a nice chat over tea and cake."

Bree shrugged. "Why, then? Do they want their boys back? We should just hand them over, really. We can't fight. What does Zulu say?"

"He won't let any of them go back. It would be like handing them over to be slaughtered. They don't look kindly on deserters."

"But surely if they just leave us here and go somewhere else, they'll take the heat with them."

"Zulu said his family and the elders will want to avenge the fact that we harboured the boys here. They aren't too strong on being reasoned with. Also, they'll try to get information out of us by whatever means they have to."

Bree snuggled back under her blanket. "They can't be that scary. Most people can be reasoned with if you choose your words right."

"No, Bree. I've seen them. Their world is cruel, and it's shaped them."

The door burst open without a warning knock. It was Boety, Number One, Zulu's brother.

"Where is Zulu?" Whites showed all around his pupils.

"Boety? What's the matter? You are almost as pale as me."

"They're coming."

"The elders from your village?"

"Yebo."

"How much time do we have?"

"Sixty minutes."

"Find Zulu. Find him now."

~*~

For all his talk of getting lost, Elden didn't use his Naviband much. He seemed to know exactly where they were. "The maintenance tunnels run separate from the general passages. This door should take us there. It should be a bit quieter on the other side."

Kai studied everything around them. It was all common office stuff. Nothing clandestine or sinister and yet his skin crawled at being in this place. He'd been telling himself to stop being paranoid, but no matter how much ordinary surrounded him, adrenalin pumped through his veins, and his nerves were shot.

Elden squinted at a sign on a door. "I think the vault is close. We need to get through this stretch of warehouses."

Elden walked with a confidence that Kai admired, but it also provoked suspicion. He was way too comfortable in this environment that had Kai twitching like an ant under a magnifying glass.

The maintenance passage ended at locked stainless-steel doors, big enough for a truck to drive through. A thumbprint reader was mounted to the wall on the right. Elden shrugged and stepped close. His thumb was enough to make the doors click open and swing backwards. Kai stepped through, expecting it all to be dark and ominous. A torture chamber of secrets designed for terrible deeds.

What he found on the other side couldn't have been more ordinary. It was like walking through a grocery store. There was a whole section devoted to cleaning products, clothing, medical supplies. They walked past shelves of toys, DVD's, games. Home goods. Blankets, bedding, towels and linen. It made no sense. Workers moved between the shelves, rearranging, packing stacks of different products onto moving conveyor belts.

"Are they stockpiling this lot?" Kai tried to keep his face in maintenance worker mode, but he couldn't help frowning. This was a bizarre collection of things for a place that was primarily offices and a laboratory.

Elden shrugged. "This room was empty when I was last here."

Kai blinked and when he opened his eyes, a green glow shone faintly around everything. The stuff wasn't quite right. A stamped release note was stuck on a stack of energy drinks that stood bigger than the shack that Bree used to live in. The sign stated that the batch was ready to go.

Two workmen stopped and stared at the four of them, heads together, whispering behind their hands. One of the two slipped out of the room, leaving the other staring at them awkwardly. His hands were busy with products, but his attention was all on them.

Elden picked up the pace. "I don't like the look of those two. Let's move."

The friends walked fast, maintenance-worker-fast, not I'm running-for-my-life fast. The workman kept pace, barely worrying about keeping up the appearance of working.

Elden dodged between two roof-high piles of cake flour, and the others followed. The workman had wedged himself in a dead end. He swore and doubled back. That bought them enough time to make a dash for the exit.

No longer caring about appearances, they ran. Alarm bells went off and they ran faster. Elden's fingerprint did the trick and they threw themselves through the open door that slammed shut behind them.

"Don't stop. They'll get through now." There was real fear in Elden's voice. "This way."

They ducked underneath an enormous metal pipe and shimmied along the wall in the tiny gap between the pipe and the wall.

The shriek of the alarm sliced through Kai's brain. It made thinking hard.

They came to a small maintenance door, and Elden used his thumb to open it. They heard footsteps coming closer just as they slipped through the door and shut it behind themselves.

Kai's chest heaved at the effort of breathing. "Why did you run? We're cleared to be here."

Elden rolled his shoulders back and twisted his head from side to side as a boxer would warming up for a fight. "We don't have time for their questions. Do you want to lose half the day being interrogated by management? Or do you want to get what we came for and get out of here?"

Zap nodded sagely. "I like the second option."

Ruaan clucked his tongue. "It was a rhetorical question, you nit."

"Don't you prefer the second option?" Zap held out his hands but Ruaan swatted them aside.

"Guys, let's do what we came here to do. Elden is right about that, we don't have much time." They led off down the passage, leaving Zap trailing at the end.

14

Elden pressed his face up against a wall of one-way glass, blocking out the light with his hands. "That's the room we need to be in. I could probably get us in, but I don't know if we'd be able to get out."

Kai leaned close, trying to see through his own reflection. This place was suffocating, worse than being in a small cave despite high ceilings and lots of space. "I thought you said we needed the vault?" The word itself hinted at dark metal and un-crackable locks. All he could see was a cavernous open space that seemed to stretch on forever. His Affinity had been zoning in and out since arriving here. He sent out a test thought to Zap. *Can you hear me, buddy?*

Zap was staring up and down the passage, looking a bit green and bouncing on his toes.

"Are you OK?"

Zap kept on bouncing. "I don't like this place."

Elden laughed, a cold hard snort. "We're deep in the other side's turf. I'd be worried if you did."

Unlike the others, Ruaan wasn't hunched over, trying to see beyond the glass. He stood as casually as a bored boyfriend while waiting for his girlfriend to finish shoe shopping. His grey eyes glowed faintly, visible even though it wasn't dark.

Kai frowned at him. "Hey, no fair! Why is your Affinity working here?"

"Some of us are more special than others, I guess." He picked at his nail but then froze. "We'd better look busy. There's a group coming."

Kai listened hard but heard nothing. "Are you sure?"

"About thirty of them. The word *harvester* is in my head."

Elden pulled away from the glass as if it had suddenly become hot. "Harvesters! That's not good. Quickly, this way."

They followed Elden down the sterile passage, hunting for a hideaway.

Ruaan mumbled as they went.

Zap tackled him in a fierce whisper, "Is that your stomach, or are you griping again?"

"I'm just saying, we're wasting our time. There's another group coming from this side."

A flash of heat passed through Kai. "So you're saying we are about to become the jelly in a Harvester sandwich."

"Weird analogy, but basically yes."

Elden stopped scurrying, and his forehead creased. "New plan. Hide the maintenance badges. We're going undercover as Harvesters. Follow my lead and shut your mouths."

The first group rounded the corner from the left. They jogged in time, moving quickly down the passage towards where the guys waited. Kai felt like a pimple on prom night.

The Harvesters halted as they reached them. The one in front stepped out from the bunch, his chest popping out slightly. "What are you all doing here?"

Elden towered over the guy by at least a head. As he spoke, he softened his spine and seemed to fold himself down until he was closer to the guy's height. "Apologies. One of my squad dropped his catch. We waited while he gathered it all up, but our squad had moved on. We were waiting here for the next passcard holder."

The man sighed as if their incompetence was a personal insult. "Fall in. You can present your Harvest with our squad. You realize that your haul will be credited to us."

Elden nodded but kept his eyes on the floor. Kai tried to copy his demeanour. Humble but productive. Invisible.

They fell in step with the group and soon lined up outside the doorway into the vault. The squad leader stuck his thumb over the fingerprint reader and two huge panes of glass slid back. Cold washed over them, turning their breath to mist. The room was kept a few degrees below comfortable, and Kai wished he'd bought a hoodie.

"Once you've secured your take, you are free to leave until your next shift." The leader checked his watch and waved them inside, looking bored. He handed out gadgets as the people passed him, skipping over five before giving out the next one.

As the group entered, they split up, covering only a fraction of the large expanse.

Kai shuffled into the vault with the others. A honeycomb pattern covered the floor that made his eyes swim.

Elden flicked his head to the right and the three followed him.

The squad seemed to work in groups of six. The bunch closest to Kai had their heads together over their gadget. One of them typed numbers into it. As he pressed a button in the middle, a single honeycomb hexagon a few steps away from them lit up. They hurried over to it and plugged their gadget into a hollow recess in the centre of the hexagon on the floor. As it clicked into place, a six-sided column rose up, a smooth shaft seemingly formed from a single piece of obsidian.

They circled the pillar, each one facing a flat side. For a moment, nothing seemed to be happening. But then a spark of green spiraled up the column. The lava glass lit up and glowed from within, turning transparent. The top layer of obsidian seemed to melt away, showing deep recesses behind. Each of the six reached into their bags and drew out a bunch of amulets dangling off a cord, just like the one Runt had claimed as her own. Working quickly, they hung the amulets in the recesses. The obsidian was slowly becoming opaque once more, and a curtain of liquid obsidian dripped down from the ceiling, solidifying as it touched the floor and growing to cover the opening.

A redhead closest to Kai fumbled and dropped her pendant on the floor. Her friend next to her hissed as she bent down to help her pick them up.

"Quickly! Get that amulet in. It's closing!"

The fumbling girl muttered under her breath, her hands shaking as she hung the amulets while dodging falling drops. One fat blob skimmed her skin, and she cried out.

Elden led the three further away from the door, around a corner off to one side. "I need the GPS coordinates for the OS."

Zap wiggled his eyebrows at Ruaan, who glared at him. Ruaan reached for the device in Elden's hand. "Let me type it in. Easier than trying to say it." He entered the digits, pressed the middle button, and waited. The device lit up emerald, the light pulsing slowly.

Kai checked the ground around where they stood, nothing. A block lit up, and a squad rushed over to claim it. The colour was wrong for the device in Ruaan's hand.

"Keep hunting, guys. It's got to be here somewhere." The lines on Elden's forehead deepened as he frowned.

They spread out, hunting for flashing light the same shade as their device, dodging other searchers. A vague sense of unease crept over Kai as they moved further and further from the doorway. The longer they looked, the more time he spent checking to make sure he could still see the others.

Zap froze, frowning at the ground, head tilted to the side like a bird. "Guys, I think this is our flashy thingy."

~*~

"Surely we can talk to them. They'll understand." Evazee held Zulu's thick wrist in her hands. His pulse was racing.

"You saw. You saw the boy die. They have no mercy. We must run."

"There are at least a hundred kids in this house. Some of them are young. How would we run? Besides, wouldn't they just keep following us?"

Zulu's head dropped to his chest. "We are done for."

Evazee's heart pounded in her throat. A headache was settling in to the base of her skull, one of those that got worse until one threw up.

"We can't run, so we wait them out. Zulu, pull your boys off guard duty. Send them to round up all the kids and take them down to the basement. There is only one entrance – through a trapdoor. It's impossible to find unless you know what you're looking for. If we hide out there and we all stay really quiet, they might not find us."

Zulu didn't look convinced.

Evazee drew herself up as tall as she could and stuck a hand on her hip. "Do you have a better plan? Because if you do, please speak now."

Zulu's face hardened, but he stuck two fingers between his lips and whistled so loudly, Evazee covered her ears.

Within minutes, all Zulu's boys were gathered around him. He hunched over and spoke to them in an urgent tone, they listened intently with their brown eyes gleaming in the gloomy light. All the boys nodded, Zulu straightened up and clapped his hands once. The boys dispersed, running at top speed in different directions.

"Friend-Evazee, the boys will bring everybody here. Then we are yours." He tipped his head in a gesture that was raw power, yet yielded to her.

Evazee wanted to throw up. "Good. That's good." A wave of dizziness washed over her and she shook it off, schooling her features to look like she knew what she was doing. Saving kids from blood-thirsty priests. Nothing weird going on here.

A full ten minutes later, all of Zulu's boys were back with groups of OS kids in tow. They reported back their headcount, and Evazee tallied it all up, satisfied that they seemed to have everybody. Zulu's boys each stood at the front of their groups, looking strong and proud—so different from the broken boys they'd pulled off the bus. Their eyes were trained on Zulu, waiting for his next command. They may be young, but there was more to these boys than Evazee had first thought.

Evazee fidgeted in front of the group, reluctant to open her mouth. Zulu checked the clock on the wall, and she thought she saw his face pale.

"Everyone, this is not a drill. Some men from Zulu's village are coming. We are going to move down to the basement to hide from them until they've calmed down. Stay in your groups, and listen to the boy who fetched you. I don't want any of you getting lost. Raise your hand if you understand."

A ripple of raised hands crossed the room. It was enough. "Follow me."

Evazee led the group downstairs trying not to think too deeply. Bree caught up and yanked on her arm.

"I don't want to cause trouble, but isn't the trapdoor the only way in and out of the basement?"

"There's a storm water drain." Evazee shrugged.

Bree's nose wrinkled. "With the way it's been raining, that is likely to be flooded. I don't think you can count that as an option."

"We just need a place to hide. We don't need to get out."

Bree had her head sideways, eyeing Evazee as if she were a science experiment gone funky. "Doesn't that sound a bit too much like a trap to you?"

"We'll just hide out until they give up and leave. It's not a big deal."

The expression on Bree's face contradicted every scrap of not-big-deal that Evazee had forced into her voice.

"C'mon. Let's get them all down."

~*~

Ruaan bent down, but before he could press the device into the hollow in the middle of the pillar, Elden swooped across and took it out of his hands.

"Here, let me do that."

Ruaan backed off with his hands up like a hostage. "Fine. Have your moment in the sun."

"Don't be such a baby. This thing was coded to me when Security gave it to me. Do you want to set off a bunch of alarms?"

Ruaan mumbled under his breath.

Zap elbowed Kai. "We should have fed him before coming."

Elden cleared his throat. "Are you all ready to grab? Get yourselves into position. You won't have much time. Here we go."

Kai shot a quick glance around the room to make sure they weren't being watched. The other groups were all absorbed in their own pillars. "Let's do it."

The device clicked into place, and the lights merged with those in the floor in a satisfying weaving of colour. As the column started rising, it let out a loud hiss before shooting upwards in a smooth swoosh.

Kai stood waiting at the one flat side, and his breath caught as the covering layer of lava glass melted away. Many amulets swung inside the pillar. One in particular caught his eye. It had Evazee's unmistakable feathery imprint. The girl had been so out of it, the thought of being able to give back whatever had been stolen from her made him mushier inside than he cared to admit. He reached in before he could change his mind. The moment his fingers contacted the surface, drops of lava glass fell from the top. He grabbed the feathery amulet and pulled his hand back just in time to miss getting scorched. A breath later, it was all sealed up. Now what?

He rapped his knuckles on the surface, already cool and solid.

Zap was staring at him. "Did you nearly get your hand singed off?" Zap pointed to Kai's side of the pillar.

"Not exactly. Maybe close, but not completely." Kai waved him back towards his side. "Get in there, Zap! There's no time to waste."

Ruaan breathed in so sharply, they forgot their squabble.

"Guys, look!" He pointed at the column. Through the lava glass they could see an amulet engraved with an open eye. "I think it's mine."

"But the thing is closed. How are you going to get it?" Zap sounded as though he'd just dropped a double scoop of ice cream.

Ruaan's face glowed, and he stared, entranced, through the lava glass. He reached for the pendant, and the lava glass drew back at his touch. He didn't seem to notice, but took his pendant while holding his breath. Only when it was safely around his neck did he breathe again. He grinned at the others, face beaming.

Zap had a smirk on his face that Kai knew well. "Pretty necklace."

Ruaan was so chuffed with his find that even Zap's sarcasm couldn't affect him. "Necklaces are for girls. This is my amulet." He shrugged and rolled the word around on his tongue. "Yep, this is mine."

"How can you be so sure?" Zap was frowning

more than Kai had ever seen him frown.

"It feels familiar in the best way possible." Ruaan's face was positively angelic.

"Zap, get in there. Yours is going to start closing soon." Kai watched his friend for a split second. Then he sprang into action, grabbing amulets by the fist-full.

The drips started from the top of the column, and Kai's heart sank. There were still too many amulets inside, each one representing a captured life.

In seconds, the column had closed up completely and sank back into the floor until it was level. The lights winked out, and the opportunity was over.

Ruaan had his back to them. "Er, guys, why are we the only ones left?"

Kai spun around. The room had emptied out without them noticing. "Where is Elden?"

Zap paled and pointed. Elden was on the other side of the closed glass doors. They ran to him. Kai pushed on the doors to open them, but they didn't budge. He waved at Elden, but Elden wouldn't look at him. He left with the other two groups, eyes downcast.

The lights in the vault switched off, plunging the vast chamber into darkness.

"This sucks." Ruaan's voice echoed through the empty space.

~*~

Bree stood next to Evazee with her arms folded. "Do you think we're over-reacting?"

They stood together at the bottom of the stairs watching groups of OS kids trooping down the steps into the basement. Each group was led by one of Zulu's boys. None of them spoke much, but they carried themselves with a suppleness and strength that singled them out as warriors in training.

"There can't be too many more to come down." Evazee glanced across the room but gave up on attempting a head count. The lights were dim down here.

"Someone's arguing up top. You should go see." Bree tilted her head towards the trapdoor.

Evazee knew better than to argue with the redhead.

Zulu and his brother were going at each other at the top of the stairs.

"What's going on?"

Zulu was so furious that there was a red tinge to his dark skin. "Number One is being stubborn."

Boety pointed at Zulu but spoke directly to Evazee. "And he's not being logical."

"Guys, surely there isn't time for this?"

Boety held up his hands as if he knew nothing, "Someone has to stay out to close and hide the flappy door. Otherwise? Men find everybody." His eyes went vacant and his voice hollowed. "They're here."

Zulu butted in with a finger in Boety's face. "I told you to go down. I'll do the door."

Boety twisted as if he were going to walk down the stairs and comply. At the last minute, he yelled, "Move, Zulu's friend!" He swung backwards, hooking Zulu's legs out from under him. Zulu tipped forwards and rolled head-first down the stairs like a human bowling ball.

Evazee stood, torn.

But Boety grinned at her and shut the trapdoor in her face.

The sound of scraping came from over her head. This kid had spunk. Not too many self-preservation brain cells, but definitely guts.

Bree was perched on Zulu's back at the bottom of the stairs. The big man raged, trying to get up to get back to his brother. The fall didn't seem to have done him any harm.

"It's too late, Zulu. Your brother is clever like you. He is small and quick. Maybe they won't catch him."

"It should have been me."

"Well, it's not. Help me get this lot settled in. Help them understand that they have to be quieter than they've ever been be—"

Zulu held a hand to her lips and pointed above. Footsteps on the wooden floor above.

Evazee's heart pounded so loud she thought they might hear.

Zulu's boys stood, one at each group, ready for anything.

Deep male voices spoke in a language she didn't understand.

Zulu tilted his head to the side, straining to hear.

"They're searching the building."

The OS kids sat on the floor, dotted in groups between the piles of boxes. They sat as still as statues, the gravity of the situation must have got through to them. Evazee stayed close to Zulu, waiting for an indication of how long they'd be down here.

"They're going to stay until we show up." Zulu hung his head, rubbing his eyes.

"What?" Evazee's fear squeezed out into that single word. "We can't keep these kids down here and quiet for much longer."

Zulu nodded. "There has to be another way out."

"I'll check the storm water drain. Maybe the water is low enough for us to get out that way."

Evazee eased herself down the stairs and stepped between all the people sitting squished together on the floor. A few of them had to move for her to get to the trapdoor. Between them, they hauled back the heavy lid. The sounds of water sloshing below echoed up the short tunnel. Someone shone a light, and Evazee sighed. Water filled the tunnel. If they all had scuba equipment, getting out that way would be great. But they didn't, and there was no way they would be leaving this basement through these tunnels.

Evazee tugged on her ponytail. Maybe the sharp pain in her scalp would help her think. She studied the contents of the room. There could even be a doorway behind one of the boxes. They'd never know because they couldn't see it. She hated the feeling of being trapped like this, with the possibility of discovery getting bigger each moment they spent down here.

There was only one thing for it. They had to examine every centimetre of this room, without making any noise. She pulled Zulu down to whisper in his ear.

"Ask your boys to look for a doorway. We have to get out of here."

Zulu nodded and picked his way between the groups of people on the floor. One at a time he made his way to each of his boys and whispered in their ears. The slow, measured steps of someone on guard duty thudded through the floor at regular intervals.

Every time they crossed the trapdoor, Evazee's heart pounded. Zulu tripped and came down on his knee with a loud *thunk*. The footsteps paused then grew louder. The walker was coming back.

A rustling sound came from a corner behind Evazee. It made her think of camping. As she turned around, she could see why. One of Zulu's boys had pulled aside a large canvas sheet. Behind it stood an open arch carved from ancient stone, cracked and dirty. A sliver of unease shot through Evazee. A stone arch seemed so out of place.

The footsteps had stopped right over the trapdoor. Two hard stamps made the door bounce. The hairs on Evazee's arms stood on end. One more stamp. Her knees turned to water. Scuffling and scratching. A shout. They'd been discovered.

Zulu pointed at the arch and held up his hands silently asking for Evazee's opinion. More scuffling above. They were out of time.

Evazee waved her hands, shooing them towards the arch. Zulu stood up tall and stuck an arm in the air. Across the room his boys stood to their feet, their gazes trained on Zulu as an orchestra would on a conductor. His hands flew in a complicated series of gestures. Then they dropped to his sides, and each of his boys stuck an arm up.

Zulu's arm swung towards the arch, dark muscles bulging under his skin. As one, the boys turned to their groups, gathered them close, and made for the opening. Those closest stepped in first. Evazee's stomach churned. They had no idea where it would take them, but they couldn't stay.

Bree wiggled through the mass of bodies, pressing through to Evazee with thunder on her face. She hauled herself up the stairs and grabbed Evazee's arm. "Do you know what that is?" She hissed between clenched teeth. "Take a good look."

"A doorway." Evazee stared at the arch. It flickered grey light as each person stepped through. A wash of cold flooded over Evazee, and she swallowed hard.

"You've seen one of these before, haven't you? You know exactly what it is and what it does." Bree's mouth pulled in a thin white line.

Not a doorway.

A testing arch.

15

"He's a snake and a traitor. I knew it from the start." Zap paced. Two steps, turn, two steps, turn.

Ruaan sighed in the dark. "Do you think there's anything to eat in here? We've been stuck here for hours."

The silence in the room made Kai's ears buzz, broken only by Zap's footsteps and the faint rumblings of Ruaan's belly. They'd walked the vast chamber flat, searched every inch for another way out. The only door in was locked tight and unbreakable. Kai had tried speaking to Tau, but it didn't seem like Tau hung out in places like this.

"I should never have dragged you two into this. Trusting Elden was a gamble that didn't pay off. I'm sorry." Kai fumbled for Elden's bag in the dark. He felt the rough canvas and dragged it closer. As he lifted it, all the contents slipped out and crashed to the floor. Four glowing tubes fell out too, giving off enough faint light for Kai to see the amulets they'd collected all spilled on the floor.

"Hey, what are those?" Ruaan bent down and reached towards a tube.

"Don't touch that!" Zap yelled. "Don't you recognise it?"

"I saw Elden pack those in." Kai reached for one and held it between the tips of his fingers. "Dark

Affinity serum. I don't know what his intention was with these. We didn't really discuss plans. He just told me to come and I did." Kai scooped up all the things on the floor and shoved them back in the bag. "I would have expected an alarm to go off by now or something." He unclipped the navigation device from the top of the pillar which had sunk back down onto the floor.

Kai opened the bag to stare at the glowing injections. The idea forming made his stomach flip, yet it seemed to be their last option. "Guys, we need to get back to the OS as soon as possible. At the moment, we could be left here for a long time. What if we tried the injections?" He braced himself for the backlash.

Zap stopped pacing, and Kai was glad for the dark that hid whatever Zap's face was doing. It wouldn't be pretty.

"I'm not even going to answer that. Do you seriously want that stuff in your veins? I think you must have bashed your head and forgotten what it was like." Zap clucked his tongue.

Before Kai could answer, Ruaan spoke. "It's a terrible idea. But it could be our only choice. Besides, it's one injection. It won't affect us forever. Just long enough to get out of here."

"Exactly. We need to get back. We can't hang around forever. This is the only way." Kai sounded a thousand times more convinced than he felt.

"You two are prize idiots. I can't believe what I'm hearing from you. Of the three of us, I'm the one who has seen this stuff developed in the lab. I've watched them destroy the boundaries to twist things out of shape to make this stuff effective. With every sane cell in my brain, I'm begging you. Don't do this."

Dread washed over Kai. Despite Zap's impassioned plea, he was beginning to think this was the only way. The thought of forcing this on his friend curdled his gut.

~*~

Stepping into a testing arch without being pumped full of serum was like stepping into an oven and sticking a finger in an open electricity socket all at once. Heat flashed through Evazee, making sweat break out across her forehead. For a moment, the pain was so intense she thought she'd burn up on the spot, but she kept walking anyway.

The heat left and with it, her strength. She doubled over, hands on her knees, and focussed on breathing with lungs that felt seared.

"Friend-Evazee, the others—"

A hook of emotion in Zulu's voice drew Evazee upright. She blinked through blinding light, trying to figure out where they were and what Zulu was trying to say.

"They're not here."

"What?" Evazee spun around. The archway had brought them out in the slums outside the OS. Lopsided shacks tilted at crazy angles, stretching into distance as far as she could see.

Bree lay on her side in the dirt, clutching her damaged arm and whimpering with her eyes shut tight. Next to her huddled another small bundle with her black hair poking out the sides. Paintbrush.

"Is that it?" Evazee rubbed her eyes and spun around. She ran to Bree and put her hand on her friend's back. "Are you hurt?"

Paintbrush rolled onto her back and stretched out,

thrashing as if she were dreaming of ants. As far as Evazee could tell, it was just the four of them. She'd watched the others walk through the arch. If they'd come out close by, there was no way of knowing.

People were coming out of their shacks, shielding their eyes as if the sun was shining for the first time in months.

"Friend-Evazee, these people are staring at you." Zulu was crouched down as if trying to be as small as possible.

Evazee laughed and patted his shoulder. "No, dear Zulu-friend. You are the star attraction here. You are quite an intimidating sight, you know."

He backed off a few steps, glanced around and shook his head. "Nope. All you."

A little boy ran out from one of the shacks and straight past Zulu. He didn't bat an eye at the two on the ground but came right up to Evazee and stood at her feet, neck craning to look up at her.

He reached out to touch her, stopped just short and snatched his hand away. "Are you an angel?"

"What's your name?"

"Sam. You look like an angel."

"Have you ever seen an angel, Sam?" Evazee couldn't help grinning at the little boy whose face glowed as he looked at her.

"Uh-huh." He nodded with his smile growing wider. "You!"

"Sam! Come back here now." An old woman leaning on a stick stood at the doorway of a shack that looked like it might collapse if someone breathed too hard.

Heat flashed through Evazee, so quick it took her breath away. Her palms tingled like the candy that pops when you put it on your tongue.

"But Nana, she's—"

"Now. Quickly."

Sam's face crumpled, but he backed away with his eyes fixed on Evazee. At the last minute, he spun away and ran to his Nana.

She shooed him inside and settled back onto her stick, glaring at Evazee through squinty eyes.

Evazee was just wondering if she should go speak to the old lady, when she disappeared inside and slammed the door behind her hard enough to make her whole shack quiver.

Bree groaned, and Evazee reached down to pull her to a sit. As their skin connected, Bree yelped.

"What did you do to me?" Bree stared at her good hand, flexing her fingers.

Paintbrush rolled over and stuck her head on Bree's lap. Her arms slipped around Bree, and she smiled before drifting back to sleep.

Bree sat awkwardly, her damaged hand across her chest. With Paintbrush on her lap, she overbalanced and nearly fell. Her hands flung out to catch herself, and Evazee gasped.

"Look at your hand. Not your good one, the other one."

Bree held up her damaged hand. The skin pulsed with light. "I'm getting feeling back. What did you do?"

Zulu tapped Evazee on the shoulder. She looked around to see what he wanted and panicked. Slum dwellers surrounded them, shuffling closer. Their faces were grim.

Evazee knew what she had to do. "Look after these two, Zulu. I'll be back soon."

Without thinking too deeply, Evazee followed the urging in her gut and ran across the dusty space to the shack where Sam lived with his Nana. She knocked on the makeshift door carefully, not wanting to risk sending the entire structure toppling.

"Go away." Sam's Nana's voice was old and brittle.

Evazee waved Zulu over. "Do you think you could make this shack more stable?"

His gaze flicked across the rusted metal sheets, balanced on each other to make the shelter. "Yebo."

"We'd like to make your house stronger. Can we do that?"

The makeshift door opened a fraction. "I don't know, can you?"

Evazee thumbed towards Elden. "He can."

"What cost?"

Evazee hesitated. There was no doubt in her mind that asking for nothing would get a no. "Something to drink. We're not fussy."

"Very well. Come on in."

~*~

"I'm sorry Zap. There is no other way. I'll do what I have to do, and you'll go along with it."

Zap stepped away from him, finger poking towards Kai's face. "Are you bullying me?"

Ruaan pushed them apart. "I say we keep going. Look. Something just lit up in the distance. It might be a door." He didn't wait for them but strode off into the gloom with his eyes glowing.

Zap sniffed, a deep, smug sniff, crammed full of I-told-you-so.

The relief that washed through Kai outweighed his

urge to punch Zap in his smug face. Anything was better than having to pump his friend full of dark Affinity serum.

Ruaan jogged faster than Kai thought was possible. His thighs burned with the effort of keeping up. Each step covered three hexagons below his feet. Each hexagon represented a column packed with countless amulets, each amulet holding a life in bondage. Stuck, not able to break free.

The further they ran, the more Kai's belly soured. He ran out of fingers and toes to count how many sections were represented.

They reached Ruaan's door. A panel of buttons ran down the side and Ruaan pushed one with an arrow pointing downwards. The doors drew back with a hiss and opened up to a rectangular cubicle, a lift.

The panel of buttons inside the lift was huge, with buttons numbered from zero all the way to one hundred. Ruaan shut the doors and shrugged his shoulders at them.

"Which one?"

A fine sheen of sweat covered Kai's body. He told himself it was from the run, but he knew the truth. A hundred floors below the surface? Might as well be buried alive. "Try one down. That should be good." His voice came out high and squeaky.

Zap was bouncing on his toes. "C'mon man. A hundred floors and you want to go one down?" He glanced across at Kai and must've seen something in Kai's expression to change his mind. "OK, fine. What about just five?"

Ruaan nodded and punched the five.

The lift glided smoothly, slipped past four floors. Beyond the glass doors on each level stretched a room further than what Kai could see, the floors all covered in hexagons like the one they'd just left.

They reached the fifth level down and came to a halt with a gentle bump. A group of security guards clustered around the door, weapons drawn.

"Don't open!" Kai yelled too late. The lift doors slid open. Kai hit the close button, nearly trapping the front guard's fingers. He pulled back with a yell and slammed his fists into the door as the lift dropped out of his reach.

Zap clutched his toe, hopping around on one leg.

The 100th floor button glowed. Kai pointed. "What did you do?"

Zap toppled sideways into Ruaan, still rubbing his toe. "I panicked and kicked. The 100 button was just there where my toe landed. It's not my fault."

Kai stared through the door as level after level slipped past them, each floor the same as the others; hexagon-laced, stretching far beyond where he could see. "Guys, are you seeing this? Do you think they're all full?" His legs turned to jelly as his mind twisted around what he was seeing.

The lift picked up speed as it dropped, and they slammed to a halt at floor 100 with a jolt that knocked them off their feet. The lift door swooshed open.

Kai saw boots, cringed as something hard smacked into his skull, and watched the ground zoom closer.

16

The woman's tiny home was hardly big enough to fit another two people. Zulu hovered, hunched over with his chin on his chest to fit in.

Evazee held her arms close to her sides to try make herself take up less space.

Sam sat on a dirty blanket in the corner with his face beaming, eyes glued to Evazee's face.

As crude and small as it was, the place was tidy and as clean as a shack built on dirt could be. Sam's nana took a deep wooden bowl from a makeshift shelf and scooped water from a bucket in the corner. She held it out to Evazee with hands that shook.

Evazee's heart pulled tight. She could only imagine the effort it took to get this bucket of water from wherever they had to fetch it from. Drinking it when they had running water from taps back at the OS seemed nothing short of a crime, yet to refuse it would be wrong.

She drank a few mouthfuls and passed it on to Zulu.

He bowed deeply to the old woman before draining the bowl and handing it back.

The lady shuffled across the small space and slipped it back onto the shelf next to an ornate black glass flask. The flask was so out of place in the humble surroundings that Evazee's curiosity flared.

"What is that?" She spoke gently to the old lady, keeping a smile on her face even though she was feeling uncomfortable.

"Tonic. It gets dropped off here every month. I don't see who brings it." Her ancient face creased into a smile. "Helps my old bones and his young ones." There were more gaps than teeth in her gums.

"Can I see what it is?" Hairs stood up all down Evazee's neck.

The woman was reluctant, but Sam shot up and whispered in her ear. She sighed and nodded. Sam gave her a quick hug before handing the bottle over to Evazee.

She took off the lid and gagged as a familiar scent tinged drifted through the room. "Are you sure you don't know who brings this for you?"

The lady's face lit up. "Somebody loves us. As a bottle finishes, we put it out and a full one is delivered."

"Do you know what you're drinking?"

"I told you already." The lady sighed as if this conversation were sucking up all her energy. She waved to Sam and he stepped forward.

"A tonic that helps us. Just what Nana said." He shrugged.

Evazee caught Zulu's gaze and handed the bottle to him. "Do you know what this is?"

He sniffed and shrugged.

Evazee turned back to Sam's Nana. "Do the neighbours get it too?"

Sam waved his arm in a gesture that seemed royal. "Everybody. Everybody gets."

"Do you like the taste?"

Sam shook his head so hard his cheeks wobbled.

"Ugly."

Dark Affinity serum. Someone was supplying them all with dark Affinity serum and they were drinking it like soda.

~*~

"I brought you some test subjects for your newest batch." A gravelly, cigar-smoking voice.

Kai lay still, allowing consciousness to return to his brain. Adrenalin pumped through him as he tried to remember how he'd ended up on the cold tile floor of this dark room.

"Who are they?" A voice as cold as the floor Kai lay on.

"Expendables. Caught them snooping in the vault."

"You know that this batch isn't safe to be live tested yet. The effects of this mutate are designed to be permanent. I'm not inclined to rush the process or the testing."

"Do you honestly think the general cares?" A fit of coughing. "Just do it. He's pushing hard now. Besides, they shouldn't have been here."

"Strap them to the beds and leave me to my work, then."

"Hey, you can't order me around like that." Bad lungs and an insecurity complex. Almost enough for Kai to pity him.

"Just get it done. I thought the general was in such a hurry."

"Fine. But I'm not doing it because you told me to."

"Ja-ja. Whatever makes you happy."

Kai's mind flew. Resist? Run? Before he could make up his mind, he felt hands sliding under his armpits, dragging him. His dragger coughed, and Kai cringed at the thought of being coughed on. The man hauled him to his knees in front of the wheeled gurney. Kai saw the straps waiting for his arms and legs.

Not happening.

He flung himself backwards. His head connected with something sharp. *Crunch.* They fell to the ground. Kai whipped himself around and backed away on all fours, looking for the others. He saw them lying in a row along the wall, not moving. Not conscious.

A slim man in a lab coat stood off to one side, arranging instruments on a metal table. He didn't seem bothered by the drama at all.

Kai's captor had regained his balance and came at Kai with his arms out like a gorilla, his face a contorted mask of rage. His nose was bleeding. So that was what crunched. Kai's Affinity sparked, and the man's eyes were solid black. The snake marking writhed on his forehead.

Kai yelled, deep and guttural. He ran, putting the gurney between him and the man. It was time to take this man out of the picture. He swung the gurney around, pulled it towards himself, and pushed. The gurney rolled across the room and smacked into the man who doubled over with a grunt.

The man sucked air into his lungs. It seemed that Kai had succeeded in fuelling the man's anger. He threw the gurney aside, toppling it. Groaning came from near the wall. The others were waking up.

"Zap! Ruaan! Get up!"

The man launched himself at Kai, catching him around the waist. The man's weight toppled them both. They came down hard.

Kai winced as his shoulder joint clicked. Pain shot through his torso, and he fought back stars.

The man hauled him onto a gurney like a sack of potatoes and strapped him down before moving on to the others who were still too far gone to resist.

Through the stars, Kai watched the man re-tuck his shirt and haul up his pants. He sniffed and wiped the back of his hand across his nose.

"That's how you do it."

The man in a lab coat sighed. "Fine. You're the man. Let me get on with my job now, please."

"If they give you any trouble—"

"I know where to find you. It's all good. Now please…"

Clunky footsteps sounded on the tiles as the man left. He must weigh about the same as a baby elephant.

Lab Coat sauntered over to Kai and shone a light in each eye. "Neanderthal."

He looked familiar.

"Me or Muscles?"

Lab Coat grinned. "I guess time will tell. You put up a good fight."

The man's face was definitely familiar. "Do I know you?"

"Doubt it." He focussed on Kai's strapped arm, trailing his fingers down the blue lines of veins that criss-crossed the inside of Kai's wrist. He reached for a syringe from a silver tray next to the gurney and filled it from a small vial. With the loaded syringe in one hand and deep frown lines creasing his brow, he leaned on Kai's gurney.

"What is that?" Kai worked hard to keep his voice neutral.

"This would be better if you were still knocked out."

Kai knew one thing for sure, whatever was in that syringe should not go into his veins. His restraints were too tight for him to budge. Keep him talking. "Is it an improved version?"

Lab Coat stopped, tilting his head to the side with an eyebrow lifted with the exact measure of are-you-crazy that Bree used. "You're Bree's dad, aren't you?"

The syringe bounced off the edge of the gurney and tumbled through the air, spinning twice before hitting the tiles with an unsatisfying *clink*.

"I can see Elden in you too."

Lab Coats' lips were moving, but no sound came out.

Kai focussed on his mouth and understood.

Shut up.

17

Evazee stood next to Zulu and admired his handiwork. "If the high priest thing doesn't work out, you can go into construction. This looks good."

A quick smile cracked his face, followed by a frown.

"I'm sorry, that's not funny. It does look much better though."

Zulu had found a bunch of weeds growing nearby with leaves as tough as leather, but bendy like rubber. He'd used the leaves to lash all the walls together and create a makeshift hinge for the door. It swung open and closed with ease. He'd tested it all by leaning on the outside wall with his full weight.

Evazee's heart nearly stopped. She imagined the structure coming down on top of the old lady and Sam like a house of cards. But Zulu had leaned and pushed, and the structure had stood.

He'd also laid a new layer of leaves over her holey roof. He'd split the topside of each leaf from the underside, using the sticky sap to glue multiple layers of leaves together. The sap would gradually harden to a solid resin that would stop any leaks.

The old lady came out blinking like an owl. She nearly fell out the door as it swung back easily instead of needing a hard shove. Her eyes misted over as she saw what Zulu had done. "How can I thank you?"

"No, thank you." Zulu grinned.

Evazee patted his arm and shook her head. "There is a way you can thank us." She led the way back into the shack. Half shocked at her own boldness, she reached for the dark bottle on the shelf. "Please don't drink any more of this."

"But it's good. It does good." The old lady's face puckered up into creases of distress.

"No, no it's not. Can I show you?" She didn't wait for permission, and she had no idea if this was going to work or not, but she had to try something to stop this woman and her son from drinking serum.

She let herself out and tipped a few drops onto one of the plants that Zulu had harvested root leaves from. Nothing. The old woman came shuffling across the dirt and hunched over even further for a closer look.

"Well?"

"Let's just give it another minute. I don't know how quickly it will take effect." Evazee began to wonder if she should have poured out more. She was just considering it when the old lady's patience ran out.

She plucked the bottle from Evazee's hand and shuffled back towards her house muttering.

Sam stood staring at the tree hardly blinking. Evazee gave him a hug. "I'm sorry, Sam. We have to go."

Sam stubbornly refused to budge. He shook his head once and kept eyeballing the tree.

Evazee rubbed his head in farewell and motioned to Zulu. It was time to leave.

They collected the other two off the dusty street and started walking.

Evazee had no idea where to go or why. As they walked through the slums, Evazee saw signs of the serum. Empty bottles lying around, some people leaned on their broken walls, drinking from the bottles openly. They were all hooked on this stuff. What would it take to get them all free? This was impossible.

Zulu rubbed his hands on his shirt as they walked. Then he started rubbing them on each other, seeming more desperate as they went.

Bree clucked her tongue at him, "You're making me itchy just watching you. What are you doing?"

Zulu held out his hands towards her. "Leaf sap. Too sticky to wipe off, itchy now."

Evazee shut her eyes and stuck out her hands as if she were trying to navigate her way out of a giant maze. She scratched her chin. "I'm sure there's a river close by here. Let's see if we can find it."

Bree crossed her arms over her chest and tapped her foot faster than a foot should move. "It's probably not a good idea to ask the only one here who used to live in this neighbourhood. That person wouldn't have a clue where to find what you need." She coughed behind her hand and stared off into the distance.

"You know where to find water?" Evazee asked. Her cheeks were hot. She should have remembered that Bree used to live here.

"It sometimes moves around, but it should be quite close. I know because I used to avoid it."

~*~

Kai sat in the cell, studying the walls, the floor, the locked door all by the light that came from him. Lab Coat had untied him from the gurney and bullied him down the stairs and into this cell. He hadn't denied it though, and the panic in the man's eyes had spoken volumes.

So Kai had been shoved into this locked room and apparently forgotten. They could try and lock him in, but that didn't mean he'd be as meek and submissive as a lamb. There was no time for this nonsense. He ran his fingers along the floor, along the join where the floor met the wall. He shut his eyes and let his Affinity kick in.

The room glowed green, and he took a moment to let his eyes adjust.

A quiet click and the door slid open just enough for a man to slip through. It was a Lab Coat—Elden and Bree's dad.

Kai stayed on the floor, arms looped around his knees, torn between the desire to bash the man on the head and run, and stay put and perhaps have some of the puzzle unravelled.

The man seemed aware of the possibility of having his head bashed as he approached Kai with his hands up. "I'm here to talk, and I don't have much time. Hear me out."

Kai waved to a spot on the floor.

The man frowned but sat down anyway. "You can call me Dr S. I'll get straight to the point. Elden doesn't know that I'm alive."

"Neither does Bree."

Pain flashed across the doctor's face, but it was gone in a moment. "They can't know that I am." His watch beeped. He reset it and took eye drops out of his shirt pocket. Two drops in each eye then he tucked them back in his pocket and blinked a few times. With a sniff, he sneaked a sideways glance at Kai's face and sighed. "My death was staged to protect them. The work I'm doing here is of the utmost importance and because of that, I have some powerful enemies. It was the only way I could protect them."

A pit of anger lit in Kai's belly, a slow burn of rage fuelled by his helplessness to free Bree, to see her whole. This man was clueless.

"I'm sorry, but in your opinion, what do you do here that is so important?"

Lab Coat leaned back on the wall and his face lit up. "Serum development. We've just made a huge breakthrough. Huge. Up until now, the serum has worn off within hours. But I think we finally have a permutation that will be permanent. A single dose will alter the user on a DNA level that won't dissipate over time."

Kai's spit dried up. "And you think this is a good thing?"

Dr S. seemed taken aback. "Yes, of course. Obviously. How can you ask that?"

"Wait, back up a moment. To your knowledge, what does your serum do, exactly?"

"I can see that you're a serum user yourself. Do I honestly have to describe this for you?" He shrugged and carried on. "Our serum is designed to integrate all parts of a person. To firstly wake up the spirit, and then connect mind, body and spirit to function in unison. Can you imagine every person on the earth functioning at their highest capacity? The world would be a very different place."

The way the man's face glowed, Kai could tell he believed every word of the sewage coming out of his mouth. Someone had short-circuited his brain.

"Have you ever tried the serum you create? Injected it into your own veins?"

"Well, no. I'm not allowed. But my field agents have told me some incredible stories. I'm part of changing people's lives forever." He deflated, and a hint of pain twisted his forehead. "I know it must be hard for you to understand how I could leave my family."

"Lie to them." *Break their hearts. Mangle their insides. Betray them in every way.*

"You're right, of course. But surely you can see that this is bigger than me, bigger than their feelings. I wouldn't abandon my own flesh and blood for anything less than this. I'm part of recreating the world as we know it."

Affinity zipped through Kai's veins, quickening his heartbeat. When he looked up, the doctor's head lit up in a solid helmet of green light. Even his eyes lit up green as if he were a cat in the dark under torchlight. Someone had done a dirty on him. This would take some delicate handing.

"Doctor, I can see you believe in what you do. I don't know how to break this to you, but you've been lied to."

~*~

Bree pushed through between two bushes and waved her arm towards the sparkling expanse of water. "There you go. Not too far from where I remember it."

Zulu ran to the edge, knelt down, and plunged his hands into the water, sighing with relief.

"Are they feeling a bit less itchy now?" Evazee pushed past the bushes and stopped at the sight of the water. The sparkling ripples made her tummy flip. Not long ago, she would have been the first one in, but now? Who knew what would happen? She settled down against a tree trunk and watched Zulu's face.

He kept plunging his arms in, even though the stickiness would have washed off on the first rinse. His face lit up as he allowed the water to dribble through his fingers. He chuckled and dipped his head under the water. Then he sat up with a gasp and shook the water off his head.

Bree sat next to Evazee, frowning at Zulu. "He's enjoying this way too much, don't you think?"

"I know, right?"

Paintbrush stood next to them for a moment, then she took off at full speed and bomb-dropped into the water, splashing Zulu. He guffawed a deep bellow laugh and scooped a handful of water over her head. She shrieked with laughter.

"The plant. It died."

The voice came from behind and Evazee spun around, ready to jump up and fight.

Sam stared at her with wide eyes, and he clutched the serum bottle from his Gran's house to his chest. He stumbled forward on wooden legs, bewilderment all over his face. "The plant is dead." He held out the serum bottle pinched between two fingers. "Please. Take it." His foot snagged a root, and he tripped. The bottle flew out of his hand, uncapped in midair, and spun. Liquid poured out in a trailing arch and landed on Bree.

"Bree! Go wash it off, quick." Evazee leapt to her feet to help her friend.

"My eyes. It's in my eyes." Bree waved her arms around like a blind person swatting at bees.

"Wait, I'll help you." Evazee put an arm around Bree and they shuffled to the water together. As they got closer to the bank, Evazee's foot slipped on a slick rock. She landed with a thump, pulling Bree down with her.

Bree slipped from her grasp and slid unceremoniously on her bottom all the way into the river. She spluttered as she rinsed out her eyes.

Evazee sat on the bank, catching her breath, keeping an eye on Bree to make sure she was fine.

Without realizing it, Bree had switched to using both hands.

Zulu and Paintbrush had quieted down and settled in the shallows to watch Bree too.

Sam pushed back onto his haunches, and tears gathered along his lashes.

Bree rubbed her hair in the water, rinsing out serum. Every movement was smooth, and her hand worked normally. Healed, so effortlessly, so easily, she hadn't even realized it.

The dropped serum bottle lay sizzling on the rocks. It was the hiss that drew Evazee's attention. The last bit of serum ran out the bottle and down the rock freely, heading towards Zulu's hand.

"Zulu! Watch out!"

Zulu turned and instinctively scooped a double handful of water from the river and tipped it on the serum. It hissed and steamed, Evazee couldn't tell if the serum was burning up the water, or if the water was dissolving the serum.

Bree waded back to the bank and climbed out, plonking herself down next to Evazee.

Zulu and Paintbrush followed, all crowding around while Bree checked to make sure that no serum had missed the wash.

"Your hand..."

Bree stopped moving and sat as still as a deer.

"I think it's working again."

"It's not possible." Bree tucked it back on her lap the way she had been doing for months. She eyed it and shivered.

Evazee found a round stone and tossed it at her friend. "Incoming."

Bree ducked sideways but reached up with both hands. She caught the rock in her once-damaged hand. The skin was smooth and whole and the fingers closed around the stone with the same strength they'd had before her run-in with the darKounds.

She threw the stone at the river and got to her feet. "This place isn't safe. We should get going." She pushed off the dark brown dirt and made her way back to the path.

The others followed in awed silence.

Halfway to the path, the dust at Evazee's feet swirled in miniature sand tornadoes. The wind was picking up.

"This is weird. I don't remember there being wind the last time I was here."

Bree tucked her arms over her chest, hands in her armpits.

Evazee couldn't see her damaged hand to check if the change was still there. She also didn't feel free to reach out and take Bree's hand to check.

The wind picked up, gusting around them with intention.

"I don't like this. Can we leave, please?" Bree shuffled closer to Zulu, tucking herself in between him and Evazee.

The wind pumped faster now, whipping Evazee's long hair into a tangled mess and pushing her along the path faster than she'd intended walking. With a loud snap, the wind shifted direction and sucked them backwards.

Evazee grabbed Sam. "Fill that bottle with river water. Make sure your Gran drinks it every day. Go, now!"

The buffeting force was too strong to resist so the friends let it take them, struggling against the awkwardness of it all.

"This is not natural wind. Guys, hold hands. Quick."

They reached for each other as the wind kicked up a notch. Zulu grabbed Ziqi as the swirling began. The wind twirled around them like water down a plug hole, and their feet lifted off the ground.

"What is happening?" Bree yelled, shrill and high above the sound.

"Hold tight. Don't let go." Zulu sounded calm enough, but Evazee knew him well enough to know that he wasn't.

Faster now, the wind pumped, spinning them in midair.

They hung weightless, and then dropped like a bag of bricks off a roof. They hit the cold stone with an *oof*.

A single clear chime rang out and Evazee knew exactly what had happened.

Somehow, they had passed the test of the arch. The task set for them was complete and the arch had brought them back.

Back to a basement full of Zulu's people, angry and ready for trouble.

18

"I don't know why you're so suspicious of what I do here. Someone has messed with your head. When I've finalized and approved my serum, it will be produced, packaged into every possible form, and shipped out world-wide. The factories are ready to begin mass-production. They're all just waiting for me to give them the go-ahead." A sense of smug self-importance settled over the man.

Suddenly Kai understood. Back in the graveyard when they'd all been serum-ed back into the spiritual realm, they'd seen Dr S's death date set a few months away from now. Bree, Evazee, and Elden had walked through rooms full of stockpiled serum. This man felt untouchable, but the powers that be were already moving on without him or his consent. It was only a matter of time until he joined the ranks of the *expendables*.

"Where are my friends?"

"They are being prepped for injecting."

Kai's mind flipped. "Why not me? Why aren't I with them?" Being in the same room would give him a better chance of freeing them.

"Calm yourself. I was concerned about the fact that you're already a serum user. I don't know what the residue effect would be if we injected you now. I'm excited for your friends though."

"Doctor S, I don't know how to tell you this or make you believe me. You are living on borrowed time. There is a factory that has been producing your serum, apparently without your approval. I hate to tell you this, but once they don't need you any longer, they won't keep you around."

"You are just saying these things to throw me off." Hot spots of colour blotched his neck. "I thought I could speak sense to you, but I see how it stands."

"Dr S., please listen. I've been under the influence of your serum. It doesn't do what you think. That stuff is—"

Beep. Eye drops. Blinking.

"What are your eye drops for?"

The doctor seemed caught off guard. "I picked up some weird allergies working here. This stuff settles it. I got it from the other chemists here. When I run out, they give me more."

"And you don't find that slightly suspicious?"

"I don't know who has been spinning fairy tales in your head. You should write books with that imagination." The doctor grunted as he pushed himself to his knees, his body popped and creaked in the process of standing.

Kai took his moment. He shot to his feet, shoving the doctor against the wall. The man bounced off the wall with a loud crack. Then he gasped and fell back, clutching his shoulder. Kai didn't hang around to check on him. He bolted from the cell, slamming the door behind him.

Now what?

~*~

Evazee fell out of the archway and rolled to a stop

at the sandaled feet of one of the priests from Zulu's village. Seconds later, Bree and Paintbrush followed. Bree screamed and clutched her hand. The priest stared, his lined face frozen somewhere between fright and elation. Zulu's entrance was somewhat more graceful. He rolled out of the archway, gained his feet and swore.

He took one look around the room and whispered to Evazee, "We're going back. Quickly."

The priest found his voice and shouted words that Evazee couldn't understand. All through the basement, priests drew closer. Zulu's hand grabbed the back of her top and pulled. She managed to stay on her feet and ran up the cracked stone steps back to the archway.

Feeling like a grape between two molars, Evazee hesitated. But Zulu wasn't having any of it. He was back down the steps, hauling Paintbrush and Bree back towards the arch. The priests were closing in, chanting with their hands outstretched.

"Go! Go now!" Zulu's voice boomed through the room, shaking the stones of the archway.

Evazee grabbed Paintbrush by the wrists and ran across the threshold. Electric shock zapped through her and she bit back a scream. She tugged her small friend through with her. Like stepping off a cliff, they tumbled and fell. Just as Evazee thought her heart might stop, they hit the ground, landing in soft sand that threw them sideways.

Evazee watched the stars dance, slowly giving way to soft, warm light. This place was beautiful, though she didn't recognize it at all.

Bree sat up, looked around and fell back with a groan. "I know exactly where we are. I just got out of this place. Stone City." Her healed hand was once again a twisted claw, damaged and useless.

Evazee rolled to her side and craned her neck. "Did we all make it?"

Paintbrush sat in the dirt and nursed a bump to her head, blinking in the light as if she was in the middle of the weirdest dream.

Zulu sat up. Then he was on his feet, crouched and ready to punch or run. He checked the area, and his dark skin paled. "They followed us. Run!"

Evazee followed Zulu's gaze. Spread out across the dirt a few feet away were the priests from Zulu's village. They were all still sprawled out on their backs, groaning as they lay. It wouldn't take long for the disorientation from being transported by the testing arch to wear off.

"Bree! We need to hide. Where?"

Bree took a few seconds to orientate herself. "Temple. Follow me."

Evazee reached for Paintbrush's hand, but the girl took off at a speed fast enough to keep up with Bree. They ran without looking back.

The crowds picked up as they got closer to the temple. It was harder to run at full speed but easier to get lost in amongst the people.

Bree gasped for air. "I think we're in time for the next service. We can hide. Wait here." Bree slipped through the crowd and grabbed a fistful of garments off a pile outside the temple gate. She kept her eyes downcast as she crossed the walkway back to where they waited. She held out the beige shifts. "Quick, slip these on. We want to blend in."

Dressed like the other city dwellers, they funnelled in through the open doorways, hemmed in by a press of people all pushing to enter.

Zulu hunched over. With his back straight, he stood head and shoulders above everybody else in the room. An easy target to spot.

Evazee kept an eye on the other three, as much as she could without being obvious. It wouldn't be good to get separated. The thought of someone actively chasing them turned her belly upside down. What kind of nightmare was this?

The quad they led into was an open-air venue, with a fully equipped stage at the front. The air was balmy and breathless, everybody waiting for something to happen. Another quick scan of the area and it seemed they'd managed to get away from Zulu's people.

Paintbrush tugged on her arm. "Why're we here?"

"I want to know where everyone else is." Evazee crouched down, breathing hard.

Evazee turned to Bree, waving a hand at the room full of people. "What are they doing here?"

"It's a healing service thing." Bree shrugged dismissively.

A quiet sliver of hope popped in Evazee. Maybe this would mean permanent healing for Bree's hand. Maybe they'd been brought here to complete whatever the Healing Stream had started. It made sense. "I'm glad we're here."

Bree looked at her as if she'd swung in from the trees. "Are you nuts? We're not staying."

"But your arm..."

"Whatever trick the arch played last time, it's been reversed. I don't care, I'm used to it. *You* need to come to terms with the fact that in real life, not everything is fixable. Nothing comes with a happy ending and nobody is looking out for us. The sooner you make peace with that, the better off we'll all be." She waved her limp hand under Evazee's nose. "This? This is a good reminder for me of who I should trust and who I shouldn't."

Evazee was fascinated by the expectation on people's faces. It almost cancelled out the acid in Bree's tone. "You're just protecting yourself, Bree. I think we should stay."

Zulu straightened up for a moment, rubbing his lower back. The shift Bree had brought for him barely reached past his belly button and threatened to pop at the seams. The people around him stepped back, and Bree tugged on his arm.

"Get back down! What on earth are you thinking? We're supposed to be blending in."

Zulu looked like a strangely young grandpa, hunched over, sweating with the effort of blending.

A commotion started up at the back of the room. Shrieks of awe and adoration oozed from the crowd. A man had entered the quad.

Evazee squinted her eyes to see who it was, but there were too many people in the way. Could this be Jesus? Kai had met him here going by some strange name. Tom? Tam? Evazee's heart pounded in her chest. She would give anything to meet him in the flesh.

Bree hissed beneath her breath. "We've got to get out of here. This guy is bad news."

"You can't let your assumptions mess with your head forever. What if you're wrong?"

"Are you kidding me right now? I've seen this guy in action. He is not on the good-guy team, Evazee. You've been lied to."

Evazee focussed on the sounds of bliss erupting from parts of the room as the man passed through. How could that be bad? Heat flashed through her, and she could feel the blood tingling beneath her skin. She was probably as red as a chili, but she didn't care.

It started as a gentle caress on the edge of her consciousness. A feather-light brush on the outskirts of her mind. A probing thought, gentle but insistent.

I know you.

~*~

Kai walked as fast as he could manage without looking like he was bolting. He followed passages without knowing where he was going, but favoured any that led up and to the right. Wasn't that from a movie?

He shook his head to clear it and carried on walking, carefully schooling his face to a calm mask of I-belong-here-so-don't-talk-to-me. As the passage widened and became more spacious, the number of people increased. Kai kept his back and his face straight. He didn't know where to start looking for his friends.

A short girl with a shiny bob of black hair cut to accentuate a jawline that didn't need accentuating popped up in front of him. "You must be the guy sent over from design. I'm Kirsten from Marketing." She stuck out her hand and flashed a practiced smile that showed off deep dimples in each cheek. She didn't wait for his name or pedigree, but swung around and walked with such meaning that her hair swished.

Kai followed Kirsten from Marketing, trying not to walk in step with the clicking of her heels. She took him into a large open office space, filled with cubicles manned by busy people in smart clothes. The guys wore cotton shirts and chinos, and the girls swapped chinos for fitted skirts that ended just above the knee. Not quite Kai's jeans and T. *I belong here. I was sent over by design. Obviously.*

They stopped at a large, rectangular arrangement of desks. Each desk was set up with a slick PC screen and keyboard. There was only one spot open, and Kirsten led him straight to it, stopping just short of pulling out the chair for him. She waved him into it and jiggled the mouse to bring the screen to life.

"This is the one that's giving trouble. I don't know who signed off on this, but I'm not sure they should still be employed." She scrolled and zoomed in on a product label for something that Kai knew well. He used it on his guitar strings to stop corrosion. The label now bore a star with the words 'new and improved' diagonally across the middle.

"I don't see the problem. This is a good product. I didn't realize it was produced all the way out here in the desert."

Kirsten from Marketing frowned and tapped on the screen with a long, sharp fingernail painted deep maroon. "There, that word."

Kai leaned close, struggling to read the small writing. "FretFree, tampered guitar string liquid."

"Tampered. Not tempered. Those two words mean very different things." Kirsten from Marketing had a suitable tone of horror in her words.

"And you couldn't just fix this yourself? It's literally re-typing a word."

Her hand was on her hip, fingers drumming dangerously. "It's a design fault. Design must fix it." Her Naviband beeped, and she tutted in frustration.

"Get it done. I'll be back."

Kai double-clicked and retyped the word, saved the file, and looked around for whip-cracking Kirsten. He could see her through the door, walking away from the office. He opened up file manager, and the screen filled with folders. Scanning the list was like scanning a grocery store's stock list. Food items, deodorants, dishwashing liquid...the list went on and on. Furniture polish, bubble bath. All of it was being reproduced laced with dark Affinity serum.

Blood drained from Kai's fingers. It was one thing to avoid injections and the odd tampered air freshener, but this?

There was no way to stop this flood.

19

Evazee's insides slipped like sludge on a potter's wheel. The oily residue of the voice in her head convinced her that this was not Jesus, but Shasta. A wave of thick nausea swept through her.

Paintbrush tugged on Evazee's hand. "I feel sick." Her lips clenched in a tight line.

Evazee gave her hand a sympathetic squeeze and pulled Zulu close. "We need to get out of here."

Zulu inched up slightly before folding himself down again. "The gate where we came in is closed."

Bree frowned at Paintbrush who'd turned whiter than a human should. "That gate is probably locked already." The pull on Evazee's insides grew. She shook her head to clear it and focussed on Paintbrush. The girl was in distress, squirming the way Evazee would before throwing up in a crowd. "Is there a restroom here?"

Bree tilted her head. "This way."

They eased their way through the mass of bodies, slowly working their way to a door on the side. Evazee had Paintbrush by one hand and used the other hand to part a way through the crush of people. Nobody moved. Paintbrush had her free hand over her mouth, and her shoulders heaved as she walked.

"Let us through, please. She's going to be sick."

Evazee kept her voice low. She didn't need the attention of the whole gathering, just the souls who stood between them and the bathroom.

Nobody paid her any attention, they all stared towards the back of the room with a vacant rapture on their faces. This wasn't working.

She cleared her throat. "Vomit. This girl needs to vomit." The word vomit worked better than if Evazee carried a live rattlesnake.

The crowd opened up before her and ushered them through without any trouble. As they passed, the pathway closed up behind them like the Red Sea after Moses.

The bathroom glowed with light from the rock walls. Paintbrush plonked herself down on the stone floor, leaned back on the wall with her eyes closed and her hands across her belly.

Bree pushed through the swing door seconds later and handed Evazee a bottle.

"Give her some water. She's probably dehydrated."

Evazee unscrewed the lid and passed the bottle to Paintbrush. She took it from Evazee and pushed herself upright. As she tilted the bottle to her lips, the gold logo on the label caught Evazee's eye. She grabbed it out of the small girl's hands.

"Wait a moment. This logo..." She twisted towards the glowing stone for a better look. Faint gold, printed tiny, it would be easy to see it as a decorative mark, but looking close it became clear. Four snakes tied at the tail, writhing outwards. The mark worn on the foreheads of those who belonged to Shasta.

~*~

Kirsten from Marketing swept back into the office with two spots of colour riding high on her cheeks, and her hands stretched out in front of her as if they'd done something to offend her. "I don't see why I'm always the one to do the dirty work. Honestly." She held out her hands towards Kai. "Take off my rings and my Naviband. I have to go wash my hands. Come on, quick-quick."

Kai shuffled over and slipped her rings off, fumbled with the unfamiliar clasp of her Naviband and watched her scuttle off on heels that were high enough to make it look as if she was on the verge of face-planting. The Naviband sat on his palm as light as a feather.

The moment her footsteps were beyond his earshot, Kai bolted in the other direction. He walked as fast as he could without looking suspicious, though everyone in this section hurried about looking worried, so he fitted right in.

He found a restroom, locked himself into a cubicle, and pressed the side of the Naviband, hoping that it wasn't somehow linked and coded to Kirsten the way Elden's had been. The screen woke up and options cycled across it. He clicked on *find* and an empty search field opened up. No letters appeared for him to type, and he frowned. How would he make this work? It nearly slipped through his fingers, but he caught it and put it on. Dropping and shattering it would not help.

If he was Zap, what would he do? They'd been friends for as long as Kai could remember, and over the years, Zap had always come up with some sideways plan that seemed to solve whatever issue they faced.

The Naviband beeped but nothing appeared on

the screen. Odd. Zap would love this enigma of a device. As Zap crossed his mind, the strongest compulsion to get up and move washed through Kai. The Naviband seemed to pulse in time to the urge in his mind.

He got up and walked through the doorway. An overwhelming urge to take the passage to the left beat inside his chest. He followed. The compulsion inside changed as he moved. Each time he yielded to it, the next direction came.

Kai found himself alone in a long passage, and he picked up the pace to a jog. Following the promptings took him down a lift and through a warren of turns and passages. It ended with a dull buzz from the Naviband.

Restricted area, not for cleared for access. He hunted around and found a security guard asleep at his station. Could it be this easy?

~*~

"What are you doing? That's perfectly good water! Why are you pouring it down the drain?" Bree had her good hand on her hip, and the other hung limp again.

Evazee held the bottle under her nose and pointed at the symbol. "Don't you recognise this?"

"It's a fountain. What's wrong with that?"

Evazee squinted at it again, turning it towards the light, this way and that. "How can you not see snakes?"

Bree frowned at her as if she was speaking Spanish. "Maybe you need glasses."

Paintbrush held out a hand to see. "Snakes." A shudder of deep revulsion ran through her. "I don't want that."

"Well, fountains or snakes, that symbol is on every product used in the kitchen."

"But that's terrible. I wouldn't trust anything with that image on."

Bree shrugged. "You and a whole bunch of radicals that live outside the city. They too have your issues."

Evazee's heart popped in her chest. It beat so fast, the noise of it filled her head. She knew this feeling. This was the Holy Spirit. "Take me to them."

~*~

The security guard's Naviband took Kai straight to where Zap and Ruaan were being held, down a passage full of tiny cubicles and holding cells. The Naviband unlocked the cells too.

They came out of the darkness, blinking wildly.

"How did you get us out? I thought you'd be locked up too." Zap's pupils were twice as big as usual.

Kai frowned and waved a hand over Zap's face. "Did they inject you yet?"

"I dunno. I can't remember much." Zap rubbed his knuckles into his temples.

Kai grabbed his arm and studied it for fresh puncture holes. The skin seemed intact.

Ruaan groaned and doubled over. "They haven't fed us either."

"OK, come you two. We have to get back home. I think this navi-thing will get us out of here."

20

A sudden sliver of light from the floor broke through the darkness. A trapdoor. They'd been following Bree blindly through underground passages, strangely dark in this city of light.

Zulu slipped in next to Bree and took the ring from her, hoisting the trapdoor higher.

"Come guys, this way. Bree dropped to the floor and wiggled through the gap. Evazee paled at the thought of where they were going. For whatever reason, they were still stuck in the testing arch, and they'd stay that way until they stumbled on the test and passed it. That thought resolved it all for her, and she dropped to her knees and slid on her rear towards the opening. Bree grabbed her legs and pulled her through, guiding her feet safely to solid ground. In a short time, the others had followed and the trapdoor had been lowered.

The room they found themselves in was small and dusty. Evazee sneezed and scrubbed at her nose with the back of her hand. "How do you know about this place?"

"Let's just say I don't need much sleep, and the after-curfew patrols seldom venture below." Bree's eyes sparkled; a creature back in her natural habitat. "No time to waste. We've got to put some distance between us and..." she pointed up and in the vague direction of everything outside of the trapdoor.

They squeezed through a doorway that led out of the tiny room into a narrow passage lit by the stones in the floor.

"This way. Come on. Don't be slow."

They followed the tiny passage as it curved and twisted, leading them down. Evazee guessed that they were heading deeper underground. "Where are you taking us?"

Bree didn't answer other than to hold a finger to her lips. They trudged on in silence. The roof of the tunnel angled down, making it impossible to walk upright. Evazee's lower back tweaked in a spasm that she couldn't stretch out without bumping her head. She couldn't imagine how Zulu felt. Sharp pain shot through her spine. The air grew stuffy. Trapped. She wanted to ask how much longer, but she'd get no answer. *Just breathe. In, out. Repeat.*

They rounded a bend and the stench of rotting fish slammed into her, an almost solid wall of odour. Evazee choked and blocked her nose. Just as she thought her heart might pack up, the passage ended. The opening at the end was blocked off with a metal grate. Wind blew in from outside, carrying the smell in with it. By the look of it, the grate had been around for a long time, rusted and buckled. If that thing didn't open...

Bree slammed her fist into the metal three times in quick succession, causing a mini rust-shower. A scurry of activity on the other side made Evazee's heart pound. Were these people like the shack-dwellers?

The grate moved to the side, and they tumbled out the end of the tunnel. It was a long drop from the mouth of the passage to the rocky ground below.

Evazee landed with a bump and toppled sideways. Her feet stung from the impact. She shook them out and shivered, rolling herself upright and back onto her feet. Grey gloom pressed in around her and over it all, the choking stench. This was nothing like the soft light of the city they'd just come from.

A company waited for them, not dressed in the standard shift that all the city dwellers wore, but remnants of regular clothes, dirty and old. They stood shoulder to shoulder, arms folded, casual but tightly wound. Evazee hardly dared breathe for fear of setting them off. Behind them stretched the cause of the choking smell. A rubbish dump that went on as far as Evazee could see.

Bree stood silent with her hands hooked behind her back, feet spread—a warrior's rest stance. She'd stripped off the city shift as she left the tunnel and looked every inch a fighter in leather pants and a tank top.

The guy in the middle eyed the newcomers up and down. He carried himself with a rugged confidence that singled him out as the leader of this bunch. "Why're you here?"

Bree shifted on her feet. "They won't use the marked products."

One of the others pointed to Evazee. "That one's marked. She shouldn't be here."

Evazee's neck flushed hot, and she fought to stop her hand going to her neck. It was easy to forget that she'd been branded like some show cow. She would do anything to get rid of that cursed mark. Shame and anger sparked through her. Who was he to assume that the mark had anything to do with where her loyalty lay? Her chin raised and she stared at him, half wishing he would say something else for which she could take him down.

Evazee stepped forward to defend herself. The leader turned towards her, and she did a double-take. Something flashed silvery on his forehead. Drawn by curiosity that nullified any fear or good manners, she stepped closer. This man was marked. Not with the twisted snakes of Shasta's folk, but with the same type of imprint that she mourned the loss of.

A slow smile tugged at her mouth. Before she could say anything, a wind from behind picked up. A slow spin that sped up and tugged them off their feet. They were being taken back through the testing arch.

Back to Zulu's people.

~*~

Zap pulled the OS van into its parking spot in the underground garage area. In spite of being hungry, Ruaan had whistled and hummed to himself all the way home from the Crux. Zap threw him an annoyed glance before turning back to Kai. "I dunno, man. That all seemed too easy. For such a hi-tech place with all the security bells and whistles, don't you think we would have been stopped along the way?"

Kai shrugged. "Sometimes these things can get too organised for their own good. You remember that time we were sent to detention, but nobody showed up because each teacher thought the other was supposed to be doing it? Kinda like that." He slapped the steering wheel and spun around to Ruaan. "Why are you so happy? What's up with that?"

Ruaan grinned at him and patted the bump under his T-shirt. He slid out of the van and shut the door with his foot.

If Zap had to frown any harder, his face would crack. "That detention was unfair anyway. I wasn't supposed to be involved in all that." He thumbed towards Ruaan. "Do you think getting his amulet back has turned him into Mr. Sunshine?" He shut and locked his door.

Kai pocketed the keys. "It's possible, but the amulet Runt had nearly wrecked her." The up arrow on the lift button glowed orange in the dim light. Kai chose the floor they wanted and shut the lift door.

"As always, you're missing the point entirely. All I'm saying—"

Ruaan stopped whistling, long enough to say, "The amulet she had wasn't hers. Obviously, it would be bad for her." He patted his chest once more. "This one? It's all mine. I've never felt this content." He picked up the tune he'd been whistling mid-phrase.

The lift bumped to a stop, and the doors slid apart. Ruaan's whistling stopped, and he tapped them both on the shoulder. "Something doesn't feel right."

Kai felt it then too, a thick heaviness in the air that pressed on his chest and made him feel like he was choking. "Come on, let's go see."

The place seemed deserted. They searched every level and found nobody. "The only place we haven't checked is the basement. Maybe they left a clue."

The trapdoor swung back easily, and they climbed down the stairs and smack into the middle of a group of waiting people who looked a lot like Zulu.

21

Kai knelt on the floor of Torn's office with his hands tied behind his back. His friends were tied up in the same way on either side of him.

Zulu knelt along the wall with them, but his hands were unbound.

An older version of Zulu paced the floor in front of them, swinging a carved ebony stick as he walked. His bald head gleamed in the pale lamplight. Glowing purple dots were painted along the crease of his frown lines and dipped to trace a circle around each ear.

He rumbled as he walked, a deep thrumming from his chest cavity that unnerved Kai much like nails on a chalkboard. The noise seeped into his skull and made it vibrate. The man stopped in front of Kai and slammed the stick down hard enough for the vibrations to shiver through Kai's legs.

"Where are my people?" he asked softly, but anger simmered close below the surface.

"I could ask you the same thing." Kai's back stiffened in defiance.

A strangled noise came from Zulu, but Kai was in no mood for tip-toeing around the whims of a dictator. He knew where the amulets were, keys to freedom for all the OS kids. They were so close to being completely free. To come back to find them all missing and then being bullied by this despot was too much.

Zulu coughed. "Will you see me?"

"I see you." The whites of the man's eyes were bloodshot and tinged purple.

"If we find the boys, will you return the others?"

Zulu's dad pointed a bony finger at Kai, though he spoke to Zulu. "Find the boys and come home, Zulumange. The curse on our village is from you. The wells are dry. You've been unfaithful."

"The wells were dry before I left home. You can't blame that on me."

The old man slammed his staff into the ground. "Your body was home, but your spirit was wandering. That brought the curse."

Zulu fell silent. The violent clash of emotions were clear in the tight clench of his jaw.

The old one stopped pacing in front of Kai. "This one, he leads here. Yes?"

A faint sheen of sweat broke out on Zulu's forehead. "Yebo."

"Let me think." He took his cohorts just outside the office where they spoke in low, rumbling voices.

Kai didn't need a gift of foresight to know where this was headed. He hadn't had a chance to examine Evazee's amulet, but if Ruaan's could make such a difference, then Evazee's might too. He cleared his throat and motioned to Ruaan to come closer. "Take this. Keep it safe until you can give it to Evazee." He tried to get to his pocket and failed.

Ruaan shuffled closer on his knees, angled himself sideways to reach in, and drew out Evazee's amulet. He'd just slipped it into his back pocket when the priests trooped back into the office in a straight line of serious faces.

Zulu's dad came in last. "We keep him as surety."

His bony finger flicked sideways and the priests moved in on Kai.

In seconds, Kai found himself with his nose on the floor, wondering what had happened. The rope around his wrists bit into his skin, but the pain sharpened his hearing. It was hard to protest from your belly on the floor.

A boot smacked into his ribs.

"Onto your feet, skinny one."

Fight or comply? Kai rolled over slowly, using the time to weigh his options. He rolled onto his knees, wobbling as he stepped up onto his feet with his hands tied behind his back.

Ten priests stood in the room, the harsh angles of their dark faces gleaming in the gloom. Faint purple rimmed their eyes.

Kai kept his eyes on priests, but spoke to Zap and Ruaan, "This is wasting time. What should we do?"

A sharp smack to the back of the head sent pain through his skull and his knees went limp. He was slung over a broad shoulder and carried like a rag doll, bouncing helplessly on the back of a priest.

~*~

Cold from the floor seeped into Evazee as she sat squished between Paintbrush and the wall. Bree sat opposite with her legs tucked tight against her chest and her head down. The room was small and as more groups arrived back from the arch, they were thrown into this same room and locked in. Evazee didn't think they would be able to fit in too many more. Her heart sank as the door opened.

Ruaan came in first, his hair more messed up than usual.

Zap followed soon after, his face grim.

"Over here." She waved them over, hoping for good news.

The guys picked their way between all the bodies on the floor and made space to sit down.

Evazee waved towards the room full of prisoners. "I'm assuming that whatever you guys went to go get to free these kids didn't work out so well."

Zap grinned, a savouring-the-moment kind of grin. "Mostly. But we do have..."

Ruaan dug in his pocket and drew out Evazee's amulet. It swung from his fingers as if he was trying to hypnotize her.

Zap gaped like a goldfish. "Were you born rude, or is it a skill you've been perfecting your whole life?"

"I'll assume that question is rhetorical." Ruaan bounced the amulet in the palm of his hand. "Do you want this?"

Evazee glanced around the room. They had caught the attention of everyone in the room. Not a difficult thing to do with nothing else happening. She dropped her voice low, leaning close to the boys. "I guess so."

Zap's face scrunched up. "Your enthusiasm is overwhelming."

"I'm sorry. Runt's pendant caused such trouble." The back of her neck itched as she thought of the events that lead to her being branded. It all started with an amulet.

Ruaan hauled his out from under his t-shirt. "If you ask me, the problem with Runt is that she meddled with a necklace that wasn't her own. That's a stupid thing to do, you know?" He bounced his on his flat palm. "This one is mine. I can feel it with every cell in my body. So far there've been no negative effects. In fact, I've never felt better."

Evazee reached for her amulet and slipped it over her head.

A guy sitting close to them with close-cropped black hair sat up straight from a deep slouch. "Hey! I also want one. Surely we've all got one. Where did you find yours?"

Ruaan and Zap exchanged a worried look. Zap answered, slowly, mulling over every word. "The amulets are being kept in a vault deep in enemy territory. You can only get your own out. Kai nearly lost his hand getting to this one."

Ruaan rubbed his chin. "Maybe we need an old-fashioned field trip."

"And maybe you need your head read."

~*~

Kai sat shivering in the sludge at the bottom of a well so deep, the sky was a tiny blue circle above that could have been the moon. Zulu's dad had been right. This well hadn't seen water for a long time. He considered climbing out with his legs propped up on one side and his hands on the other, but the thought of breaking a few bones when his muscles failed was a little off-putting.

Impatience and frustration burned through his veins. He'd fought on his captor's shoulder, but all he had to show for it was a swollen egg on the back of his head that had knocked him out for the entire trip. He'd woken up in this hole in the dark and yelled until his throat burned, but nobody came. Hours—*days?*—later, the sun turned the sky a blushing pink, then orange, settling into the moody blue that hovered over him now.

Being able to see felt better for a little while, but then it all seemed much worse as he was fully aware of how deeply buried he was.

The atmosphere was heavy, yet his Affinity was off the charts. Every second blink brought a wash of green over everything that surrounded him. Was it even possible for a place to be this broken?

Right now, he should be back at the OS, dishing out amulets and watching chains fall off. Instead he was stuck down here, more useless than pond scum. He slammed his foot into the well bricks in frustration. Instead of a solid *thunk*, the sound bounced around inside the well wall as if it were hollow.

Kai got onto his knees and pressed each stone carefully. Running his fingers along the grooves, he felt for anything that would give way. It didn't feel like the spiritual realm, but he'd long ago stopped expecting anything to be what it seemed.

He'd been trapped in rocks before, and he'd sung his way out. The rock had exploded, which would be disastrous in this situation. He would end up buried. Kai rubbed his temples. Things were so much simpler when he was little. See the green, follow his gut, and sorted. It was all more complicated now.

Or was it?

He shoved aside the frustration and panic of being stuck. Took a deep breath and thought of Tau. Jesus. Tau melted through rocks with his fingers in the spiritual realm. But this was normal life. Rocks don't melt unless there's lava-inducing heat involved.

Kai placed his fingertips on the stone in front of him and leaned in close with his ear against the cold stone. He hummed, a middle-pitched vibration from deep in his lungs. He raised the level, going higher, but nothing happened. He drew a deep breath and dropped the hum low, and his chest vibrated against the smooth surface. A vibration rippled through the side of the well, a mere dragonfly breath on a lake. Was it real? Or imagination?

Another deep breath, and Kai shut his eyes, allowing the sound to come out. The rocks trembled violently, and Kai stopped, fearing a cave-in that would bury him alive. All around him, bright green cracks showed around each stone. He touched one and it shot open, not just a rock, but a drawer.

Hardly daring to breathe, Kai peered in. The inside of the rock drawer was a midnight-sky velvety-shade of black. An amulet lay tucked inside the rock drawer. Kai peered in at it as if it were a live snake. There were markings on the amulet, but they didn't mean anything to Kai.

He moved over to try another one. This one popped open within seconds, another amulet tucked away inside. This was not an ordinary well, this well was a cupboard. A safe. A vault much like what they'd found at The Crux. Without warning, the first rock drawer he'd opened slid shut. Within a minute, the second one did too. They seemed to be on a timer.

His insides crawled at what each of these harmless-looking amulets represented. He opened a drawer again, and a sideways thought hit him. That drawer was just big enough for him to step on. He hooked his foot up and lifted off the ground. The drawer carried his weight. This was promising.

Slamming his hands against the rocks, he buzzed open a row of drawers, each higher than the last. If he timed this right, he might just be able to make it out. If not, he might fall to his death. By the look of it, they were leaving him in this hole anyway, so what did he have to lose?

Kai rolled his shoulders, clicked his neck to the side and hit the wall. Five steps, working clockwise around the well, each higher than the last. He climbed up, cautiously at first, but soon feeling more confident, hitting more drawers open as he went.

He kept his focus down, swinging between the drawer beneath his feet and the next drawer in. About two metres up, the amulet in the drawer caught his eye. The mark on the front matched the scar on Zulu's face. All of them glowed green, broken—but this one pulsed and shone. He hesitated for a split second before dipping down, grabbing it, and shoving it in his pocket.

The wait was a split second too long, and the drawer slid shut, pushing his foot off. Kai scrambled for the open drawer above, but he missed, slipped and fell, crashing to the floor of the well, landing on his knees in the ooze with enough force to topple him sideways. His head hit the side, and he landed with a smack that knocked his wind out.

~*~

The door opened. It was a priest—the one built like a warrior. He sauntered through the room, studying each person up and down before moving on. When he got to Evazee, he stopped.

"You. Come." He didn't wait for her to comply but just leaned down and lifted her by an arm. His fingers were cold steel on her muscles, numbing them. There'd be no quick pull away from this guy. She caught Zap's eye and shook her head. She could see his mind working overtime in his gaze. Now didn't seem like a good time to pick a fight.

His face dropped and took on a resigned look that she'd seen sometimes when he lost an argument. He must have eavesdropped on her thoughts, and he didn't seem to like what he'd heard.

A second priest came in. The warrior motioned towards Runt, Paintbrush, and Peta, calling them out with a hooked finger. They came out willingly, no doubt to keep their friends safe. Well trained by this harsh environment.

The two priests marched them all down to the basement where the other priests waited in a semi-circle around the testing arch. A low, rumbling hum came from their chests that made the walls quiver.

The Warrior forced the three to their knees and half the other priests left their arch-guarding duty to surround those on floor.

The other priest pointed at Evazee. "You. Go fetch boys. Come back. Otherwise..." He motioned to the younger ones and ran a thumb across the base of his throat.

Evazee knew exactly what he meant.

The thought of stepping into that arch again, only alone this time, was enough to make Evazee break out in a cold sweat. But it was that, or the little ones would suffer. She stepped towards the arch, her legs quivering like jelly.

The priests gave her no time to think or hesitate.

A firm foot in the small of her back persuaded her it was time. She toppled through the opening and fell for what felt like forever.

When she finally landed, it was dark and soggy. She came down with a splash of cold water that instantly soaked her jeans up to mid-thigh. Thick darkness pressed in, lit purple in the distance by dotted, glowing splodges too far to be identifiable, but Evazee knew exactly where she was.

She'd stepped out of the arch straight into the marshes of the village of Benan. Zulu's own village. The testing arch was so far beyond broken, Evazee nearly laughed, but then she thought of the sand worm that had tried to eat her the last time and she wanted to cry.

22

Kai lay on his back in the mud watching the stars dance across his vision. Breathing hurt. Getting out of this hole was not impossible, but the pain in his shoulder and ribs made him nervous to try again. If he'd been higher when he fell, he'd be a broken bag of bones right now.

Tau—Jesus, if Evazee was right—He could help. But for the fact that he was more silent now than before Kai had met him face-to-face. He wouldn't show up and he probably wasn't listening, but Kai spoke to him anyway. "Do you want to give me some clues here, please? That serum distribution isn't waiting for me to get out of here."

Kai groaned as he lay there in the sludge, cold slowly knotting his back. He felt the bulge in his pocket. The injection full of Affinity serum. His belly twisted at the thought, but it was an option.

~*~

Evazee sloshed along, stepping slow then fast, hoping to keep her movement irregular enough to avoid waking the worms. But the water was cold and it cramped her muscles. It lapped at her armpits, splashing her face if she moved too fast. In the distance, she saw a rough, wooden platform. The stilt houses must be close. Getting out of this water couldn't happen soon enough. It might be close enough to make a dash for. Steeling herself, she waded fast, focusing on reaching her goal.

Bubbles rose from the sand beneath her feet. Evazee slowed slightly to see if the bubbles stopped, but they increased until it felt like a a pot of boiling water around her. High pitched shrieking started up from behind. The worms.

Throwing off caution, Evazee ran. The thigh-high water slowed her and her frozen muscles didn't want to co-operate.

Gurgling, the water sucked her backwards, a tide going out too strong to resist. It dragged Evazee along, pulled her off her feet. Icy cold stole her breath and she fought to keep her head above the surface. She tumbled sideways and screamed underwater. The bubbles rose as a cavernous mouth opened up over her. She was being sucked into a sandworm. Panic blistered through her veins and she scrambled frantically. This was a big one. Its mouth closed over her, the churning water stilled and she floated in the eerie blackness of a cave.

Her mind darted wildly. This couldn't be happening. A deep wave, a convulsion, started at one end of the worm, working its way to the front. A tidal wave of swamp water carried Evazee on its crest. Dim light flooded over her as the worm reared up, it's skin translucent. She fell on the backbone of a waterfall from the thing's foul gut, only to ride the wave deeper into its belly once more. Over and over, each time it bucked and reared, Evazee was thrown forward and back. A scream fought its way out, and she clamped her jaw hard to keep it in.

~*~

Icy sludge slipped through Kai's veins like venom. Shouldn't have done this. But it was too late. Short of bleeding out, there was no way to remove serum from one's veins. This was his rodeo bull to ride now, and he just hoped he'd be alive by the end of it.

His eyelids weighed a baby elephant each, but he forced them open and wished he hadn't. The walls of the well had turned see-through, and he could see water beyond the glass, though it was tinged luminous purple. He rubbed his fingers along the wall, feeling the shape of stones that had been there seconds before. This wasn't glass, but rather something like tough old jelly. Not quite slimy, but close enough to make his belly heave.

The ground below his feet was visible through the murky water, shifting with the odd tides in the river water. A bubble popped through the sand and scurried to the surface, quickly rising beyond where Kai could see. The blue sky overhead was now greasy green, turgid and brooding.

Another bubble popped out of the sand below his feet and face-planted on the bottom of the tube. It scurried to the side and slipped out to rise to freedom. More bubbles. There were so many, Kai's head spun. He sat down quick before he fell over. The water churned all around and his heart pounded.

Water droplets on his skin. Was it raining? A sudden torrent drenched him and he shot to his feet in shock at the cold. Something solid smashed down on top of him and pain spasmed through his back.

Whatever it was, it had arms and legs and was screaming loud enough to curdle his blood.

~*~

A ring of teeth gnashed further down the worm's throat, slicing inwards with the sound of a thousand swords. The teeth moved as the worm did, in and out as the body constricted and stretched.

Evazee grabbed for a handhold, but the inside of the thing's mouth was a smooth, slippery wall. The worm constricted, and the teeth pulled close together, blocking off the throat. It raised up and bucked, depositing Evazee onto the meshed teeth.

Her mind spun. This could not be happening. She imagined getting to Heaven. *Welcome! How did you die? Well, I was eaten by a giant freaky worm. And you?*

The worm bucked hard. A torrent of swampy water gushed from the worm's belly with a force that toppled Evazee head over heels. Fresh air washed over her and she fell. Panic flashed through her, and she grabbed for something—*anything*—to hold onto. But her fingers closed on nothing but wet air. She fell.

A scream built in her belly, and she came down hard, slamming into something solid that buckled at the impact. A torrential dump of water crashed down, and Evazee gasped for breath.

Whatever she'd landed on pushed her off, and she rolled on the floor, coming to a stop against a wall made of jelly. She watched the worm move away. Then she breathed.

"Evazee, is that really you?"

She pushed back her soggy hair, and there was Kai, as drenched as she was, his eyes wide with a touch of panic. No, there was something more. Something dark.

"What is that thing? It's hideous."

Evazee did a quick body check. Everything hurt, nothing seemed broken. "That blasted worm nearly ate me." All at once, she wanted to scream, punch something, and sob her heart out. They were at the bottom of a deep jelly tube with see-through walls, somewhere in the swamps of Benan.

"Hey, come here." Kai crawled over to her and pulled her to his chest. It was an awkward angle, and her arm poked him in the ribs, but she needed arms after slimy worm insides. Kai seemed to be at a loss for words, and she didn't blame him. They were both shivering from cold after their unintentional shower.

Kai pushed her away, holding onto her arms as if she might run away if he didn't. "How did you get here? Why? And that worm?"

"Testing arch. The priests sent me to look for their boys. Kai, we have to get back. They are going to..." She couldn't say it. "They've got Runt, Peta, Paintbrush...the little ones who are too small to fight back." Panic knotted her throat. Breathing was hard.

"I've been trying to get out, haven't quite nailed it just yet. What is that worm-thing? Do you think it's coming back?"

Evazee shivered and crossed her arms. "Mutated from living in poisonous, mushroom infused water. Zulu told me. My best guess is that it's dumped us here to rot. A tastier snack than fresh, I suppose. How do we get out before it comes back?"

"Well, that's a tricky thing. There is a way, but it probably means falling to our deaths."

"What are you talking about?"

"Look. Let me show you." Kai kicked three drawers, and they popped open, quivering. "One can climb out on those, but they go so high, a fall would break bones."

Evazee prodded the squooshy drawer with a

reluctant finger. It wobbled at her touch. "Other than looking too bendy, I don't see what the problem is." The drawers snapped shut with a *shlurp*. "Oh, I see."

"There's something else too. Each drawer holds an amulet like Runt's. I feel like we should take them out. Look here." He fiddled in his pocket and pulled out a charm. "I think this might be Zulu's."

Evazee took the heavy object from Kai and turned it over, feeling the jagged groove that slashed through the surface. "This is his scar. No doubt."

"The only problem is, taking them out could literally kill us." Kai leaned back on the jelly wall, scratching his chin.

"Not if we work together and time it right."

"Aaah, Zee. Ever the optimist. We would die. Honestly. Even with this jelly goo, a fall from that high would do bad things."

Evazee felt warmth from her amulet against her skin. "Kai, we have to do this. I'm pretty sure these amulets belong to Zulu's boys. Imagine being able to hand them their freedom? We could take away the hold that the priests have over them. It's all right here at our fingertips."

"Or we could die trying. That would be fun too." Sarcasm laced his words like arsenic.

Evazee frowned at Kai. He didn't sound normal at all. "Listen, Boy, when did you get so sour?" She reached over and pulled his eyelid up. There was a greenish tinge to the whites of his eyes. "What did you do?"

He pulled away from her hand. "Zee, this whole thing is worse than you could ever imagine. I've seen it with my own eyes. They are lacing everything with dark Affinity serum. Everything. Even toilet paper. We don't stand a chance. There is no way to stop this."

"So I'm assuming you picked up green eyeballs from seeing all this toxic stuff."

"It gets worse. This latest batch of serum? It doesn't wear off. It's designed to be permanent. Once it's in you, that's it. Forever."

Evazee heard Kai, but his words wouldn't settle in her head. "I don't know about that. Surely there must be a way? Anyway. What is going on with your eyes?"

He slipped his hand into his pocket. Evazee could see him fiddling with something. What was he about to show her? But he kept his hand tucked away and shrugged. "Trick of the light, I suppose. I'm glad you're here."

23

Evazee backed down, but Kai could see her staring at him when she thought he wasn't looking. None of those sneaky looks escaped Kai, but he pretended to be oblivious. The empty syringe in his hand became a silent accuser; his jury, judge, and executioner.

They'd argued back and forth about waiting or trying to get out. In the end, a worm swimming past had decided it for them. Who knew when their particular worm would be back for his snack? There was no point hanging around to find out.

They'd practiced a drill on the lower drawers. Evazee went first, tapping drawers open with her feet. Kai followed behind hauling out amulets and climbing the drawers as he went. After some fumbling, it all seemed to work. All they had to do now was psych themselves up to keep going all the way up and out.

"Are you ready for this?" Kai couldn't read Evazee's face. She seemed to hover between anger and determination.

"Are *you* ready?"

"I guess we'll never know until we try." He waved her towards the wall and she stepped up and got moving. Kick, climb, kick, climb.

Kai followed, hauling out amulets and climbing.

The two of them were sweating by the time they reached halfway up. There was no time to pause. Kai felt the thick double thump of his pulse through his system. This was exhausting. The amulets he'd retrieved hung around his neck and weighed a ton, making climbing harder. There was no telling how much time had passed, other than his screaming muscles.

Evazee was breathing heavily up ahead, and her pace slowed slightly.

"Keep going, Zee. I'm on borrowed time." Kai stepped off a drawer as it pulled shut. They needed to move quicker. The timing was getting too close.

They made it all the way to the last circle.

"Faster, Zee! We're nearly there." Kai glanced down. That was a mistake. The ground was a long way down. To get this far and fail... His head swam a little as panic trickled through his veins.

Evazee stepped off the last drawer onto the safety of the rim. Kai reached in for the last amulet, hung it around his neck with the others. As he stepped up, the last drawer snapped shut. His other foot slipped off the edge, and he lost his balance. Zee grabbed his arm. For a moment he thought they might be safe, but her weight was no match for his and he pulled her with him.

They clung to each other as they fell, yelling as adrenalin raced. Kai held Evazee with one hand and clung to the amulets with the other. The jelly walls rushed past faster. Their screaming would surely bring a worm. But did it matter since they were about to die?

They dropped like rocks. Suddenly Kai felt gravity shift as if they were being sucked sideways, much faster than before. Everything around them blurred and the colours smeared and ran into each other. They flew between two pillars, hit the ground hard, and rolled, carried along by momentum. Kai bumped up against an immovable force, dressed in sandals.

He lay back and checked his body for injuries. His ribs ached, his legs felt like jelly, but he was still breathing, and he didn't seem to be bleeding. Death, it seemed, wasn't as painful as he thought it would be.

Evazee prodded him. "Kai, wake up."

"You're here too! That makes me happy." He patted her arm and lay back, pleased to see a solid roof over his head and no jelly walls. Wait, what? Kai pushed himself up on his elbow, blinked away stars. The basement of the OS settled into view as the stars dwindled.

Evazee whispered, "The testing arch brought us back. We must have passed. I think these people are a bit shocked to see you."

The priests from Zulu's village surrounded them, as wary as if they were seeing a ghost.

Kai sat up and the amulets around his neck clinked like music.

A ripple of shock shot through the men. They backed off, whispering to each other.

The circle opened up, and the chief priest stepped forward with Zulu at his side. He pushed Zulu to his knees before turning his attention to Kai.

"What is this *imilingo*? My people locked you up in our village. How can you be back?"

Zulu stared at Kai with the intensity of a cat stalking a bird. "He wants to know what magic this is that brought you back. *Imilingo* means magic."

Evazee said nothing, and this dictator would not put up with silence.

Kai pushed himself to his feet with the amulets clinking around his neck like sports medals. He reached into his pocket and found the amulet with Zulu's scar. He held it in his palm as he spoke. "I have some things that will help us find your boys." *I think.* "Zulu, this might be yours." He walked over to give it to Zulu and caused another ripple of muttering and back-stepping.

These priests were scared.

Zulu took the amulet, ran his fingers down the groove that matched his scar. He slipped it over his neck and popped it open. His eyes rolled back in his head, and he rose to his full height. He seemed taller, broader, larger than life. A deep roar started in his belly and worked its way up, building intensity, growing, filling the room. It tore from his mouth as an angry growl aimed straight at the priests from his village. He stepped towards them and they crumbled before his anger. Another step. The roar grew deeper, louder, rattling the windows.

Kai blocked his ears and shot a worried glance at Evazee. She shook her head and shrugged.

The priests around them howled and ran from the room, tripping over each other to get up the stairs and through the trapdoor.

As they left, Zulu snapped the amulet shut and as it clicked, he shrank back to his normal self. He held the amulet clutched in his enormous hands and shook from head to toe. He grinned at them both, swaying on his feet. "I'm going to rest now." He left the room with one hand trailing along the wall to keep him upright. The amulet's effect on Zulu was both awesome and terrifying.

"Maybe we shouldn't have done that." Kai put an arm around Evazee, more for his comfort than hers. This serum was different to what he'd had before. The last batch had shifted him entirely into the spiritual realm, but this batch seemed to bring both the natural and the spiritual into sharp focus, like some warped new dimension.

"I don't understand. What did we just see? The result of what he did is amazing, the priests are gone. But I won't lie. It scared me, more than a little. Restoring what has been stolen from someone should be a peaceful thing. I didn't think it would be quite so dramatic." Evazee's hands were shaking.

"I think we witnessed Zulu expressing his talent."

"Which is what? Roaring?"

"No, man. He's a protector and a helper."

"Oh! That makes sense."

Now more than ever, Kai regretted his impulsive decision to inject the serum. Under the influence of it, he couldn't trust what he saw. Before, he could easily discern broken from whole. Right from wrong. Now? He couldn't trust his Affinity. He couldn't trust himself.

~*~

Evazee ran the options in her mind. "Come on. We need to go find Runt and the others. I don't think we can help Zulu right now, he just needs to rest."

They ran up the stairs and through the trapdoor into the main section of the building. The place seemed deserted.

"Torn's office. Let's go." Kai led them through deserted passages. As they got closer to Torn's office, he heard banging and shouting. The key was in the outside of the lock. Kai turned it and the door swung inwards, depositing Zap and Ruaan in a heap on the floor.

The others sat in a row along the wall, all squished up. There was no sign of any of the priests. Peta flew at Evazee and squeezed her tight. Paintbrush did the same with Kai, while Runt waited with her arms crossed.

"Did they hurt you? You're not being guarded?" Evazee stretched her neck to see around the corner.

Runt shook her head, but her lip quivered, and she bit her lip again.

Ruaan rolled Zap onto the floor. "They took off in a hurry. Strangely, they didn't think it necessary to explain themselves to us."

"Is everybody back? Have you done a headcount?" Evazee glanced around, but there were too few in the room. Most of Zulu's boys were still gone too. Those that were there were sweaty and tired. "You guys must be hungry. Go find something to eat. Maybe go lie down and rest once you've eaten."

As the room cleared, Boety stood up from the corner.

Relief washed through Evazee at the sight of him. "Boety! Did they catch you?"

Boety shook his head. "This room was my hiding spot. I didn't know they were going to lock everybody in here." He grinned and his face lit up.

Seeing his smile warmed Evazee inside, and she wanted to hug him. His face reminded her of Zulu downstairs alone. "Boety, your brother is downstairs. He chased away the priests, but now he's worn out. We don't know how to help him."

"I'll go." The boy shot out of the room and disappeared down the passage.

Evazee sat back and let the wall hold her up.

Kai had been quiet since they'd sent everybody

out. He stood off to one side, staring out the window, chewing on his thumb knuckle.

Zap ambled over and stood behind Kai with his hands on his hips. He leaned in close with his head cocked to one side. A minute later, he poked Kai in the shoulder. "I can't hear what you're thinking anymore, but I can see all sorts of nonsense going on in your head by the way your face is scrunched up. Are you going to tell us what's going on?"

Kai leaned close and whispered.

Zap's eyes went wide, and he thumbed towards Kai's back. "Our boy here wants to go blow up the serum storage at Bree's old school. Now that sounds like fun. Who's in?"

~*~

Kai heard his plan coming out of Zap's mouth, and it sounded like pure lunacy. In his head it made so much sense. He turned to his friends. "What do you guys think? I know it's only one fraction of a worldwide problem. But that stuff is going into everything and it's going everywhere. It's lethal. Once they've started distribution, it will be too late. We have to do something now." He considered the enormity of the problem and his heart raged. "We can't stop it, but maybe we can slow them down."

Anger burned through him. He felt the serum in his body like cancer. Invisible but deadly. And this time, it wouldn't wear off. It was in him for life. A death sentence in his blood. Just because there was no hope for him, didn't mean that he couldn't make a dent in the enemy's plans for the others.

Zap still had his hands on his hips, but his eyebrows bunched in the middle of his forehead. "I'm all for a good explosion or two, don't get me wrong. The thing is if you blow up the building and all the serum in it, there's a good chance that all you'll be doing is releasing it into the atmosphere. The heat of the explosion would make it evaporate and in gas form, it's heavier than air."

"So you're saying it will be in the air that we breathe, and it won't dissipate but hang around?" Evazee wiggled her fingers in the air.

Zap nodded, "That's what I think."

"But wouldn't it thin out and become ineffective?" Ruaan had the sceptical slant to his eyebrows that seemed to happen often around Zap.

"Do you really want to take that risk?"

Evazee cleared her throat. "Apart from the fact that it's illegal to blow up buildings. There's always that small fact that you might want to think about. Just maybe."

Kai's mind spun. "You're right. We can't do that." A breeze ruffled some papers on Torn's desk, and Kai moved a paperweight onto the pile to stop it. "If we can't destroy the serum, the only other option is to neutralize it. Zap would need to get back in the lab and figure it out."

Zap shook his head. "Don't even go there. I don't know enough. Even if I did, the lab here at the OS is a dismal little thing. It's not equipped for that level of investigation. We'll have to think of something else."

Kai's head felt like it might split in two. "Seriously though, if you can't neutralize the stuff, then we have to get ourselves someone who can."

Zap shot up straight and stared at Ruaan with eyes so wide he looked a little crazy. "Are you serious right now?"

Evazee waggled a finger at Zap, "Please stop doing that."

Zap shrugged, "What?"

"Dipping into people's brains the way you'd eat yoghurt with a spoon. We all need to hear what's going on, you know."

Zap sank into the corner of the couch muttering. "Well, fine. I just think kidnapping some scientists from a high-security building out in the middle of the desert may just get us locked up. But, whatever."

"Ruaan? Please tell me he's making that stuff up?" Evazee's face paled a few shades.

"The way I see it, we don't have a choice, and we're out of time. And we need to move now before Zulu's priests decide they're brave enough to come back and face the *Imilingo*. They might know how to get the amulets free without us having to bring along all these small people."

"How are you planning to get back inside? From what I've heard, you don't just go waltzing back in through the front gate." Evazee's voice had raised a few notches.

Kai reached into the back pocket of his jeans and pulled out a crumpled piece of paper. "I took this off a notice board. They're looking for test subjects for their serum."

"Did it hurt when it died?" The scorn in Evazee's words stung.

"What are you talking about?"

"The last brain cell that contained any common sense at all. It must have hurt when it died."

"It will get us straight to the scientists. Straight to Bree's Dad. They are the ones we need."

Ruaan fiddled with the pendant hanging beneath

his t-shirt, scuffing the floor with his shoe. "Do you know how much red tape you have to wade through to be accepted as a test subject? There are forms to go through and sign, tests to be done, physicals... It could take weeks before we even see a scientist." His face crumpled in a frown as he scratched his chin.

Zap frowned at Ruaan. Then his eyebrow popped up, and he nodded. "That's not a bad idea."

Evazee threw her hands up in exasperation. "Will you stop it! What now?"

Zap pointed at Ruaan. "He's thinking we should try St. Greg's."

"For what?" Kai's nose pulled up.

Ruaan shrugged. "It's just a thought. They're working with the Recruiters. Just because we shut down their operations at the OS doesn't mean they're not still going strong elsewhere. Bree and Elden's old school is being used for storing serum, why wouldn't there be something dodgy at St. Greg's?" Ruaan's stomach growled, but he patted it and turned his attention back to their conundrum.

Zap scratched his head. "Should we find you some food before—"

"I'm fine, really. You've been trying to force-feed me all day. I'm hungry, but I can wait."

"You're sure?"

"If you keep asking me that, I'll probably get angry."

Zap flung his hands up in surrender. "No, it's all good." He shot Ruaan a puzzled look. Since getting his amulet back, the boy had been as meek as amicable as after a full meal. Judging by the way Zap was eyeing Ruaan, he clearly didn't trust the change. Zap turned back to Kai. "I'm beginning to wonder if these schools are connected." He waved a hand in frustration at his clumsy words. "We know that they are *connected* with all the recruiting and stuff, but I'm thinking physically. Secret roads, maybe?"

Kai sat up straight. "There could be an entrance to Brio Talee or something similar."

Zap looked both chuffed that someone understood, and a bit sick at the mention of Brio Talee. "Exactly. Though I'm hoping for something less, uh, spirit realmy."

"You remember how we used to hear rattling in the middle of the night? Sometimes our windows would shake, and we were scared of earthquakes..."

"Except now we know that we don't get earthquakes here." Zap's face lit up with conspiratorial wonder. He clicked his fingers.

"You might not be as insane as you sound right now." Kai grinned at his friend.

Evazee stuck her hand in the air. "So while we are all out hunting for secret earthquake-inducing roads," thick sarcasm laced her words, "who will be watching over this lot and those who come back from the testing arch?"

24

Kai found Zulu's boys sitting in a circle around him in the sleeping hall. They'd covered him with a blanket and sat talking quietly amongst themselves. From the outside it looked as if Zulu lay fast asleep, but Kai wasn't sure what to make of it all.

He joined their circle, and they shuffled sideways to make space for him. He'd brought the amulets from the well in their village. He'd watched the change in Ruaan and seeing Zulu rise up and take a stand against the bad things the priests of his village wanted him to do, convinced him this was the right choice. Between the Healing Stream water that they'd drunk and getting their amulets back, Kai couldn't wait to see how much these boys changed. If their response was anything like Zulu's, they'd have some serious power on their side.

"Guys, we've got big trouble. We have a plan to fix the trouble, but I'll need to ask you a favour."

They bum-shuffled closer and bowed their heads. When they looked up, there was steel in their eyes. "Our swords are yours, Bright One."

Bright One. He had a name? He didn't know what to make of that, so he ignored it and moved on. "Will you watch over the people here? We need to go do something. I hope that what we find out will free all the people of your village."

"Even the priests?" Boety waved towards the boys that were back. "Priests are bad for most these boys. Village traditions are broken. Very bad. You make magic to fix?"

"Yes, I hope so. It's not magic, though, just..." Kai didn't know how to explain it. "It doesn't matter. We want to fix it, but we have to go away to find the cure, and we can't leave them alone."

Boety banged his chest twice with a clenched fist. "On it. Go in peace."

"Are you sure? It's dangerous and they aren't your problem..." Kai withered to quiet under the gaze of the young man who seemed to have no problem babysitting a bunch of messed-up OS dwellers. "Will the men from your village come back?"

"They will do many rituals first to break the *Imilingo*. Not back for many days."

"We'll be back as soon as we can."

Boety pointed to the bag. "What's in there?"

Kai patted the bag and fumbled over what to say. "Necklaces, like Zulu's. From the well in your village. I have a feeling they are yours."

Boety reached for the bag, tucked it on his lap and folded the sides down to better see inside. He shut his eyes, reached in, and dug around below the surface. In a moment, Kai saw his face change. A blissful glow crept into his features and Kai had the strongest feeling that he'd found his amulet.

He pulled his hand out the bag, clasped around an amulet. He breathed deeply in through his nose and out through his mouth. "My gratitude burns hotter than the sun." He slipped the cord over his head.

He called his group close around him and they whispered in a tight huddle. They passed the bag around, each reaching in and coming out with an amulet. Once they'd each found theirs, they sat grinning at each other.

Boety passed the bag of leftovers to Kai for safe-keeping.

They all whispered quietly to each other, until Boety clapped his hands once and the group dispersed, running in different directions.

Boety stood, and he seemed taller and broader than he'd been before. The whites of his eyes glowed, not grey like Ruaan, but pure white.

One word burned in Kai as he looked at the young man: dreamer. "Do you dream much, Boety?"

Boety grinned, his teeth flashing against the darkness of his skin. "I walk in my dreams. I see things. What I see happens. Bad things can be changed."

"You're a dreamwalker."

"That is what they call me. But when they took me to train as a priest, the dreams stopped. I had to let go. But now," his fist bumped his chest, "now I feel them all come back. Thank you." His hand slipped around his amulet, and his face shone.

Exhaustion rolled over Kai, but now was not the time. Words failed him, so he patted Boety's shoulder and ran downstairs to find the others.

~*~

Evazee had a foot in the van, but her heart was still torn. It was all very well to leave Boety and his friends to watch over the OS, but leaving Peta, Runt, and the others felt like leaving a newborn on a doorstep in the middle of a tsunami. Besides, if there had been one bottle of healing stream water that had made such a difference to Zulu's boys, there might be more. Maybe between her amulet and a bottle of healing stream water, she could get her imprint back. This would buy her some time to go hunting. "I'm sorry, guys. I can't leave. Just go without me." She backed away, feeling the haunting sting of indecision glow red hot in her belly.

Kai pulled her to one side. "Are you sure about this?"

"Runt, Peta...even Zulu. They need someone. If I went with you and something happened...I don't think I could live with myself. You know?"

Kai's mouth drew into a single, sharp line. "I understand." He turned back before shutting the van door. "Don't get caught."

Evazee swatted his words away. "Same to you."

Kai laughed, but he dipped his chin enough for her to know that he'd heard. He gave a quick salute and climbed into the vehicle.

Evazee watched the dust billow up from the van's tyres and rubbed her arms against the cold dread that crept over her. She shook it off and ran upstairs, telling herself that staying behind was the right thing to do. Now she just had to find the healing stream water. Maybe even get her imprint back.

She made it to Torn's office without anyone stopping her. She knew something was wrong the moment she stepped through the door. A cold shiver passed through her, followed closely by a delicate, probing thought that sliced through her brain.

I've missed you.

~*~

Twilight took on a darker shade as they pulled up

outside St. Gregory's school.

Zap glanced behind the car. "Do you think someone followed us?"

"Doubt it, why?" Kai's cheeks were flushed like he was running a temperature.

Bree put a hand on his forehead. "Are you OK? You don't look so good."

"Being back here is weird, that's all." He looked away before she could examine him too closely.

Kai directed Ruaan around the back to a separate entrance where Phil lived. The ancient caretaker had less hair than Kai remembered, and what he had was even whiter than Kai thought possible. He hugged Kai. Through his threadbare jersey, Phil's bones felt fragile beneath Kai's fingers.

"Come in, come in. Are you still fixing things?" He waved the friends into his stuffy apartment. The windows were all closed up and the curtains drawn. One look at the man's hands, and Kai could see why. Thick, ropey bands of green laced through and around the tendons. Arthritis had taken a deep hold in his old joints and robbed the strength from his fingers. Window catches were no longer manageable. It made Kai sad to see it, but some things were beyond fixing.

"I try." Kai felt the heat in his face.

"You always had a talent for that. Remarkable." Phil's hands might have been broken, but his mind was as sharp as ever. He studied Kai with sharp eyes, and his gaze slid over the bunch of them. Then he nodded once as if satisfied with what he saw. "I'm glad to see you full of light. I knew they wouldn't succeed with you."

"You know what's happening here?"

"I've watched for many years. I've seen many

things. Now I'm sure you didn't pop in for tea with an old geyser like me. How can I help you?"

Kai drew Phil over to the kitchen corner of the small space. How much would Phil understand? "You know every inch of this school, right?"

"More than any living soul."

"Would you know what I'm referring to if I say Brio Talee?"

"Maybe. Maybe not. I know of a door that has been sealed up from before I got here. How come? What is it you seek?"

Kai sat quiet, weighing up how much he could tell Phil. The old man had covered for him so many times in the past. Apart from Zap, Phil was the only other person Kai had ever felt safe with. "We want to bring down the system. The recruiting, the serum. It's all wrong."

Phil stared at Kai for so long without moving that Kai started thinking he'd made a mistake confiding in the old guy. But then he nodded gravely. "Follow me. I think this might help."

Phil shuffled over to a hook on a wall and took down a ring of keys that clanked and jingled. He fumbled, trying to hook them on his belt loop, clucked his tongue, and stuffed them in his pocket. His hands were giving him so much trouble. He popped a headlight on his head, straightened the light, and waved them out of the back door. He led them around the back of his house, down a garden path between overgrown flowerbeds that spoke of hands too stiff to weed.

As they stepped onto the dark sports field, a thin breeze picked up, and Kai shivered.

Zap scooted up close. "I can't shake the feeling

that we're being followed. It's so much worse out here in the open. Look at me. Dude, even my forehead is sweating. I'm going to look like I showered by the time we get across this field."

Phil shuffled ahead of them towards the hall. They found a door labelled *stage entrance*. Phil led them offstage down the wooden stairs on the right. His knees creaked at the effort of bending and straightening, but he kept going.

Zap grabbed Bree and pulled her close. "Does it feel like somebody is following us? I really feel like somebody is following us."

Bree pointed down the steps that angled downwards into inky shadow and held up a flat palm millimetres from Zap's nose. "Stop being creepy."

Phil fumbled with the ring of keys and Kai stepped in to help. Together they unhooked the chains that fell to the side in a shower of rust. Phil passed the headlight on to Kai. "You'll need this more than me. Don't think too much. In you go. May the secret things show themselves to you as you need them."

Kai hugged the old guy.

Phil shuffled off into the darkness and soon disappeared from view behind the overgrown bushes.

Kai adjusted his headlight and stepped down into the shadowy gloom of the stairwell. "Come on, you lot. I'm not going down here by myself." He plunged into the inky blackness that the headlight did little to break.

"I'm coming. Wait! Don't leave me behind." Zap came down the stairs two at a time to catch up. This place seemed to be working on his imagination.

Judging by the state of the door, Kai expected the room to be dusty and dingy, crammed full of old stage props and costumes. He took the stairs with blood rushing over his eardrums, stepped off the last one and let out a low whistle. This was not the dank storage space he was expecting.

~*~

They stood in a vast circular room with smooth walls dotted with doors. In the centre of the room stood a lone, square desk, manned by a woman whose hair was pulled back into a bun and kept there by an overstretched elastic band. She was working through a pile of papers and marking things off on her tablet. As she worked, she rubbed her nose as if it were permanently itchy. She showed no sign of having seen them yet.

Kai squeezed his eyes shut, wishing he could flick a switch to turn off his altered Affinity. This was not Brio Talee, just an underground system of tunnels that he'd lived on top of for all his young life without suspecting a thing. He'd been expecting back alleys and country trails. This was like a five-lane highway. With his serum-Affinity sight, everywhere he looked, bits glowed green. It made him uneasy.

As Kai stepped forward to talk to the woman, a loud alarm bell went off and all the doors swung open at the same time. From every side, people streamed into the central space. Some walked in groups speaking softly, others came through the doorways alone. They flowed around the friends as water around a clump of rocks. The lady at the desk stood up with a resigned look on her face as the crowd all converged around her desk, making three wonky queues at each side. She worked her way from left to right, receiving papers, glancing through, scanning and depositing them on a pile in the middle of her desk before issuing new ones.

The questions were the same every time. Where from? How long? Where are you going now? Stamp. Next.

Kai and the others moved closer, blending in with the crowd. He strained his ears to hear where people were going. There were a bunch of names he didn't recognize, but one that he did. He waved his friends close. "Guys, they seem to handle this in batches. Maybe we can hitch a ride to Crux."

They hung back until they heard someone going the right way. Kai pushed forward. "We're going with him."

The lady behind the desk tapped a fingernail. The guy they were attaching themselves to was large with a mass of curly hair as black as Kai's. He swung around slowly with a deep frown. "I don't..." He studied them like bugs until he got to Bree. She smiled at him. He swung back to the lady and thumbed over his shoulder. "My squad."

Her finger tapped faster, but a quick glance at the waiting queues swung it for her. "Fine. Crux through door eight. There's a shuttle waiting, it's nearly full enough to leave. Go."

There was no time for chatting as they filed through the doorway. It was dark on the other side, but the track under the shuttle glowed slivery white. The seats came in rows of two and their black-haired ticket made sure Bree sat next to him.

The shuttle made Kai think of roller coaster car, but slicker in design. Once the car was full, a plexi-glass cover slid from behind and locked in place. Before Kai had time to panic, they took off at such a speed, the walls blurred to nothing. Even the nothing blurred.

Kai reminded himself to breathe. Each dip and turn was smooth and quick and within minutes, the shuttle slowed down and drew to a stop. Kai's legs felt like jelly, and the eight of them shuffled through the doorway out into a lit overhang in the desert. There were desert buggies lined up but no buildings visible through the thick, heavy darkness.

"Where are you guys headed?" The big guy had a voice to match his size. He smiled at Bree shyly.

Kai forced nonchalant confidence into his voice. "The labs. We have an appointment with a scientist there."

"Oh, I see." The smile faded from his face. "I'm sorry about that. I'm off to packaging. We'll have to take separate buggies."

Kai hadn't factored in the size of this place. "Hey, I've never come out at this stop. Could you tell us which way to go? I feel like a right nit for having to ask." He chuckled and felt heat creep up his neck.

"Sure, give me your Naviband."

Kai fished around and handed over his band from Kirsten in Marketing with his heart in his throat. This could get ugly.

"This isn't your Naviband. What's going on?"

Kai rolled his eyes, "IT guys. They didn't have any new ones, so I got a recycled one. Can you believe that?"

"You need to get your profile updated. This is out of sync. It has you as some chick in marketing." He nodded sagely. "It's them fools up in the IT block. They think they're above us all. Bunch of incompetents. Anyway, I've loaded the co-ords for the entrance that you'll need to access." He stared at Bree, "It was good to meet you guys. All the best with the tests." He shuddered a little, before climbing into a desert buggy and taking off at such speed, dust clouds flew up and made them all cough.

~*~

Evazee turned slowly in the middle of Torn's office, looking for a stash of Healing Stream water. What Torn would be doing with bottles of Healing Stream water was another story, but right now all that mattered was finding it.

A scent lingered in the air. She sniffed deeply, trying to place it. The long wooden bookshelf got the once-over. None of the books were her type, and there didn't seem to be any secret hidey holes for bottles of water.

Desk drawers were a good place to look next. Paperclips and pens top left. Scrap paper bottom left. Wads of forms tied together with elastic bands filled the top right drawer. She slid the last drawer open, feeling hopeful. Instead of Healing Stream water, the last drawer held empty syringes and vacuum-packed needles. Evazee's belly flipped, and she shut the drawer fast.

The desk rattled as the drawer slid shut. She tried it again. Open, shut. There was something loose. She pulled the drawer right out and fiddled with the bottom. A section gave way and slid back. Nestling in a rectangular space were two small bottles filled with clear liquid that gave off the slightest blue glow.

Tears pricked Evazee's eyes. This could be the start of getting her life back. She reached for in and took them both. She slipped one into her pocket and was about to uncap the other when the door creaked. Instinctively, Evazee dropped down and crawled in under the desk. If this was Peta or Runt coming to look for her, they would never let her hear the end of it. She bent right down to see who'd come in.

One pair of feet, in black boots.

~*~

Ruaan drove the way a granny would in fear of tipping a Sunday casserole; painfully slow and cautious.

Zap rode up in the front next to him and kept feeding him ginger biscuits. Ruaan took one each time Zap shoved one towards him without question, but by the fifth one, he was nibbling at the edges.

Kai sat behind them, and watched the biscuit exchange. "Why do you keep forcing those on him? It doesn't take much to see he's had enough."

Zap twisted around. "Are you forgetting what happens when this guy gets hungry? The whole Jekyll and Hyde thing. It's ugly, man."

"Yeah, but if you keep force-feeding him, he's going to be sick. That's not particularly attractive either."

"You're just grumpy because you're worried about Evazee. You're wishing you didn't leave her back at the OS, but you also didn't want to bring her with because it's also dangerous." Zap grinned, a broad smile that lit up his face. He turned back to Ruaan. "Also, I think he fancies Bree."

Ruaan shook his head. "I thought you said you couldn't read his mind anymore."

"Dude, I don't need to read his mind to know this stuff. He wears it all over his face." Zap chuckled.

Kai clucked his tongue. Nothing he said would convince Zap otherwise, mostly because Zap was right.

It was a prickly thought that he shoved down deep. He stared out the window, attempting not to think anything that Zap could pick up on and throw in his face. Now he'd have to poker-face too. Exhausting. The buggy's lights hardly lifted the shadows above the endless sand that slid past as they went. But every now and then he'd see shapes that flew past too quickly to be identified. In a flash, they flickered between physical reality and serum-induced visions of the spiritual realm. At times, the two images settled awkwardly into each other in a split-second that left Kai's belly swimming.

They'd been following the Naviband's instructions for nearly an hour when their desert buggy choked and died.

Ruaan slapped the steering wheel. "We're out of gas. No, man!"

Kai squinted ahead, something gleamed ahead just over the rise, rippling in the dirty light. "That looks like the entrance gate. I think we're close enough to walk. Come on. We'll fry if we stay here in this heat."

Zap grunted. "I thought deserts were supposed to be cold at night? Why is it so hot? I swear I'm melting."

"I don't think this is a natural desert, not with all the weird things going down here." Kai swung his legs out of the buggy, and the moment his feet hit the sand, a shock of pain washed through him and his view flipped. He shook his head and when he looked again, the sky had reddened and the gates in front of him were burning. Instantly the wailing started. This was straight back to just after his run-in with the bus.

The flames licked up the metal, blackening it further and making it sizzle.

He stood frozen as adrenalin pumped through his

veins. A jagged shard of memory shook loose. The squeal of the bus brakes a breath before pain shut down his mind.

A hand on his back. Bree's voice in his ear.

"What's going on?"

He shivered and tore his gaze away from the fire. As he blinked, the scene switched back to black skies and his people. "It's all good. Let's go." He led the group towards the gleaming gates. As he walked, his view flickered between the natural and spiritual until they blurred into one. He could see the gates ahead, cold metal gleaming, and the flames. DarKounds paced along the perimeter fence just waiting to be let loose.

His mind screamed, adrenalin pumped through him. How could he keep walking his friends towards this disaster? Yet there was no other way.

They had to go. They had to face whatever lay waiting for them beyond the burning gates.

25

Evazee's pulse raced. Zulu's boys didn't wear boots. She ran through a mental checklist of the OS dwellers. None of them had boots like this either. The feet came closer, sauntering as if they belonged. Unhurried. No fear of discovery. Who was this?

A slow whirlpool started in her thoughts. It grew, making every scrap of logic spin slowly. Emotions hooked and pulled along too. Swirling down and around. Thinking through a mind of sludge became impossible.

I know you.

~*~

Kai didn't dare blink as they walked up to the gates. For the moment, they were just ordinary gates. No flames, no smoke, no screaming souls. Kai's eyes watered by the time the gate guard strolled over.

"What is your business here?"

Ruaan pulled back so that Kai could do the talking.

"I have a new batch of volunteers for testing."

"You walked through the desert?"

Kai waved over his shoulder. "Our desert buggy ran out of gas. You might want to send someone to fetch it." The guard held out his hand. "Naviband."

Kai coughed to cover the red heat climbing his

neck. The Naviband would probably have been reported and blocked. Handing it over could well get them locked up. He unhooked the band and handed it over. He watched the guard's face waiting for the change. Waiting for him to shout for backup. There would be guns and blood. This was a stupid idea.

The guard stared at the device, pushing buttons down the side. "I'm sorry, but this isn't going to work. I should probably call somebody."

"It's a recycled band. Probably the IT guy's version of dumb joke." Stupid, stupid idea. "Is there a problem?"

The guard nodded his head knowingly. "That bunch in IT are beyond lazy. They just didn't bother to do it right. I'd advise you to get it sorted out immediately. Not all the guards are as understanding as me. I've put in the co-ord's for where you need to go. You can use that spare buggy over there." He clicked a button and a pedestrian gate built into the main gate popped open.

Kai took the band back and forced out a conspiratorial snort as he snapped it back onto his wrist. He didn't trust himself to throw out any further comment, so he waved his friends through the doorway. Together they climbed into the buggy. Kai patted the dash and motioned for Ruaan to drive on.

They chugged past a number of different sections of parking bays and entrances. Kai tapped the Naviband to make sure it was still tracking. This place was enormous.

As Ruaan pulled to a stop in the bay that the Naviband led them to, Zap poked his head between the seats. "Seems to me, the IT guys aren't the only incompetents employed here." He cricked his neck to the left and right, laced his fingers, and pushed, making all his knuckles pop. "Right. What's the plan?"

Bree spoke up from the back seat of the buggy. "The fact that you haven't already brain-dipped to know the plan, means he probably hasn't got one."

Zap frowned long and hard at Kai. "For some reason, our boy's head has become a no-go zone to me. I'd love to figure out why." He poked Kai's temple with a finger.

"Stop that." Kai batted his hand away. "Besides, I do have a plan. Sort of."

Bree's lack of expression said it all. "Sure you do. We believe you." She shrugged, and Zap grinned at her.

Bree hung back as the guys climbed out of the buggy.

The Naviband had guided them right to the back of the building. If a laboratory had a service entrance, Kai imagined that this is what it would look like. The rest of the building was all glass and shiny metal, but this side was a long stretch of solid grey brick and cement. The only break in the wall was a single door, closed over and unguarded.

Bree slipped out from the back of the van and shut the rear door. It swung closed with a loud crash that echoed and made Bree jump. "Are you sure this is a good idea?"

Kai's face was a mess of concern. "I don't know. Maybe you should just wait out here? It won't make much difference to have you come inside."

Bree drew herself up and got so close to Kai he tottered over and had to back step to catch himself. Her fury was tightly contained in her small frame. "You can't leave me behind again. That won't happen." Kai opened his mouth, but before he could say anything, Bree shoved her finger in his face. "And don't tell me it's dangerous."

Kai pinched his face with the effort of not saying what he was thinking.

Ruaan looped an arm around Bree's shoulders. "Our Bree deserves to see her dad as much as any of you. Anyway, there's nothing you can do now. It's not really any safer for her to sit out here in the parking garage. What's the plan?"

Kai clenched his jaw so hard, his cheeks rippled. He stalked back to where Zap was puzzling over how to unlock the door.

Bree and Ruaan jogged to catch up.

"I can't believe he was trying to leave me outside. My only family is right here," Bree whispered.

"Don't hold it against him. He still hasn't forgiven himself for leaving you behind in the desert." Ruaan shrugged. "And I think Zap is right. He fancies you."

"Oh, that's rubbish, did you see how he looked at me right now?"

"Believe me, don't believe me. I don't care. It doesn't change the fact."

Kai called out over his shoulder, "I can hear everything you two are saying. I hope you know that."

Bree stifled a giggle and Ruaan scratched his head.

Kai turned away and held up his Navibanded arm as a magician would demonstrate his empty sleeve. He aimed it under a small beam of light, and the lock clicked. The door swung back on its hinges. "That's how you do it. Brains."

Zap shot out a fist for a bump, but Kai pushed past him through the doorway and left Zap hanging. Kai waited inside for them all to get in before pulling the door shut, cutting off the sunlight from outside. The passage was dimly lit by faint fluorescent tubes dotted at intervals. The one over where they stood flickered and popped before winking out.

A cold shaft of dread slid through Kai. He should have come alone. As much as he'd bragged about having a plan, he wouldn't tell them how half-baked it was. It was a relief that Zap couldn't scoop around in his brain and spell it all out for them, as puzzling as that was.

The passage they were in offered three options: left, right, or straight up the stairs in front of them.

Kai hunched over the device on his arm. He shut his eyes, breathed deep, turned right, and led them down the passage. They walked in single file, trying to look as if they belonged.

The first person to pass them was a woman in a white lab coat. She walked with clipped footsteps, absorbed in the tablet in her hand with a deep frown on her face. She grunted as they passed.

Kai got the feeling she didn't particularly notice that they were there.

They came to a break in the wall on the right. A gloomy stairway led down and around. Further down, some of the lights were out, making it impossible to see what they were walking into.

Kai flinched as he took the first step, but he kept going and they all fell in behind him, taking the stairs in single file.

The gloom filtered through Kai, laying a dark cloud in his heart and mind. He breathed in the thick odour of chemicals and it choked him.

Bree's face pulled tight as it would if she were trying to wear jeans a size too small. She caught Kai looking at her and grimaced, shaking her head. She felt it too, this oppression.

~*~

Evazee sat under the desk with a frozen bottom. Whoever had come into Torn's office didn't seem in a hurry to leave. She could tell by the creak of a swivel chair and low rumbling hum of some unfamiliar tune. Her insides were in complete turmoil. She couldn't keep two words straight, and fear ran rampant, paralyzing her. She didn't have time to be stuck under the desk, freezing from the cold tiles. This was nonsense.

Evazee had to know. If she was hiding for nothing, she could have a good laugh at herself and get on with life; drink her water, get back on track. Maybe even save the day. She eased her weight onto her hands and knees, careful not to squish the bottle in her hand, and crawled as quietly as she could out from under the desk to peer around the corner.

The chair by the window swivelled around, and Evazee sucked air through her teeth. It was Shasta, draped across the seat as if his spine was made of warm wax, his long, silvery hair caught in a leather tie at the nape of his neck and his pale eyes luminous in the gloom. Shasta, who'd run the Affinity training program and messed up so many lives. The same one who'd got under Evazee's skin and into her head in a way she couldn't escape.

~*~

Kai's mind spun. Having Bree here shoved their mission to new levels of risk that made his head ache. He led them down the corridor with a growing sense of dread weighing him down. A staircase led off the passage to the right, and his belly twisted at the thought of going into such a shadowy place, but the Naviband was clear—that was the way to the laboratory.

As his foot touched the first step down, his sight warped, showing the stairs but overlaying the spiritual realm. The stairway was littered with DarKounds. At the sound of his foot connecting with metal stairs, the creatures' heads popped up as one, tracking their movements.

Kai cringed as he stepped between them, thoughts flying. He had no time for their nonsense. The lab was at the bottom of these stairs and nobody would keep him away, but to put the others in danger was not something he wanted to do.

"Guys, you can wait upstairs. I'll check this out." He could tell by their faces that none of them were seeing what he was.

"Don't be daft. Just go." Ruaan waved him on with a flinty look to his face that he didn't have time to tackle.

As he picked his way between the hideous animals, his heart shrank in his chest and his palms sweated. The others followed without hesitation. A glass door waited at the bottom of the stairs with the word *Laboratory* sandblasted into the glass. A printed notice hung below it. *Authorized Personnel Only. Keep Out.*

He lined up the Naviband with the scanner, and the door slid back with a quiet *whoosh*. Strange for a marketing employee to have access to a top-level lab, but Kai didn't stop to question it. He stepped through the doorway first, peered around.

Many scientists were dotted around the room at different workstations, peering into microscopes, decanting liquid into test tubes.

One from the workstations closest to the entrance stared at them as they entered. He set the test tube into its holder and rushed over to them. His shoes tick-ticked on the tiled floor. "You're not meant to be here. All visitors are to go straight to reception. What is your business here?"

The others shoved Kai forward as their volunteer spokesperson. He tripped over his own foot and caught himself just before face-planting. "I've been working with Doctor S. He asked me to recruit some more test subjects." He thumbed over his shoulder. "These are them."

The scientist didn't look convinced, but then Dr S. stepped forward from the back of the lab. "Yes, yes. Thank you. I'll take it from here." He came over to the group and grabbed Kai's elbow. "Follow me."

By the time they reached his office, sweat rolled down Dr S's. temples. He waved the five of them inside, checked up and down the passage, and shut the door. "You've got some nerve coming back here. I should lock you up right now. I still have the bruise from the last time you pulled that stunt and got away."

"Have you stopped using the eye drops?" Kai had to get through to the man.

"And why would I do that?"

Bree stepped forward with her hands tucked into her armpits. "Well, maybe it will help you see some of the things that you've forgotten about." She pulled the tie from her hair with her good hand and shook out her curls.

Dr S's eyes blinked fast as if someone had flicked

the turbo switch. "Bree?"

"I thought you were dead." Her face remained wooden.

"How did you know?" His eyes darted wildly. "You shouldn't be here."

Kai stepped forward, slipped a hand onto Bree's back. Her whole body was ice cold and trembling. "We've come for two things."

The doctor passed a shaking hand over his eyes and waved for Kai to continue.

"Your life is in danger. Unless you change something, I doubt you'll still be alive in another few weeks."

The corners of the man's mouth pulled in the effort of suppressing a laugh. "And the second thing?"

"This serum you're working on is bad news. You might think you're doing the world a favour, but you need to understand what the serum does."

Dr S. scratched his head and held his hand towards Bree. "You lot have complicated things by coming down here. The whole reason we spun the story of my death was to keep you out of all this. You and Elden. I believe in the work I'm doing here, but that doesn't mean it is without risk. Any new thing comes with challenges and growing pains. I didn't want either of you caught up in any of it."

Bree's lips pulled into a tight line. She spoke in a small, bitter voice. "You're a fool for thinking you could protect us by lying. That's not how it works. You won't believe Kai that the serum is bad, then believe me. I was stuck in that world, under its influence for months. This happened there too." She drew back her sleeve and held out her mess of a hand.

Dr S. blanched at the sight of his daughter's

mauled hand. He covered his mouth. Blood drained from his face. "What happened?

"DarKounds. Somewhere in the desert surrounding this place."

"DarKounds? You must mean our Stalkers? I like the sound of darKounds. More creative than Stalkers." He frowned at Bree's hand. "They did that to you? They were never designed to be violent, just vigilant."

Bree waved her damaged arm towards him. "Oh, for sure. Vigilant. Who are you trying to kid? You can't even look at it."

Dr S. took her hand and ran his fingers over the puckered scars in her skin. "I don't know what to say." He seemed to be struggling to swallow.

Kai took his gap. "Doctor, I think there's a whole lot more going on here than what you know about."

"Now that I think about it, there've been some things that didn't make sense. But if what you're saying is true, then it would all fit right in." He looked around suddenly as if paranoia overwhelmed him. "I'm so sorry. I thought it was for the good."

There was a brief knock on the door, and a security man came in without waiting for an invitation. "I believe you need some assistance. Would you like me to escort this lot to the lab for prepping?"

"I didn't call for you. I need to interview them and document it all first. You're dismissed."

"They told me you might say that, and that I should insist most strongly." The man grinned as if he enjoyed the power he was wielding in this moment. He didn't wait for consent, but moved in on them.

"Craven! Think about your daughter. She wouldn't still be here if I hadn't stepped in. Are you sure you want to cross this line with me?" Dr S. stood quiet with his arms folded. Only the tick in the corner of his eye gave away his heightened emotions.

"Aw, Doc. I can't argue with that. I'm just trying to do my job." The big man changed at the mention of his little girl.

The doctor patted him on the back. "But you are still doing your job, just outside. I promise I'll call you when I need you. Now off you go." He shut the door behind the big man and paced the room, wiping at the beads of sweat on his forehead with the back of his hand. "I need to think this through. Something's definitely not right. This is my life's work, you know? If what you're saying is true..." He buried his head in his hands.

Kai stepped in close and whispered, "We need your help. An antidote. Will you do it?"

"It's not that simple. This new batch is designed to be irreversible. It—"

"Are you willing to try?" Kai asked for the world, but for himself too. Even standing there, he could feel his cells changing.

The doctor glanced at Bree, and pain crossed his face. He shut his eyes, rubbing his forehead as if that would somehow reverse time. "I'll try."

"That's all we need. We'll figure out how to distribute it."

"I must be crazy." Dr S. glanced at Bree. "But listen to me. You can't come back here. There are powerful people here who think nothing of using the guns they've been issued. Let me get you guys safely out of here. Give me your Naviband."

Dr S. frowned over the buttons, muttering. Another doctor pushed through the swinging doors. "Craven's looking particularly thunderstormy today.

What's happening in here?"

Kai looked up at the sound of his voice and stared. Kai had seen him before. In visions and dreams. "Roland?"

The doctor swung around. "I haven't been called by that name for a long time. Oh." He stopped dead at the sight of Kai. "What are these people doing here?"

Dr S. floundered. His mouth worked wordlessly, and his head swung between Kai and the doctor who'd answered to Roland.

Kai hadn't really thought through what would happen if he met his dad face to face here. He should have. Faced with him now, he only wanted to leave. He took the Naviband from Doctor S. "We were just on our way. Come on, guys."

He pushed past Roland on legs of jelly, hoping the others would follow.

~*~

Shasta pushed himself out of the chair and sauntered across the room to the window. Even with his back to her, Evazee felt invaded. His presence had a way of undoing common sense, of infiltrating all her defences. He was in her head, and every second spent in this room melted more of her resistance.

Evazee crawled back in behind the desk, her mind raced. It was only a few steps to the door. Maybe she could make a run for it before he saw her. Moving a hand, a knee at a time, she moved around the far side of the desk, the side closest to the door. She tucked her toes under, a runner getting ready for the gun. She had to get out of there. She eased herself forward enough to see that Shasta still had his back to her. One quick inhale and she launched herself upright and towards the opening.

With a flick of his finger, the door slammed shut. He turned just enough for her to see his grey eyes glowing in the semi-gloom. "Don't rush off. We've got a lot to talk about, you and me. Come here." He stood up straight.

Evazee's breath caught. There was no reason to listen, or obey. She resisted.

Her foot slid forward.

~*~

Kai half-walked, half-ran to keep up with Bree. She'd overtaken him and was stalking down the passage. Her hands were shaking.

"How are you?"

Bree grimaced. "Not sure, to be honest."

"Come on guys, keep up." Zap and Ruaan were falling behind. Bree set a mean pace.

"I suppose I was hoping for more. That was just awkward." Bree sniffed and a wiped her face.

"He's got some choices to make. That's for sure."

"Kai, wait!" It was Roland, the black-haired doctor who'd walked in on their meeting with Dr S. Kai's father.

Kai's steps faltered, and he halted and came to a slow stop. He ran a hand through his hair but didn't turn around.

The doctor slowed as he got closer, he reached for Kai before letting his hands drop. "I'm sorry—"

Red flooded Kai's cheeks. "For what?"

"For how things turned out, I suppose. For many things."

His apology left Kai cold. "Just make it right."

An alarm went off deep inside the building.

Roland paled. "You need to get out of here. Move, now."

Kai waved them through the doorway. "Let's go."

All the unspoken things between him and his dad would have to stay unsaid for a while longer. Things were going downhill fast.

~*~

Shasta said nothing, but he studied Evazee with his head tilted to one side and a look in his eye that made moths swim in her belly. His eyes locked on hers and his wordless voice filled her mind, drowning out doubts and fears. It was a deep hum of white-noise that blocked out reasoning, and Evazee faced it helplessly.

Logical thoughts were compressed and squeezed into the tiniest back corner of her mind, and all she could think was how obeying Shasta was what she'd been created for. Evazee had longed for a life of significance, and he was holding it out to her in his pale hand. She stood so close now, every breath filled her with the scent of the man. That's how close she was to all her dreams coming true.

Maybe a few steps closer wouldn't hurt.

He reached out and touched the amulet hanging around her neck. It slipped into his hand with the ease of familiarity. He traced the feathery pattern on the front, and Evazee felt his fingers on her soul. He gave a sudden tug and the amulet slipped off her neck. He slipped it into his shirt pocket right next to his heart.

Evazee's heartbeat shifted. The rhythm slowed and deepened as if his heart had replaced hers.

He cupped her cheek in his palm and a slow smile spread across his face.

"I think you're ready. We've got some work to do."

26

The Naviband led them to a loading dock—a broad space with room for goods that currently stood clear. The outside wall was lined with huge truck-sized garage doors that could roll up to open, but were closed and kept locked.

Dizziness washed through Kai, and the serum burned through his veins. The room, once a clinical, clean space, suddenly writhed around them like demons captured in stone. The once-smooth floor spread away from them, chipped and pock marked— half-buried under countless sleeping darKounds. Kai thought he might throw up.

He shot a glance at Bree. There was nothing in her expression that showed she could see what he was seeing. Somehow, he doubted he'd get her across if she could.

Kai tiptoed between the black lumps, leading his troupe to the opening. Kai cringed each time someone's knee creaked, and he shot up a hand to halt them as he watched a ripple of consciousness sweep over the darKounds. For endless moments, he stopped breathing.

Kai waited until all their heads were down, their closed eyes invisible slits against their blue-black skin before moving on. Crossing the room took an eternity. The floor levelled out beyond the doorway and Kai stopped to wait for his friends.

Bree got out first. Zap made it through next, and together they watched Ruaan crossing the floor. The relief on his face was almost comical.

Together, they ran to the desert buggy that had brought them in from the gate.

No sooner had they cleared the gateway and an external alarm went off, an ear-splitting metallic scream that bounced up and down the deserted passages.

Ruaan swung around, his eyes stretched wide and glowing in the gloom. "They're coming. It's too late."

Seconds later, they were surrounded. Kai saw an opening in the crush of guards and took his chance. He put his foot flat on the accelerator and prayed that the guards would have enough sense to move.

Beyond the gate stretched the desert and freedom.

~*~

Evazee stood in Torn's office. Shasta was so close that if she breathed in too deeply, her back would brush against his chest. It was like paddling on the edge of a black hole. Any moment she could slip into oblivion. It wouldn't be too much longer until she lost a grip on real life and got sucked into his reality. His fingertips traced circles in the nape of her neck, and he hummed an unfamiliar tune.

"Well, what do you know. I come back for my things, and I find you too. It doesn't get better than this." He breathed heat down her neck. "Somewhere in this stuffy building, is a stash of important things. You will help me find them."

"I don't know what you're looking for."

"Hmm, I can fix that." He cupped the base of her

skull in one hand, and clamped the other over her forehead. Images filled her mind. Images of faces. Her friends. A deep rebellion burned in her belly.

Her fingers traced the bottle in her fingers. Thinking through sludge. Options. Try to drink it? Or throw it in his face like holy water at a vampire? His thoughts threaded through hers like weeds. Choking them, dragging them down.

His mouth moved next to her ear. "I can read your mind, love." His hand slipped down her arm, fingers closed around hers, his skin as cold as marble. With a quick snap of his fingers, he crushed her hand, shattering the bottle. The glass sliced through her skin. Blood and water flowed. Broken glass dropped from Evazee's bleeding hand. The water was wasted. Gone. At least she had one more bottle. Pain sliced through Evazee, and she fought back tears.

Shasta's fingers entwined her hair at the base of her neck, gentle at first; then he grabbed hold with a yank that made her eyes water.

"Let's go find my things." He yanked her out of the office and down the passage.

It was all Evazee could do to keep her feet underneath herself. If she could send thoughts she would. *Run, friends. Run.*

~*~

They shot along the passage fast enough that the tunnel walls blurred. Bree was squashed into the seat next to Kai. "What's the plan?"

"We need to recruit." Kai stared dead ahead without looking her in the eye.

"From where?"

"We start wherever this rattletrap takes us."

Bree's nose wrinkled, "That doesn't sound like a plan."

Kai squinted at the GPS built into the dashboard. "There's a junction coming up ahead. We're taking the left track. The switch is on your side of the dashboard." Kai glanced at her face as she searched for it. Her nose was the most perfect thing.

"Got it."

"And switch...now."

She flicked it hard and the shuttle jerked left, into a tunnel lower and closer than what they'd been in.

Bree settled back and pulled her knees up to her chest, pensive and sad.

"Did you see anything in that last room we came through?"

Bree peered at him from under heavy lids. "It was an empty room. What are you talking about? What did you see?"

Nothing would make him tell her. "I was just wondering. I thought maybe with your gifting you'd see something different."

"What about your gifting? Shouldn't you be fixing things?"

That whole thing hasn't been working for a while now. Maybe I'm burnt out. I don't know. "I'm trying."

Bree caught his eye and grinned. "Well now, that's an understatement." She laughed and for a moment the gloom they'd been living under lifted.

"That is such an old joke. Couldn't you at least try to come up with something new?"

Before Bree could answer, their transport ground to a halt. The cover drew back and a soft glow washed over them.

With what Kai knew now, it curdled his insides.

He hoisted himself over the edge of the shuttle, and his feet landed on gritty sand. The transport had brought them to a quiet section of Stone City, but for the first time, they were seeing it in the natural not the spiritual.

"What is this place?" Zap scratched his head.

Ruaan stared at it, his eyes glowing faintly. "It's a city within a city. A commune of sorts, and this tunnel brought us right into the middle of it."

Bree frowned hard. "It's so familiar but so foreign. The buildings look so cold. They look dirty even though they're not."

"Things look different without light." Kai felt much like the buildings looked.

Ruaan sighed. "At least the food here is good. Didn't care much for the fashion, though."

Zap snorted. "Oh, I dunno. I thought you looked rather fetching in your seamless dress. Dashing in a way."

"I'll dash your face with my fists." Ruaan puffed up, shifting his weight from side to side. It was the first time Kai had seen him anywhere close to grumpy since he'd put his amulet on.

"Shut it, you two. We have company." Kai put himself between his friends and the group approaching.

They were dressed in tired, dirty versions of Kai's jeans and T-shirt with no sign of Stone Cities' strange garb amongst them. Thick dust caked their skin, collecting in the wrinkles and creases.

The man in front stepped forward flexing his fists, muscles rippling through the fabric of his T-shirt. His head was shaved and tattooed. "You shouldn't be here."

Bree pushed past Kai. "They're with me, Roach. Can we talk?"

Zap elbowed Ruaan, and his lips were a stiff line as he repressed a giggle. "Roach," he whispered. "Seriously, like cock*roach*?"

Ruaan shuffled sideways as if he could disassociate himself from Zap and his misplaced humour.

The man named Roach stared Zap down with his pale grey eyes all flinty as Bree spoke to him too softly for Kai to hear what was being said.

Zap coughed and swallowed, rubbing the back of his neck.

Bree finished her speech with a shrug, Roach checked out the rest of them and nodded once. "Follow me."

Kai had never been this close to an actual garbage dump. The stench was enough to make his eyes water. He blinked and choked down a cough. The fishy-ness of it all took him by surprise. He didn't have enough time to investigate to find exactly what could smell that strongly as Roach led them between two high mounds. Kai kept his gaze on the ground at his feet.

Zap still chuckled as he walked.

Kai wondered if he wasn't seeing any green because of the serum in his blood, or more strangely, because nothing here was deeply broken. How was it possible that a beautifully designed, glowing city could be green to its core, but this garbage dump made from everything that was discarded was fine. It wasn't logical.

They walked for at least two minutes through unending piles of rubbish. They came to a halt at a particularly large pile and Roach whistled, low and hollow.

Kai blinked and rubbed his eyes.

The garbage was rolling to the side. It took Kai a few moments to realize that this particular pile of rubbish was fake, nothing more than a front for whatever lay beyond it, which turned out to be more garbage.

By the third sliding door, Kai was losing patience. But it drew back and they walked out of chaos into order. They walked on a neat road of pressed sand, compressed and polished to just short of shiny. Grassy fields stretched away on both sides of the road, clipped short to a rolling lawn, dotted with tidy wooden structures. After breathing garbage-dump air, this felt like it was washing his lungs out.

Zap slipped next to Kai as they walked. "The light feels different here, don't you think?"

"I was just thinking that. The buildings aren't glowing. There's no sun, but I can't see where the light is coming from. It's a bit like that other place we were at. The one made from glowing stones. That was beautiful yet rotten inside. So weird."

"It's all around us." Ruaan's eyes glowed faint grey. "It's the moisture in the air that's carrying the light."

"I see it now." Kai blinked in wonder. The air around him sparkled in rainbow colours as each droplet glowed as if lit by inner light.

Their rough host paid no attention to any of the wonder that had Kai's head spinning. He walked them over to a wooden structure set into the side of a bank of land tall enough to be called a small mountain. A house built into the mountain—surely the insides would be dark and close.

Roach stood to the side and waved them through the doorway. There was a strange elegance to how he moved that seemed at odds with his rough appearance.

The entrance hall was as gloomy as Kai was expecting. The only decor was a map pinned up on one wall, unlike anything Kai had seen before. No place names, just co-ordinates. A few of the places were lit up in different colours.

Ruaan got stuck staring at it, but Roach led them through a partition into a lounge area.

Kai gasped. One length of the room was glass, overlooking a vast body of water similar to what they'd seen at the Resonance Pools, yet distinctly different. The water sparkled and shimmered, sending up the fine mist that lit the atmosphere. The glow from the water lit the room brighter than sunshine on a summer's day.

Bree hung back, rocking back and forth on her feet and frowning at the water. Roach grinned at her, and it changed his face. Ignoring the rest of them, he placed a hand gently on her back and led her forward. At their approach, the glass panes clicked and drew back.

The fresh air washed over Kai. After the biting stench of the slums, the freshness was so sweet, it made him a little tearful.

Roach spoke softly to Bree in words Kai couldn't hear. He took her right out on the deck and sat her on the edge, hovering close in a protective way that made Kai want to shove him. He went closer to see what was happening.

Zap and Ruaan stood transfixed, staring at the water with their mouths open.

Roach scooped up the water and let it run through his fingers. It tumbled from his hands as if it were alive.

The reflections played across Bree's face, softening the hardness that Kai had grown used to seeing. She was so beautiful, and it made his heart ache.

Roach spoke softly. "Wash your hands, and I'll get us something to eat while we chat."

Bree reached down, hesitated at the surface and plunged her hands in. She rubbed the dirt off her damaged hand with the good one and stopped. She sat still for a full minute not moving. When she drew her hands out of the water, her damaged hand was whole again.

~*~

The door hissed open and a short messenger fast-walked to Roach. Two guys waited at the door, they had the look of rugby players with bunches of muscles tucked under their skin in each arm.

One pulled Roach over to the side and whispered in an urgent voice, casting furtive glances towards Kai.

Roach nodded. All the softness that was on his face while speaking to Bree was gone, and he pointed at Kai. "You have to leave. Now."

Bree left the water and moved closer to Kai, who wasn't saying anything. "Why do we have to leave?"

"Not all of you. You're welcome to stay. Just him." He flicked his head at Kai, and the two strong guys were on him in seconds. They grabbed him, and Ruaan and Zap flew at them.

"Wait! Ruaan, no. I'll go."

Zap inserted himself between Kai and Roach. "If one goes, we all go. But before we do, there is something you need to know. If you're against what's happening, the take-over, then we're on your side. I don't know what you've got against Kai, but you're wrong. We're doing everything in our power to shut this operation down. If that's what you stand for, then I urge you to hear us out. You're making a big mistake." The vein in Zap's temple pulsed and red flooded his cheeks.

Roach considered him in silence for a moment. "As I said. You all can stay, but he goes. Now."

Kai went with the two without putting up a fight.

"Kai! Say something." Bree turned to Zap. "What's in his head? Why isn't he saying anything?"

Zap's face was a mask of confusion. "Beats me. His brain has become foggy to me. I can't read his thoughts anymore."

Ruaan shook his head. "I'm going. You lot coming?" It came out as a question, but the underlying tone gave no room for arguing. The others scuttled to the door.

Bree was already out when she turned around and ran back to Roach. Standing on tiptoes, she whispered in his ear. He frowned at her, but she patted him on the arm and he nodded.

They were taken in a different direction to where they'd come from. The garbage seemed so much worse after the clean beauty they'd just experienced.

Kai shook himself free from his captors, who seemed to be less fierce because of his compliance. "Is this really what you want? Living cut off, secluded. Hidden in the middle of this." He waved his arms at the stinking heaps around them. "You've made it work, no doubt. But is this all you can imagine? All you can hope for? What use are you when you're hiding?"

Roach glared at him, fists twitching. "You are

tainted. I will not listen to another word from your mouth." He turned to the two escorts. "This is as far as I go. Take them to the edge. They must not be able to find their way back here." He turned to go but stopped and motioned Bree closer. He slipped a piece of paper in her hand. "If you need anything, anything at all, just let me know. How's your hand?"

Bree slipped her hand out of her sleeve. The skin was still whole and smooth. She held it out to him and he checked it carefully, bending each finger and stretching it in turn. "There's a world out there that needs what you have. You shouldn't keep hiding here."

"You're a walking miracle." He grinned at her.

"I could be one of many." She shook her head at the rubbish and shrugged at Roach. With one last smile, she turned away and fell in line with the boys.

27

Blood ran down Evazee's fingers as Shasta walked her through the OS. A small, detached part of her mind worried about who would clean up the drips before they stained.

Shasta made straight for the basement where Zulu's boys waited for the rest to come back through the testing arch. They squatted with ease on flat feet with their arms looped around their knees.

A strange ripple passed through them as Shasta entered the room. One by one, they stood and turned towards him. Their eyes emptied and they tracked every movement he made.

With a single flick of his hand, they lined up in front of him like soldiers for inspection. He paced down the line, examining the boys as he walked. He turned to the first one in the line, held his chin and stared at his face. "What is your ability? Wait, don't tell me. Let me guess. I think you are a breaker." He nodded sagely and patted the boy on the head. He moved down the queue and came to the shortest one of the bunch. The boy was lean, but strong. His ropey muscles bunched beneath his skin. All of them pulled taut as the grey man stepped close.

Shasta planted a hand on his forehead and the boy swayed. Shasta nodded knowingly as he moved on to the next one. He hummed as he went as if he was choosing fresh veggies for supper.

Evazee stood frozen and watched the boys succumb to the same compulsion that had her trailing after him like a puppy. All except one. The smallest who hadn't been given an amulet. He stood off to one side, wringing his hands, staring at his friends as though they'd lost their minds.

Shasta pointed at him. "You, there. Come here."

The boy refused. He was shaking so hard, Evazee could see it from across the room.

A slow smile crept over Shasta's lips. His fingers coiled around Evazee's hair and pain prickled across her scalp. He leaned in close and whispered, "You tell him."

Evazee's lips moved and she heard herself say, "Come here. Don't worry. You're safe." She wanted to bite her tongue. It was all completely beyond her control.

Shasta eased his fingers out of her hair and chuckled softly. The moment his fingers broke contact with her skin, she felt a sliver of willpower return.

The boy stared at her, then Shasta, clearly conflicted.

Evazee stared at him with wide eyes. Behind Shasta's back she shook her head, willing the boy to resist and run. He frowned at her, puzzled.

Shasta swung around and caught Evazee in the act of prompting the boy to say no. She froze and her hands dropped to her sides. A rolling wave of hopelessness flooded through her.

He tsked once and shoved her out the way, extending his hand to the boy once again.

The boy stuck to his guns and backed away as Shasta came closer. Shasta reached the boy in two steps. He stuck his hand on the boy's forehead. The boy writhed, twisted, and fell in a crumpled heap. Shasta nudged him with a foot, but there was no response.

Evazee's heart pounded in her chest.

Where was Zulu? If he could chase the priests, surely he could stand up to Shasta?

~*~

Their escorts were silent and strong, never letting their guard down for a moment. Even so, they were not cruel or unkind. They left the house and went straight back into the garbage dump, the stench doubly overwhelming after the clean freshness of the house they'd been in. The guards led them to the left, deeper into the mounds of rubbish.

Kai slid in next to Bree.

Her eyes were watering, and she blinked hard to clear them.

"So what was going on back there?"

Bree squirmed. "Nothing."

"I'm not so sure about that. How's your hand?"

Bree shoved her hands in her pockets, a clear sign that she didn't want to talk about them. She ignored his question. "Part of me would love to stay there. Didn't you feel it too? I'm conflicted. Anyway. Enough about me. Why did they say those things about you?"

Kai shrugged. *Defiled*. It made him want to run and never go back. Fine tendrils of mist appeared in the air as they walked, thickening every few steps. Blowing gusts of it rode the wind blocking off the road ahead forming a thick bank that brooded over the road like a hungry animal.

Their guards slowed. "This is as far as we go. The

way back is just beyond this bank of mist."

Zap rolled his shoulders as if he had an itch he couldn't reach. "Is this mist burny?"

The guard shrugged. "I guess so. I've never been through. You need to leave now."

Kai paled at the memory of the pain the mist brought last time. "I'm going to run. I don't care for the slow burn, I just want to get it over with."

Ruaan, as amicable as if his tummy was full, nodded. "It's a good plan, let's all go."

They braced themselves and sprinted. There was no pain from this mist. Just the cold, clammy wetness from the ordinary kind. They would be soaked through by the time they reached the other side. The ground sloped downwards and they picked up speed. The moisture made the stone slippery and before they could stop, the angle sharpened and Kai slipped and fell. He slid and shot off the edge, heart pounding in his chest as he fell. The others screamed next to him, he wasn't falling alone.

Kai hit the water so hard, the impact smacked through his body and stole his breath away. He shot beneath the surface like a stone. The water was cold, and it clenched his head in a vice and made his teeth ache in his gums. A moment of breathless waiting, then slow floating in the same direction as the bubbles. Up.

~*~

Zulu appeared as Evazee thought of him. He stopped with a jerk as he stepped into the room, blinked hard, and rolled his head. He crossed the floor as if his feet weighed a ton, fighting this compulsion hard. His eyes slipped from normal to milky and back.

Seeing one of his boys get hurt was testing Shasta's hold over him to the limit.

Shasta turned to watch him cross the floor with his thumbs hooked in his denim pockets. Zulu got within a few steps and swung his arm back. If the punch had landed, Shasta would've been down, but he side-stepped and touched Zulu's forehead with one fingertip. Zulu flew back, smacking into the wall hard enough to knock his wind out. Shasta closed in on him, pressed his palm to Zulu's forehead and held it there, cracking and sizzling. Electricity zapped through Zulu, and the stench of burning flesh filled the air.

Evazee choked and fell to her knees, her mind swimming. The conflict between Shasta's compulsion and rebellion against it clashed inside with a force enough to shatter her consciousness. Feathery blackness danced around the edges of her vision. She toppled sideways and hit the floor hard.

~*~

Kai hadn't known about the waterfall that had deposited them into an icy cold pool. The pool was in a secluded part of an overgrown urban forest on the outskirts of town. The longer it took to navigate their way out, the more antsy Kai grew. He didn't like the thought of being away from the OS this long.

Ruaan had taken the lead to get them out from amongst the trees. He trudged up in front now, humming to himself. Looking at the change in him, Kai was absolutely convinced that reuniting kids with their amulets was his first priority. The amulets seemed to enhance and strengthen gifting. A group of kids all operating at top capacity would be a formidable force. They just had to make sure that each one got their own amulet, otherwise it would be a disaster.

The sun had started setting when they finally cleared the trees. They trudged down another street unfamiliar to Kai. It gave him no means of judging how long it would take to get back, and that soured his belly.

He kept going over their rapid eviction. The only thing he could think of is that they must have been able to pick up on the serum. He owed his friends an apology. He coughed before breaking the silence. "Guys, I'm sorry. I don't know what went wrong back there. Not exactly a great start to our recruiting."

Zap drew himself up tall and spoke in his most earnest for-the-good-of-all-mankind voice. "Those guys are something else. I don't know that we can trust them anyway. Probably better that they weren't interested."

Kai plucked a blade of grass as they walked and swatted his leg with it. "I don't know, hey? We need everybody that will listen to us."

Zap slowed down until he was next to Bree who had gone all quiet at the back of the group.

"So was your mom a cheese fan?"

Bree wrinkled her nose at him. "What are talking about? You make no sense at all."

"Your name. It's like the cheese. I like cheese."

Bree huffed, "That's b-r-i-e. Not even close to my name. What is wrong with you?"

Kai called over his shoulder, "Really? Do we have to do this now?"

"Yes, Dad." Zap rolled his eyes and shook his head. "You're just annoyed because we're lost."

Ruaan turned back with a fierce look on his face. "You might be lost. I am not. I happen to know exactly where we are."

Zap pointed at a building. "Oh, really? What's that then?"

It was a long, rectangular brick building with lights mounted at intervals along the wall, one positioned over a sign that read *Comm Centre*. Ruaan turned a slow circle as they walked, rubbing his chin and muttering. "It's a community centre. Obviously. We should go inside."

Kai itched at the waste of time. "Do you think we can recruit some people from here?" The sarcasm in his voice was unveiled and deliberate.

Ruaan stuck a fist on his hip and frowned at Kai. "It's just a community centre. Are you daft?" Apparently Ruaan didn't speak in fluent sarcasm.

"If it's just a community centre, why are we going in there?" The urge to get back to the OS overwhelmed Kai.

"I'm allowed to have hunches too, you know. It's just a feeling. Intuition." Ruaan wiggled his fingers over his midriff and nodded as if he were a fountain of pure wisdom.

Zap snorted. "More like indigestion in your case." He pointed at a rusty sign stuck up on the wall. "Today was soup kitchen day. Sounds fun. At least if any of us get hungry," his eyes shifted to Ruaan, "there's food close by."

Ruaan sighed, a deep painful sound. "I'm not hungry. Besides, it doesn't look like they're still running, but I still think—"

Kai pushed between the two of them and knocked on the door. A hollow echo bounced down the hallway beyond. A flock of birds flew overhead, swooping in low over where they stood on the doorstep.

Bree clucked her tongue and pushed past the boys. "I'm not hanging around here waiting to get eaten by the birds." She banged on the door with meaning, hunted around, found a doorbell and pushed long and hard.

The intercom buzzed and a male voice spoke. "Key is under the mat. Let yourselves in."

Bree was standing on the said mat. She jumped off as if it were lava. Kai lifted it and peeped underneath. He found a key and unlocked the door. He hesitated for a second, but Bree stamped her feet while watching the birds circle, and Ruaan sighed loudly. Kai twisted the knob and the door swung back on rusty hinges that groaned.

The hallway was a cavernous wooden space lined with black bags stuffed full, three rows balanced on top of each other.

Zap waved at the bags. "That's a lot of garbage."

Kai sniffed the air. "Doesn't smell like garbage."

Zap prodded him with his bony elbow. "And we've got tons of experience in that department."

"I say we take a quick look around and then we get out of here." Kai didn't wait for anyone to agree. This felt like a waste of time, and they had to get moving. The passage branched off to the left and right. The left led to an enormous dining room, the external wall lined with windows that let in the last rays of the setting sun.

Zap's face sagged. "If there was a soup kitchen today, I'm not seeing any sign of it."

"But you don't even like soup. You'd always skip if that was dinner at St Greg's. Why are you obsessed?" Kai frowned at his friend.

"I don't know. I like the thought of hungry people

getting free food. Why it has to be soup...I'm not sure, but I like the idea of it."

Kai had no words. This boy was always on a different mission. "Soup or no soup, let's see what's down the side passage."

They moved off to the right and into a waiting room full of comfy bean bags. The temptation to sit was high. A circular staircase curled down from the middle of the floor. He checked his companions. "Down?"

Ruaan flicked his hands, "Lead on."

~*~

It was the dream of snakes biting her hand that woke Evazee. The pain from her slashed palm burned like a pulsing, living thing. She lay on her side in the dark basement, lit only by the flickering glow from the testing arch. Shasta and Zulu's boys were gone. Three small bundles slept at her feet, curled up together for warmth. They stirred as she moved. Runt, Peta, and Paintbrush.

Then she saw Zulu, lying like a felled tree in a pool of his own blood next to the body of the small boy who'd resisted. Zulu's breathing was shallow and his dark skin ashen.

Evazee crawled over to him, wincing each time she tried to put weight on her injured hand.

Zulu's eyes followed her, but he didn't speak. Couldn't. A single tear slipped down his cheek. He was losing this battle, his life slipping away. The three small girls gathered around him with looks of deep concern on their faces.

Evazee felt for the last bottle in her pocket, praying it'd still be intact. She eased it out awkwardly with her left hand, popped the lid, and dribbled some of the liquid between Zulu's stiff lips.

He nearly choked swallowing it, but Evazee persisted until the bottle was empty. It was hard to judge from the light of the testing arch, but Evazee thought his colour seemed better. His breathing evened out and he slept.

It was too late for the small boy next to him. She covered him with the tarpaulin that had come off the testing arch. Deep anger burned inside Evazee. There was only one thing she could do about this.

She called the three small girls close. "Will you watch him while I'm gone? I'm going to fetch what he needs to get better."

They nodded and earnestly slipped in next to him to watch over him while he slept as if their presence could delay his body failing.

Evazee washed the wound across her palm in the kitchen and found some cloths to bind it with. The bleeding had slowed, but it was still a messy, tender wound. While she was there, she dug out the biggest empty bottle she could find and stuffed it in a backpack. She was on a mission for more Healing Stream water.

Back in the basement, Evazee checked on Zulu. No change. The three girls huddled together, close enough that their knees touched him. Evazee couldn't think of anything to say to them, so she flashed a quick smile that sat false on her face. She lined herself up at the Testing Arch with her stomach churning at the thought of stepping through. She sent up a quick prayer, not knowing if it would be heard. *Please lead me, take me where I need to go. Let me meet the right people. Not for me, but for Zulu.*

~*~

Kai led the others down the stairs feeling like an intruder. This whole setup felt vaguely familiar, though Kai knew he'd never been there before.

A guy sat at a desk with his back to them, bent double over a laptop. He pushed away from the desk and spun around on his chair before bouncing to his feet and holding out a hand. "Beaver's the name. It's good to meet you."

"Hey! We met before, though it wasn't for long." Kai shook his hand, feeling a deep peace wash over him. He waved towards the others. "This is Bree, Ruaan, and Zap."

Bree dipped her chin. "We've met too."

Beaver nodded. "Yes! I remember you." He grinned at them all, holding out his hands in welcome. "Can I make coffee? Come and sit. I've been waiting for you."

Kai stepped forward, away from the rest. Beaver had helped him once before, but he didn't know him well enough to trust a statement like that. "What do you mean *waiting for us*?"

"You don't have much time, am I right?"

"Well, yes, but..."

"I'm here to help. Do you want to show me your plan?"

Kai looked at the very ordinary Beaver and couldn't help himself. "I'm sorry if this comes across as rude, but you run a community centre. How much would you honestly be able to help us?"

Beaver blinked a couple of times, his face blank. "Oh, you read the sign. That makes sense now. It's an easy mistake to make. Follow me, I want to show you something." He led them through a door into a larger room full of equipment. One entire wall was taken up with a map identical to the one they'd seen at the Stone City Rebel's house. No names, just co-ordinates.

Beaver turned around with his hands spread wide. "Ladies and gentlemen, welcome to the Communication Centre. We track and help Spirit Walkers, Water Workers, and Seekers. We are the metaphorical finger on the pulse of everything that moves underground, including yourselves."

28

Kai, Bree, and the two guys arrived back at the OS as the sun was rising and armed with coordinates to all the entrances to the underground transport network and all of the places they would need to go.

They found Zulu man-down in the basement. He was sleeping with Runt, Peta, and Paintbrush glued to his side, taking turns to pat his face with a tissue. They'd tucked a pillow under his head and covered him with a blanket.

Paintbrush ran to Kai and hugged him. She'd found clips somewhere and attempted to pin down her paintbrush ponytails. Runt had pink warrior stripes on her cheeks. Someone's blush had been raided for the cause. She wouldn't hug Kai, but fist-bumped him instead. Peta stood off to one side, her large eyes seemed to be holding in a flood of emotion.

Kai crouched down close to her. "Peta, do you know where Evazee is?"

Peta sniffed hard and pointed at the testing arch.

Runt sighed and hugged the girl. "Evazee went to find healing stream water for Zulu."

Zap patted Zulu on the cheek. "He's so pale. What happened?" Zulu still had his amulet around his neck, but it was securely closed and tied with a purple hair elastic.

Runt shrugged. "The grey man came. He made

many problems."

Kai looked at the others. "The sooner we make this plan happen, the better."

Kai waved the three girls closer. "I want to send you guys on a mission. Would you like that?" Their sparkling eyes said enough. "Call everyone to the main meeting room. Go as quick as you possibly can."

Runt crossed her arms. "Aw, no, I wanted a real mission. This one is stupid."

"OK, Runt, here's a special one for you. You know the storm drain in the basement? Go check if it's still flooded. Go now."

The three of them stood staring at him with wide eyes.

He clapped his hands once. "Go!" They shot off like greyhounds from their stalls.

~*~

Evazee barely flinched at the pain that danced across her skin as she stepped through the arch. By now, she should at least land on her feet but she still tripped, bit the dirt, and rolled before pushing herself upright.

She blinked against the brightness, her eyes still used to the dim light in the OS basement. The arch had brought her back to the slums outside Sam's house. It was a small victory, but it made her heart pop a little. This was the right place for the Healing Stream.

Evazee turned in a slow circle, figuring out where she was. If she remembered correctly, Sam's house was diagonally to the left and the Healing Stream to the right. She found Sam's house easily, but it made her heart ache to look at it. All the repairs that Zulu had done had been undone by the plants withering and turning brittle. If they'd been using Healing Stream water, there was nothing to show for it.

Her backpack bounced as she walked up to the door.

Sam swung it open, and his face lit up when he saw her. "You're back!" He hugged her so hard, it took her breath away.

"How are you, Sam?" His face was sunken and hollow.

"Not good. My nana, she can't get up anymore." He looked so small and lost.

Evazee wanted to hug him and never let go. "Have you been giving her water from the river we found?"

Sam shrugged. "The river is gone."

"That can't be right. Take me there."

Sam ducked out of the shack on bare feet.

Evazee followed him, walking so fast, her T-shirt quickly soaked in sweat.

The shacks thinned out, replaced by patches of weeds and the odd struggling tree.

They reached the spot where Evazee thought the river should be, but there was nothing but a dried-up sandy channel. "Sam, are you sure this is the right place? I don't remember it looking like this last time."

The boy nodded. "The water stopped coming."

Using the weeds as leverage, they lowered themselves down the dry bank onto the riverbed and kicked up dust. Now what? Together, they followed the dry bed.

Evazee's mind ran options. Something pale glinted at her feet. Before she could get it, Sam swooped in and picked it up. He handed it straight to her as if it were something she'd dropped. It was a scroll much like the one Kai had carried around the first time he'd been stuck here.

"Thank you, Sam. Isn't this for you?"

"No. It shines the same colour as you. Yours." He grinned briefly before his face fell. "Can you fix this?"

Evazee pocketed it and started looking for a good spot along the bank to climb out before answering. What could she say to this boy?

"I don't know, Sam, but I'll try." The words were barely out of her mouth when the wind started. She braced herself, knowing what was coming. Maybe this time she could land on her feet.

~*~

Kai sneaked a sideways glance at Zap as he turned the kettle on. Zap was spreading peanut butter on bread, whistling quietly. It seemed like Kai's thoughts were still veiled from him. This was good. The guys knew about half the plan in his head. The other half, he intended to sneak off and do by himself.

Runt ran in and tapped him on the shoulder. "Somebody is watching us." The girl was dripping from the waist down. "Also, I checked the storm water drain. It's freezing cold, but we can get out that way now. The water has dropped enough." She shivered so hard, her teeth clacked.

"Back up a step. How do you know we're being watched? Show me."

The two of them slipped up onto the roof.

Runt bent herself over double to sneak along the low wall and Kai copied her. She peeped over the wall and stopped.

They crouched together.

Runt thumbed over towards the building across

the road. "Watch the windows one floor higher than where we are. You'll see."

Kai followed the direction of Runt's thumb and picked out the glint of binoculars.

"There are more of them. They don't leave."

It was obvious they were under surveillance. And Kai thought he was being paranoid. Somehow it was a relief to see the glint of the binoculars. "I have a plan. We need to get everyone into the storm water drain."

~*~

Evazee landed back in the basement and kept her feet under her for all of three seconds. The edge of her foot overstepped the stairs and she overbalanced. She pitched forward and rolled down the stairs, landing so hard the wind was knocked out of her.

Zulu lay on the floor in the room, all alone. She checked on him, no change one way or the other. This was no good. She'd have to go back.

Her legs shivered as she approached the arch. This never felt easier. There was a slide and blur and she was through, landing with a roll that made her back click. She sat up and rubbed her head, waiting for the spinning to settle before opening her eyes.

The air was different here, fresh and alive. Colours played across her eyelids. Resonance pools. Her heart sank. She loved this place, but the water in the pools was not Healing Stream water. She didn't have time for vision gazing that may or may not be reality. As far as she could see, she was alone.

Her only choice was to play along. Do the right things to crack the arch and get back to the OS. With a deep breath, she turned in a slow circle waiting for a pool to stand out. Her eyes took in the beauty of the living lines of colour flung upwards, dancing and twirling.

Amongst all the moving lights, one pool simply sparkled. It sat alone, quietly shimmering in a shade of blue that stole Evazee's breath. It was as if a ton of glitter floated in the air above the water.

This one appealed to Evazee and she hurried over and settled at the edge. The sparkles drew her in, capturing her imagination. She might as well be watching the night sky on a moonless night, each light individually sparkling and twinkling.

She saw herself reflected in the water surface. Small and insignificant, almost invisible. From deep inside, a tiny figure of a man formed. She saw no features or markings that she could identify him by. The man grew and grew until he enveloped her completely. It settled her heart, filling her with a sense of wholeness that she hadn't felt since losing her imprint.

In a moment, the water in the pool stirred, creating a mini whirlpool. Evazee hung onto the bank to stop herself falling in. The water gathered inside the image of her, leaving the rest of the pool scooped out and hollow. Evazee stopped breathing for a moment. The water seemed to compress in on itself and then exploded outwards, aimed directly at Evazee. It landed on her with enough force to throw her backwards onto the grass. She lay there, soaked through to her underwear.

As she regained her breath, the sky overhead started to spin. She clung to the grass and rolled down the stairs once again. She was going to be bruised from head to toe if this kept happening.

Evazee coughed water from her lungs and sat up

to find Zulu staring at her. He was still weak, but upright.

"Friend-Evazee, Kai has taken them all to retrieve their amulets. This is bad. Very, very bad. I found this." He handed her a piece of paper with a set of coordinates scribbled down in rough, and the words "the Crux."

"Oh, no. He doesn't know. I have to stop him." Evazee rolled the paper in her fingers with her mind racing.

Zulu rolled himself onto all fours and slowly regained his feet. "I'm coming. Let me get my things."

Evazee looked at him and knew one thing for sure. That would never happen. The way he'd gone at the priests from his own village had been terrifying. To risk that level of power being harnessed for bad was not a risk Evazee was willing to take.

She waited until he was out of sight, tucked the co-ordinates into her pocket, and sneaked off to the garages to get the OS bus.

~*~

The shuttle flew through the tunnel at a speed that made Kai's head spin. To think they'd been living on top of one of the underground stations and never knew it. The storm water drain in the basement led to a door that ran to a station.

Before they'd left the OS, Kai had briefed them on the buddy system and divided them up into groups of five. No matter what happens, stick together.

They'd all trooped past Zulu and the Testing Arch, down through the manhole cover and into the storm water drain.

Kai'd done a quick headcount before they got to

the shuttle and then it was just a matter of getting off at the right place.

They skipped the first stop and got off at the second. The exit came out within the security fence of the Crux, close to the backdoor entrance he'd come in last time they visited.

Tau, please let this Naviband still work. The thought of walking all these kids into a trap soured Kai's belly, but there was no other way.

They avoided the pools of light thrown down from lamps mounted high and crept from shadow to shadow.

Kai's heart nearly stopped as he lined up the Naviband with the beam. But with a click, the door drew back and they were in.

They lined up in quiet rows along the dim passage. It was unthinkable that they could make it this far without being discovered, but so far it all seemed to be working. Maybe Tau was listening after all.

Kai left them there and ran on silent feet to the lab where he'd found Dr S. The lab was quiet, a gentle hum the only noise in the air. Not a single scientist in sight.

Now what?

His Naviband beeped and cycled through options. It came to rest on the vault that he was trying to take these kids to. Kai could follow it and end up exactly where he needed to be. There was definitely someone looking after him.

He led his troupes along silent passages and they worked their way deeper into the the Crux. They turned down a passage that was familiar but with more twists and turns than Kai remembered. Before long, they stood outside the same vault where he and his friends had been deserted by Elden.

Kai shook his head at the memory of Elden. They'd all been taken in by the guy. One day he'd like to have a conversation with him and find out what he was thinking. Or punch his lights out. Probably punch more than talk.

The Naviband opened up the vault and they all trooped in.

"Guys, sit along the wall. We've only got one device, so this is going to take a while. Be patient, we'll get to you all."

He picked out Peta who sat closest to him and put the device in her hands. He slid her thumb onto the fingerprint reader in the centre and the whole gadget lit up neon pink. A hexagon on the floor lit up in the same colour a few metres from where they stood.

"Click the device into the top of the pillar." Kai watched her small hands fumble. But then she got it right. There was a collective gasp from the whole room at the click. The pillar shot up and Peta walked around examining the amulets through the lava glass. Her face lit up as she saw one she knew was hers.

"Go ahead, take it." Kai spoke gently but his insides were boiling with impatience. This was taking too long.

~*~

The OS bus ran out of petrol in the desert outside of the Crux. Evazee's determination faltered as it jerked to a shuddery stop. The building glinted in the lights rigged all along the fence. The desert still gave off shimmery heatwaves, which was odd because deserts were supposed to be cold at night.

She had to find Kai and stop him before he started dishing out amulets.

She hopped out, shut and locked the door, and pocketed the keys. Sweeping her hair off her face, she walked. By the time she reached the high perimeter fence, Evazee's thighs were on fire from crossing on the soft sand. She hadn't thought through how she'd be getting past security.

She rubbed her palms on her jeans. Sweat and sand was a gross combination. Sand had been trickling into her shoes steadily and was rubbing away the skin in a few places. Everything about this place made her skin crawl.

Evazee needed to talk to Jesus. Whether He was listening or not. She tried to frame her thoughts into words. They twisted away from her as if her mind was covered in soap. She took a deep breath and tried again. "Please help."

It was all she had right now.

~*~

The process was working, but it was slow. Every hour that passed increased their risk of discovery and they'd already been in this room for over two.

Kai found Bree. "Tell the other two to keep going with this lot. I'll be back as soon as I can."

"Where are you going?" Bree's hands were on her hips. Not a good sign.

He waved and left quickly before she could ask any more questions. He found his way back to the labs and Doctor S., who was working quietly by himself.

His face dropped when he saw Kai. The doctor shooed Kai into a side room. "What are you doing here? You can't just keep waltzing in here as if this is your lounge. That Naviband will be deactivated and setting off alarms any moment now, if not already." The doctor looked all shrivelled like a prune that needed soaking.

Kai waved his concerns aside. "Have you found an antidote?"

"The truth? Not even close. This last batch...seems to have a life of its own. It has developed the ability to adapt, to defend itself from substances that would cause it harm. Or for our purposes—neutralize it."

"How is that possible?" Kai felt the blood drain from his face. He'd known all along that what he'd injected into his veins was permanent. He'd felt the effects of it seeping into his flesh from the inside out, fought the growing darkness in his mind. But through it all, he'd held on to the tiniest thread of stubborn hope. Hope that said one day he might be free from the death sentence inside. But if it was a living, mutating thing? There was no fighting that without doing permanent damage.

"This won't sound very scientific, but it feels as if it's being manipulated from the outside." The doctor pressed the heels of his hands into his eyes and rubbed hard. "I don't even know what I'm saying. Get out of here, Kai. Go be with the ones you love. The world as we know it will be changing forever real soon." Invisible weight crushed the doctor. "And I've been part of creating this." Guilt was eating him alive.

~*~

Evazee approached the guardhouse, feeling like her legs might give way beneath her. The uneven sand sucked at her feet. The truth was–she was scared silly. She prayed as she walked, each step a simple *help*.

The security guard put down a cup of coffee as she knocked on the glass. Some of the hot liquid slopped on his hand, and he cursed. This was not the best start to her attempt to get into the Crux.

"What is your business here?"

"I'm one of the Doctor's test subjects. He told me to come back after a week. He needed to check if my levels had stabilized." She coughed behind her hand.

The guard stared at her, annoyance clear in the set of his eyebrows. "Which Doctor?"

Evazee hunted for a memory of what Kai had said, what had been on the gravestone. Nothing.

The security guard's finger hovered over a call button.

Something with an R. Roland. She blurted it out, "Roland."

The security guard pressed buttons. "Sure. Let me check if he's expecting you." He waited for his call to connect and mumbled too quietly for Evazee to follow the conversation. He leaned through his window. "Give me your marking number."

Evazee flushed. This would end badly. She turned and got as close as she could to the light from the window, holding her hair up for the man to see. She'd never seen her marking, and she didn't know if it had numbers, but it was the only thing she could think of. The scratchy tip of the man's finger poked her skin as he read off her marking. He listened in silence, then answered, "Sure. This is on you if it backfires." He ended the call and issued her a strap for her wrist.

"This is your Naviband. You must have used one before. Head on over to the vehicles on the right. Someone will take you to the labs."

~*~

Doctor S. escorted Kai to the lab exit. "I'm assuming you know how to find your way out from here." He leaned in close, whispering, "I'm being watched. Don't come around here again."

"What about Bree?"

Pain clouded the man's eyes. "Look after her. Tell her I loved her."

"You're giving up. Listen to me. You were duped. Your noble intentions exploited. Now you get to fix it. You just can't back down, not now."

It was a broken man standing before Kai.

Green-infused Affinity pulsed and Kai counted six darKounds sitting around the doctor, close enough to touch him. Their eyes—deep pits of emptiness—followed every move Kai made. The one closest to Kai stood, and his acid paws steamed prints into the tiles where he stood. His eyes locked on Kai, and the onslaught began. It was different this time. Not words that Kai's mind could comprehend and reject, but a silent pressure that rolled over him with the weight of an elephant, crushing his soul and extinguishing hope. There was only one who could counter this attack. *Tau.* "Tau can help you." Silent screams battered his insides, filling his head like a million bats, all teeth and claws.

The doctor clung to the doorframe as if it was the only thing holding him up.

Kai backed away on wobbly legs. "Jesus can help you." Kai forced the words out between teeth clenched against the pain inside.

"Get out of here."

"Talk to Him. He's been waiting for you."

The doctor clutched the sides of his head. "Get out. Please."

All the darKounds were on their feet now, circling

the doctor's legs, but their eyes stayed fixed on Kai.
Kai turned and ran.

29

Kai expected to be stopped any second. It made breathing hard. He made it to the car without an incident. So much for high security. His stolen Naviband was servicing him well. He could only hope that the guys were doing well with the kids and amulets. Plan A to neutralize the serum had failed. Now Kai was scrambling for a Plan B.

He turned away from the road and aimed the vehicle deeper into the desert. He'd seen something on the map back at Beaver's place that had made his heart pound. He had to take a closer look at what it was. He'd begun to wonder if that change in heart rate was a sign from Tau. As much as Dr S. was convinced there was no antidote for the serum, Kai wasn't ready to give up yet. To give up was to sign his own death warrant.

The sand was soft beneath the wheels. The car felt swimmy, and he knew he'd have to turn back. Just not yet.

He shut it off and sat in silence in the dark. His ears buzzed with the lack of noise. No, not silence. A deep thrumming came from underneath the sand. He got out and felt the vibrations tingling through the soles of his feet. It pulsed in waves, rippling further into the desert. Something was happening below the surface.

A vague, green shimmery line ran from beneath

his feet, and he followed it. His footsteps created a rhythm and the line pulsed in time, growing brighter. He walked until sweat dripped down his back even though the temperature was dropping by a few degrees each minute.

The line ended abruptly at a circular ring of stone at his feet, a manhole wide enough for a single person to squeeze through at a time. His belly writhed at the thought of lowering himself into the darkness, but to come this far and stop? That wouldn't do. The serum ran thick through his veins. It was difficult to say what was real and what wasn't.

Tau, help me.

He swung his feet over the edge, hooked his toes onto the metal rung of the vertical ladder and began to climb down.

~*~

Evazee pretended to walk over to where the vehicles were waiting, but the moment she was out of the reach of the light, she stood still and prayed, whispering quietly under her breath. "Jesus, do You remember when Kai was in hospital and every time I prayed, I'd be taken to wherever he was? Well, that would be rather useful right now." She took a step and then another. "If you don't lead me, bad things will happen. I'm absolutely lost without You. And scared. Don't forget scared." A few more steps. Another few followed after that. Soon she was heading off, without knowing where her feet would take her. The dark became a living thing that swirled around her hungrily.

It was all she could do to keep walking deeper into the shadows. Evazee had never felt more alone. She kept up her running commentary to Jesus, not expecting Him to answer but taking comfort in pretending. "This place feels off. I don't like it." Evazee rubbed her arms against the cold air. It was hard to tell how far she'd walked in the gloom. "I don't really want to ask, but do You think someone is following us?"

She should know better than to ask questions out here in the dark alone. Evazee's teeth were beginning to clack, she was shivering so hard. "I'm beginning to think this might not have been my brightest idea. Also, this whining is driving me nuts."

Evazee rubbed her ears. "Maybe it's a migraine coming on." She tilted her head and listened. "That's odd. It's like I'm seeing the sounds I'm hearing. Is that You, showing me something, Jesus?" She dropped to her haunches and put her hands on the ground. She felt a vibration through the sand, then saw a line of glowing green light starting beneath her fingers and leading away into the distance. "This glowing sand is a little freaky."

She didn't want to follow the line, but she knew she would. Every trembling footstep made the light pulse brighter. Evazee couldn't see where she was going. It shook her. "I don't think Kai is out here. He's the whole reason we came, right?"

She hunched over, following the invisible trail, picking up speed. "I don't want to go out into the desert. There'd better be Kai or something important out here." She picked up speed until she was running to keep up with the streaming light. She could hear footsteps behind her speeding up too. The sound was too much.

She spun around with her hands clenched into

fists, the ones she'd practiced in boxer-cize class at the old gym. "I'm warning you. Show yourselves."

~*~

At the bottom of the ladder, Kai's feet hit the floor and he stumbled to regain his balance. The floor seemed metallic, polished to a slick, high shine, pulsing gently with an inner light that made Kai's head woozy, shifting through a cycle of colours.

The room had a high, vaulted ceiling, curved and organic as if he were inside an oyster. He'd never really thought of himself as a pearl before. The thought made him want to chuckle. The irritation that became something valuable. He could only hope for the latter. A loud buzz followed by footsteps came at him from behind. It was a person in a bio-hazard suit, and they waved their arms as they ran towards him, yelling a muffled warning that he couldn't understand a word of.

"I'm sorry, but I can't hear you."

The person pulled off the helmet. It was Roland, Kai's father. He looked flustered and angry all at once. It almost made his face blotchy-purple. "What are you doing here? It's not safe." An alarm sounded and panic flooded his face. "Come with me, there's a pocket that we might get to in time."

Kai's feet slipped underneath him as if he ran on ice. Roland hit a button on the wall and a panel slid back, revealing a shallow room, just large enough for the two of them to fit in next to each other. A violent wind blew through the room, but the man pushed Kai, threw himself in, and shut the door as the strong wind slammed into it.

"What was all that? And why are you wearing a

biohazard suit?"

Kai's dad ran his fingers through his hair just the way Kai did. It was eerie to see such a familiar mannerism on someone else.

"No. You don't get to ask the questions. What are you doing down here? Do you have a death wish?"

"Well, that's two questions. Which should I answer first? Though why don't we start with why you abandoned me when I was a baby? Yeah, I know all about that."

"We just have to figure out how to get you out of here safely." Roland's eyes held a wild look. Panic had apparently blocked his ears. His face showed no sign that he'd heard Kai.

"Are you even listening to me?"

Roland grabbed his arms. "No, you listen. You shouldn't be down here. Any moment now the room outside will be flooded with serum. The final ingredient will be injected before it gets pumped into containers and shipped out. Do you have any idea what that amount of serum would do to you?"

Kai's mind spun. "So if one wanted to alter the serum, this would be a good place to do it?"

Roland halted, his head tilted in puzzlement. "Theoretically, yes. But I'm more concerned about getting you out of here alive and in one piece." The question shifted his thinking to the cerebral, and it seemed to calm him.

"Now? You choose now to start playing the interested father? I don't get it."

"Trust me, there's a lot you don't get. Now is not the time for a heart-to-heart." He pressed his ear up against the door, listening to what was happening on the other side.

"Can I ask one question that isn't about..." Kai cleared his throat, "you and me?"

Roland propped his shoulder against the door. "Sure. But I might not answer."

"Why the amulets?"

"I don't know what you're talking about."

Kai couldn't tell if he was playing dumb deliberately or if he genuinely didn't know. "You know, the necklace thingies. Each one has an image that somehow links to the person it's attached to."

"Oh! You mean receptacles. Simple, really." The man's face lit up as he shifted into teacher mode. "If you want to pour something into a container that is already full without wasting anything, you have to decant some of the original contents to make space. The receptacles are a way to keep things safe but out of the way."

"What things?" It all sounded caring and kind, but Kai's skin crawled.

"Sometimes it's a memory. Sometimes hopes, dreams. We try and get to the essence of the person. It seems to work better that way. The extractor pumps the essence into a receptacle. The receptacles are designed to analyze the contents and create a mark on the outside that is a reflection of the essence of the person it came from. Each receptacle will resonate with its owner."

"What would happen if the owner tried to access what is in the receptacle?" The picture of Zulu chasing the priests and Ruaan growing so easy to please slid through his mind.

"That wouldn't be a good idea. Reversing the process is not something we've had opportunity to investigate heavily just yet." Roland tripped over the words and coughed. "We were persuaded to make sure the first part worked. There was no importance placed on the second part."

Kai reeled. There was so much wrong with everything that came out of Roland's mouth. One thing snagged at him, a burr not to be ignored. "How do you," Kai faltered over the word, "*extract* what you need?"

Roland was positively glowing. "We devised a few different methods. We even built some extractors with the ability to fly. I was particularly proud of those. Flying extractors.

"You mean the bugs. LightSuckers?"

"Yes! Exactly. What did you call them? LightSuckers. That's quaint. I like it." He rubbed his chin as if rolling around a new taste on his tongue. "We always just called them the airborne extractors. I should rename them."

Kai's blood boiled. His father had developed the bugs that had nearly killed him. The man was both blind and cruel. "Those bugs nearly killed me."

~*~

Evazee braced herself for soldiers. Or guards, or scary homeless people, but when the followers stepped out of the shadows, her jaw dropped.

It was Runt, Peta, and Paintbrush. Peta rolled her eyes at Runt. "I told you we were too close."

"So you'd prefer getting lost in the desert, is that it?" The two girls were the same size and Runt took full advantage, glaring at Peta hard enough to bore holes in her skull.

Paintbrush watched the exchange with a pained expression on her face. The small girl did not seem to like conflict.

Evazee's mouth dried up. "You shouldn't be here. How did you find me?"

All three girls started talking at once, hands flying and fingers wagging. Evazee tried to follow, but they were too loud.

The bag on Runt's back meowed.

"Guys, shh. You're too loud. I don't want anybody finding us. Runt, what is in your bag?"

Runt looked at the other two and shrugged. "I didn't know how long we'd be gone. I didn't want to leave them."

"You brought the kittens."

Runt nodded as if it were the most obvious thing in the world to do. "Kai brought us all here to get our amulets. But he's got mine, and he hasn't given it back to me yet. Paintbrush doesn't want hers, and Peta..." She stopped to think and rubbed her chin. "Why are you here, Peta?"

Peta frowned. "Because I don't like that place." She thumbed back towards the enormous building behind them and crossed her arms.

"But girls, why aren't you with him? Why are you out here in the dark all alone?"

Runt shuffled from one foot to the other, and Peta developed a deep interest in her cuticles.

"Girls..."

"Kai left us all with the crazy one and the hungry one. We decided to follow him. Just in case he needed us, you know? Also, we're not really alone. Three isn't alone." Runt grinned at Evazee.

Paintbrush tugged on Evazee's hand. "You weren't alone either. I saw Him walking with you. Where's He gone? I like Him."

Before Evazee could ask Paintbrush who she was talking about, a deep shudder passed through the ground below their feet. It felt like an earthquake but over a much smaller area and more intense than any Evazee had felt before. It shook them off their feet and they huddled together, shaking.

When it subsided, Evazee turned to the three. "Girls, you have to go back. This place is dangerous. But first, tell me which way Kai went."

Runt leaned towards Peta and whispered at a non-whisper volume, "I told you she'd say that."

~*~

"Oh, no, that's not possible. You don't have to fear them. They are quite harmless. I can imagine a swarm of them in the dark being a little scary, but honestly? It might sting a little when they first attach, but there are no harmful side effects."

Kai's stomach turned at the memories of swollen sores weeping black goo, the fever that nearly drove him out of his mind. This man was clueless. "Get me out of here."

"Wait, what's the matter? I don't understand."

"There's a lot you don't understand." Kai's teeth clenched so hard his jaw ached.

Roland blinked. The man looked puzzled, but any trust that Kai might have had in his goodness was annihilated. "Kai, when this project is complete," he waved a hand that took in the entire expanse of the Crux, "I want to hang out." He shuffled awkwardly. "With you, I mean. I've always done what I thought was right, but I can see now that I might have missed a few things along the way. Made some mistakes."

"We probably won't survive this." Kai didn't have

the heart to speak his full thought...*because of you.*

Roland's face twisted in puzzlement, but he didn't argue. Instead, he pressed his ear against the door. "There's a lull. Come on. Now is your chance." He breathed for a moment, threw back the door and ran out, pulling Kai with him.

The room was empty, but there were residual traces of serum collected in pockets along the edges.

"Quickly now. There's no time. The batches come through in quick succession." Roland escorted Kai across the floor back to the ladder.

"Are you telling me that this entire space fills with serum? This whole room?"

"Mostly, yes. At regular intervals."

Blood drained from Kai's face, his skin prickled with pins and needles. The volume of altered serum being produced was overwhelming.

They reached the ladder, and he grabbed the side to swing himself up and climbed. He crawled out at the top and stopped dead.

A man stood, waiting for him with arms folded. Shasta.

"It's been a while. You can't stay away, can you?" He paced across the desert and covered the distance between them in a few short steps. "What's this I see?" He reached out and pulled Kai's bottom eyelid down, away from his eyeball. "You've already had some of the good stuff. Eager, are we?" He chuckled as he walked a slow circle around Kai. "This is an unexpected development."

Kai stood frozen. His mind scrambled for an escape route, while the rest of him was paralyzed by Shasta's closeness. He wanted to vomit.

"Do you know what I find most interesting about

this batch of serum? The moment it enters your system, it begins to change you. It gets to work on your DNA. Isn't that phenomenal? Rewriting things you thought you'd be stuck with forever. My man here, Roland, he's been leading the research. He is single-handedly responsible for this latest development. We wouldn't have been anywhere close if not for this one."

Roland had climbed out behind Kai and stood off to one side with his head down, staring holes into his boots.

Kai would have given anything to read his thoughts, especially if the conflict on his face was anything to go by. Kai's mind took it all in, still hunting for an escape.

You should really just yield. A gift like yours would be a terrible thing to waste. I can see that you get everything your heart wants.

30

Evazee walked blindly, feeling her way forward with her toes. She kept hoping her next step would be a bump into Kai. Something shifted in the air and invisible heaviness dropped over her like a cloak. Standing upright was hard. She felt exposed, vulnerable. A bug kept in a glass jar. Thoughts like eels probed her mind. She knew this silent voice. A shudder ran through, and she nearly tripped. Each step took her closer to where she didn't want to go. But she couldn't abandon Kai.

She touched her throat where her imprint had been, felt the empty chain where her amulet used to hang. She'd been stolen from, cut down, and shoved aside. Right now, she was nothing but a blob of fear with a bunch of hang-ups and issues thrown in.

She couldn't bear the darkness any longer. She had to run. Kai was nowhere in sight. She rounded a bend and smacked hard into a muscular arm. It snaked around her, covering her mouth and pulling her into the shadows. She fought like a crazy person, elbows aiming for soft targets.

"Shh! Stop fighting me. I'm trying to help you."

The voice in her ear was familiar and brought back an instant memory of stolen peaches. She stopped struggling and his arms relaxed. The moment they did, she swung around and rammed her fists into his chest. "You're a traitor! Get away from me!"

Elden coughed at the impact to his chest. "There's a trap and Kai and your precious OS kids have walked straight into it. Stop fighting me."

Cold fear ran through Evazee. "How do you know?" A shockwave of panic washed through her, and she didn't wait for his answer. "We have to get them out. They should never have come. They're not meant to be involved in this mess."

"You have to trust me. Now is not the time." He held a finger against her lips.

Evazee's skin crawled. Between letting her be marked and abandoning the other guys, she didn't trust Elden as far as she could throw him.

"I can read your eyes, Zee, and I understand. But I don't think you have any other choice right now. Your marking got you in the door. Think about that for a moment."

"Touché. But it doesn't excuse what you did." She was torn. Her thoughts and feelings were a tangled mess, a ball of thread left at the mercy of a bored cat. She wouldn't figure it all out right now. She shut down that train of thought and flicked her fingers at the darkness ahead. "What is out there?"

Elden met her eyes for the first time since grabbing her. "Let's just say, it's not safe. Not safe at all. Kai is out there, we have to try find him." He held her hand in his and together they walked into the darkness, following the faint glow of the line at their feet.

~*~

Shasta towered over Kai with his arms folded as if mulling over his options. His phone beeped once and he took the call. He listened without blinking, a slight lift in his eyebrows the only indication that he was hearing what the other person had to say.

Kai watched the subtle play of emotions on Shasta's face.

Roland eased himself between Kai and Shasta.

Shasta ended the call and rubbed his hands together. "I needed some volunteers and what do you know? They came to me. If the universe is giving you a sign like that, you're on the right track. Don't you agree?" He chuckled at his own joke. He flicked his head towards Roland. "Take him to the amphitheatre. I'll be along shortly."

"The amphitheatre? But we're not at that stage yet. Our deadline is still weeks away."

"I decided to speed things up a bit. Don't question it, just do what I tell you." Shasta didn't hang around to make sure that Roland did his bidding. He walked off into the dark in the direction of the Crux.

Kai watched the conflict play across Roland's face. If he spoke carefully, he might just be able to get through to this man. Harmless question first. "What is the amphitheatre?"

Roland didn't answer, but the fine sheen of sweat across his forehead spoke volumes.

Kai patted his shoulder, and Roland roused as if he'd just woken from a nightmare.

"What?"

"The amphitheatre. What is it?"

"You'll see for yourself soon enough. Please don't resist. I don't want to have to restrain you."

"But he's bullying you. You're the expert, and he should be listening. Not doing his own thing in your area of specialty. Surely?"

Roland hunched as he walked, looking sinister by the glowing green light that lit their path. His shoulders bunched tightly as brown stained his cheeks.

The sand was hot enough for Kai to feel it through the soles of his sneakers. Temperatures dropped rapidly in the desert at night but this place was different. The midnight dark dome of sky curved away from where he stood and for the first time. Kai realized there were no stars. Under different circumstances, his mom would have loved taking this walk.

"Why did you do it? Why did you abandon me?"

Roland kept his gaze down and stayed silent long enough for Kai to think he hadn't heard the question. "That's not what happened."

"From my side, that's exactly what happened. You dumped me at St Greg's and left. Never to be seen again. Who does that with their own child?"

"What you could do scared me. You were a baby, and you had healing powers. That's terrifying. It's not like you'd been to Bible school or had any proper training. You just did it. That's not how it works." He shook his head. "I found a school where you'd be safe, and I offered my services as a researcher, hoping that I'd find a cure. All I wanted was for you to be normal so that I could fetch you and go back home."

"You abandoned TrisTessa."

"I tried to go home, but she wouldn't have anything to do with me. She threatened to get the police involved, and that would have been an enormous mistake. I tried to make her see sense. I wouldn't tell her where you were, I just told her that you were in good hands, but she wouldn't believe me. Sometimes I know what's best for my family. This was one of them."

Kai stopped walking and stared at the man. He wore a green turban of brokenness around his head.

The glow was so large, that it looked like his neck might snap. "You are completely deceived."

~*~

"Here it is."

Evazee squinted into the blackness. The moment they'd stepped off the end of the green line, it had faded away to nothing, plunging them into deeper darkness.

"I don't see anything. Are you sure?"

He led her over a sandy rise and down the other side. At the bottom of the mini-hill steps disappeared deeper into a tunnel under the sand. As they followed the short flight down, Evazee could see light glowing from below. It grew brighter as they got lower. The stairs bent to the left at the bottom. Evazee nearly tripped over her feet from shock.

The amphitheatre was just that—a huge, hi-tech underground arena, with the seating area blocked off from the open space in the middle by what looked like one-way glass.

Elden led Evazee away from the door, and they crouched down behind a wall. They huddled there, trying to be invisible in the hollowed out, empty venue.

Evazee's foot started to cramp. She eased her weight off, overbalanced, and fell. She caught herself.

Something in her back pocket poked her. The scroll she'd picked up from the dry riverbed. She slipped her hand into her pocket to take it out. No longer a scroll, now it was a small book. A Bible. She opened it to where someone had slipped in a bookmark. A single paragraph was highlighted:

"Whoever believes in me, as Scripture has

said, rivers of living water will flow from within them."

One of her favourite verses. She hadn't thought about it in a long time.

Elden seemed distracted by what was going on down on the floor of the amphitheatre, people were leading in and being separated into groups. But he must have noticed because he turned back and asked, "What have you got there?"

Evazee quickly closed the book and slipped it back into her back pocket. "Nothing. Just a book." She stared ahead, wishing he'd focus on something else. As much as Elden seemed like the old Elden she remembered, she couldn't bring herself to trust him. Sure, the branding on the back of her neck had bought her entrance into this place, but he couldn't have known that she'd need it. It was all too convenient. She sat with adrenalin pumping through her veins, waiting for him to betray her again.

Rivers of living water will flow from your innermost being. She could do with some of that right now.

Jesus, help.

~*~

Kai was seeing spots from staring at the glowing green lines in the sand—the only light in the deep darkness of the desert. The lines stopped abruptly, and Roland led him past two stairways going down into the sand and came to stop at a third.

"I have to get back. This is your entrance to the amphitheatre. Head straight on down, and there'll be people to help you." Roland was twitchy, an ant on a hot plate.

"Can you at least give me a clue what happens here?"

"It's a simulation, just on a bigger scale than what you're used to. You've been through them at the OS. Just keep your wits about you, and you'll be fine."

"I was never in a sim. I was trapped in the spiritual realm. If I died there, there'd be no regeneration, no resetting of my mind and moving on." He passed a hand across his face. Trying to get through to Roland was like trying to speak clearly with one's cheeks full of marshmallows—it just didn't work. "I can see why TrisTessa was frustrated with you. You won't hear anything that doesn't fit with the messed-up picture in your head."

Roland winced. "You've got this. Go do what you came here to do. Now get down there. I've got things I need to get back to."

Kai took the stairs two at a time, just to get away from Roland. A single narrow passage led away from the staircase, and Kai kept walking. The buzz of conversation grew louder as he walked. The passage was dimly lit but better than the absolute darkness of the desert. It opened out onto a holding room full of people. It didn't take much to pick out Ruaan. He stood head and shoulders above the rest. Zap was next to him, but all Kai could see of him was the top of his head bobbing up and down. In between them stood a swaying sea of OS kids.

Kai began to push his way through to get to his friends. As he walked, he checked the necks of those he passed. Most of them seemed to have found their amulets and were wearing them happily.

He managed to push through to his friends. Bree stood with her arms crossed just behind Zap, thunder on her face.

"Guys! What are you doing here? You should be on your way back home. What happened?"

Zap's shoulders sagged. "We came so close to making it out. They stopped us at the last gate."

31

A door opened at the far side of the arena. People started leading in, and Evazee squinted to see if it was anyone she knew. It was hard to tell from such a distance, but she could swear she saw Kai's black mop of hair. She tilted her head, blinked a couple of times. It was definitely Kai. Ruaan and Zap were with him. They were huddled together, furiously discussing something. Zap's hands were flying as if he swatted bugs, and Ruaan and Kai shook their heads.

She poked Elden with her elbow. "What is going on here?"

Elden's jaw clenched. "Human trials. The latest batch of serum is supposedly ready to go live. This is where the testing happens."

"Supposedly?"

Elden avoided her eyes. "I overheard a conversation. The scientist working on the serum asked for another three months at least. The powers that be aren't prepared to wait."

Evazee could read between the lines. She knew exactly what he was getting at. "We have to stop it."

Elden grabbed her arms and pulled her towards him until he was right up in her face. "Listen to me. Going down there will do no good. You cannot stop this. You can't change anything or fix it."

"I refuse to sit here and watch my friends be

poisoned. That might work for you, but it doesn't work for me."

~*~

"Stop flapping your arms. You'll hit something." Ruaan swatted Zap's hand away from his face.

"We can't stay here. I don't like this setup at all. We need to make a run for it before it's too late." Zap was obviously freaking out.

Kai checked the door they'd come through. It was shut tight. He knew it was locked because he'd tried to open it the second it swung shut behind them all. There wouldn't be any getting out that way. As far as he could tell, that was the only door into the strange dome-thing they were trapped in. It was like being stuck in a bubble. The walls stretched from sand, to high overhead, then back down into sand again, in a smooth surface criss-crossed with veins of light that glowed enough to light the cavernous space. Kai imagined being in a fish's belly would feel like this.

He shuddered and was about to start a roll call when the lights shut off. Thick darkness swallowed up the room in an instant. A single beam of light flicked on from across the room. By the faint light, he could clearly see that there were no longer any walls surrounding them. They were out in the desert under the glow of a rising moon.

"Do you think the bubble popped?" Zap asked.

Kai swiveled around, trying to see everything all at once. "Looks like it did. This breeze is refreshing. Should we go see what's over the hill?" He raised his voice, loud enough to be heard over the chatter. "Light would be better than the darkness."

Ruaan was turning in circles, craning his neck.

"We aren't being guarded. We should make a run for it."

"You might be right. Could it be this easy? Zap, what do you think?" Kai's heart was pounding.

Zap clucked his tongue. "Have I not been saying this all along?"

"True. But if they know that their bubble popped, they'll probably send someone to fix it." Kai grimaced. "There's probably someone on the way already."

"All the more reason to get a move on." Ruaan spoke as if Kai had half a brain.

"So we run?" Kai looked at the other two. Their heads were nodding in time with each other.

Kai waved to all the others to come closer. "Everybody, we are going to make a run for it. Buddy-up, aim for the light. Let's go."

~*~

The lights went out in the arena below. The dome was built to allow those on the outside to see what was going on. It must be a live video feed onto the surface of the dome as the images seemed to shift, zooming in and out. One of the close-up shots showed Runt, Peta, and Paintbrush huddling together. Runt clutched her bag to her chest, protecting her kittens. Zulu was there too, but he seemed smaller than before, folded in on himself.

Evazee shoved the back of her hand in her mouth to stop herself yelling out. So they'd been caught too.

Elden slipped an arm around her and moved in close. "Don't move. Shasta is close enough to see us." He pointed to a control booth situated a stone's throw away from where they were hiding.

Shasta was presiding over the events below with a

dark gleam in his eye. He held a joystick in his hand and every time he moved, he changed what they were seeing on the outside of the dome. A wide shot of the whole group running up a dune. With a click, the image zoomed in on one girl.

Shasta stood up, breathed deep and closed his eyes. Evazee watched in horror as the girl he'd zoomed in on grabbed her amulet. Her eyes rolled back in her head, and she stopped running. A stone in the path of a living stream of humans.

Shasta shifted his focus to the next victim and the same thing happened. He was manipulating them through their amulets.

Evazee had to stop him.

Elden grabbed her hand and held on so hard, his fingers made white marks in her skin.

Evazee fought him. "I can't just sit here and watch this happen. I have to help them." She was whispering through clenched teeth.

Elden shifted his weight and his arms locked around her like a safety bar on a rollercoaster. "Too soon, just wait."

Hot tears ran as she struggled against him. More and more of the OS kids were giving in to Shasta's compulsion through their amulets. Less of them were moving. "What is wrong with you? I know you are working for Shasta. I trusted you. I was a fool. So tell me, how deep does this double agent thing actually go?"

Elden grew still. His arms stayed around her, but his chin dropped and he shut his eyes. "If you must know, I haven't been completely honest."

~*~

Kai ran with a spark of hope. The desert sand sucked at his feet, and it didn't take long for his thighs to burn with the effort of running. He slowed down to check on the others, but they were gone. He spun around, but he was alone. Nothing stirred in the deep dark all around him.

This can't be happening. Tau, what's going on?

A wisp of mist drifted past him, and he wanted to shout his lungs out, but he didn't dare make a noise. He willed his heart to slow, focusing on every noise coming from around him. The silence made his ears sing.

Then the voices started.

~*~

Evazee crouched, paralyzed. Elden had just admitted to everything she'd been suspecting all along. She wanted to remove herself from his arms, get as far away as possible. But she couldn't move. Now was not the time.

She focussed on the screen, her heart in her throat as she watched her friends buckle under the onslaught. It played out across the surface of the dome; the reality of where they were and the forces unleashed against them. Serum pumped into the dome like heavy fog, and with it, Shasta's influence over them grew.

In a moment, she knew. This was no simulation. The fabric separating the physical world and the spiritual had been shredded in this place. Her friends were at the mercy of a cruel dictator who was interested only in their submission. And this was only the start. From here it would spread. This confusion and isolation. The dominion and control. It would grow, multiply like cancer.

Elden shook as he held her, his arms like vice grips.

Evazee inhaled deeply. As she breathed out, she shut her eyes and turned her focus inwards. She was empty, bereft, and broken. Then her focus slipped upwards. She cringed at the thought of bringing all this *nothing* to the feet of God, but He was the only one who could help. If she could see His face now, what would she find? Disgust? Disappointment? Her heart poured out through her lips in a silent prayer. *Not for me, Jesus, but for them. They need You. You are our only hope.* The warmth on her skin took her breath away. She kept her eyes shut tight, too scared to look.

"Psst! Up here."

She knew this voice. Curiosity won and she opened her eyes.

Jesus sat on the top of the dome with His legs crossed and His feet bare. She'd never actually seen Him like this before, but her heart knew it was Him. Her Jesus, the one Kai called Tau.

"Come, I have something for you."

She breathed in and as she breathed out, she sat next to Him on the very top of the metal structure. Yet she was still vaguely aware of Elden's arms around her. This must be a vision.

"Give Me your hand."

Fear constricted her throat, but she met His eyes and they sparkled with delight as if He was sitting on secrets that He was about to start sharing. There was no trace of punishment that she was expecting.

"I'm sorry..."

"Shh! Give Me your hand." He held out his and it was easy to slip hers into it. "My Evazee. You've been through so much. You think all of it has bent you out of shape so much that you no longer fit into My heart."

His hand was warm. The tears that slid down her cheeks were the hot tears of shame.

"There's something that belongs to you. Stay right here, I'll be back." He sauntered over to where Shasta sat hunched over the controls of all that was happening down below. He waved his hand in front of Shasta's nose, but Shasta carried on as if completely unaware of Him. Jesus leaned over the man and frowned at what Shasta was labouring over. Jesus rolled His eyes and shook His head. With a shrug He leaned forward and plucked Evazee's amulet from Shasta's top pocket. He bounced it on his palm and patted Shasta on the head. Shasta went right on sweating over what was happening below, apparently oblivious.

Jesus jogged back to Evazee and sat cross-legged in front of her. He held out a hand, and she slipped hers back into His without hesitation.

"My Evazee. My heart is not small or brittle. My heart has room for you, no matter how bent out of shape you think you are. Take what is yours." He placed the amulet back in her open palms.

A sliver of fear shot through her. Shasta would use this to gain control over her again. She was done with all that. "But getting this back didn't help me before. Why would it work now?"

"Only I can restore things that have been stolen. That's my job." His hands folded around hers, warm as the sun. "Here, let's finish this." He drew breath and breathed over their hands.

Evazee felt the amulet crack, shatter. It dissipated to nothing between her fingers, but the warmth of His breath on her skin remained.

Jesus grinned at her, kissed her hands, and drew

her to her feet. He slipped one hand to the back of her neck and placed a thumb of the other at the base of her throat. Her skin tingled under his touch. "My girl. Mine. None of this was ever taken from you, you know. You just believed that it had been. Now get down there. There's work to be done."

~*~

Evazee's eyes shot open. She was still held tight in Elden's arms. The mess below was getting worse. A fog of serum hung thick in the air. Evazee's mind flew back to Sam and their tonic. She'd seen the serum-tonic sizzle and evaporate at a few drops of healing stream water. They needed healing stream rain. That's all it would take to sort this mess out. Yet there was simply no healing stream in the desert. She waited for the hopelessness to roll over her, but warmth still lingered on her fingers. Nothing seemed different. And yet nothing was the same.

It was time to engage Heaven.

~*~

Voices. No, only one. *You can save your friends. Stop resisting me.*

It echoed and came back at him over and over.

Save your friends. Stop resisting.

Kai felt Shasta's mind bend towards him like a piercing spotlight, searching hungrily. It was coming closer, only a matter of time until it locked onto him. He stopped running and stood, wondering what he'd been running for. Thinking through the sludge in his brain was virtually impossible.

Standing there, he felt greasy approval. His heart rate slowed right down. Maybe if he stayed quiet, the tension in his skull would unravel and he'd be able to think. He couldn't figure out what he was meant to be doing. And why?

Like some weird throwback, he began to stumble onwards. The light over the rise flickered and smouldered. A compelling curiosity burned inside of him. If he could just see the light, it would all make sense.

A bright flash split the air in front of him and he halted, blinded.

"Boy, what are you doing? It's not your time!" It was Evazee, as bright as the first day he'd met her in the desert. "You can't give in to this! He has no real hold of you. He thinks he does, but he doesn't. You belong to One much greater."

"Zee? What are you doing?"

"I get it now! The serum is neutralized by Healing Stream water."

The imprint at the base of her throat was back, it gleamed in the darkness. This was the shiny girl he remembered. Radiant and free. It made his heart ache.

Her words washed over him like a stream of living water. They made his skin tingle, but they couldn't get through the thick layer of muck bogging him down. He'd worked on an engine with Phil once and his hands had been dirty like this. The water couldn't budge it.

"But we're in the desert."

"Tau is here. He is dancing circles around Shasta." Evazee laughed and the sound filled his mind with light.

A thick wave of darkness rolled in to oppose the swelling light, and Kai felt his head might splinter in pieces. "But the amulets..."

"Give them to Tau. He is the only one who can give back what has been stolen. He says whoever believes in Him will have rivers of living water flowing from within them."

"What? I don't get it." His mind was a breath away from breaking.

In a flash as blinding as her arrival, Evazee was gone.

~*~

Fog rolled in thick around Kai. He couldn't see more than a meter away from himself. Evazee's words trickled through his muddled brain, slowly at first.

Whoever believes in Him ...

Kai stopped running and stood. Him. Tau. *I believe.*

Streams of living water ...

Healing stream water?

Will flow from within him.

A spark of hope popped in his belly. It gave him enough courage to turn around. His friends were lost in the fog, cut off and alone.

He couldn't save himself, but he could help them. He started running. Evazee's words built in his belly, an uncontainable force ready to explode. He yelled as he ran, "Guys, can you hear me?" Silence.

There had to be a way to get through to them. Wait. There was that army-thing that Runt had done. It was a long shot but it might work. He sucked air into his lungs and sing-songed so loud, his throat hurt. "We've been lied to and misled."

A breathless moment of silence, then a few voices echoed.

We've been lied to and misled.

"Shasta kind of wants us dead."

Shasta kind of wants us dead. More voices joined.

"But he forgot to factor in..."

But he forgot to factor in...

"Tau slash Jesus is the King."

Tau slash Jesus is the King.

The cadence fit in with the rhythm of his feet. Not exactly the deepest lyrics he'd ever come up with, but it was getting through. The call and response of an army on the move.

"Sound of..."

Sound of...

"Freedom..."

Freedom.

"Sound of..."

Sound of...

"Healing..."

Healing.

"Let me hear you say YEBO!"

YEBO!

Each response grew louder. More kids were hearing and responding.

"To me, to me. Rally to me." Kai belted it out so loud, his voice cracked. He'd reached the top of a rise and began to shout. "For Tau and for His kingdom." His voice rang out clear and true, echoing through the space.

The response around him swelled.

For Tau and for His kingdom.

~*~

Something smacked into the side of Evazee's head and she fell. One moment she'd been praying for Kai, the next she found herself flat on her back staring up at

Shasta.

Elden sat doubled over, blood on his hands.

"So my pet, you are causing problems for me." Shasta loomed over her, tall and imposing.

Evazee waited for the whirlpool slide that always sucked her sideways around him. Nothing. She pushed herself up onto her elbows. "What you're doing is wrong."

"You're lecturing me on right and wrong?"

There was an edge to his voice that pricked a warning all across Evazee's scalp. "You have no rights over me. I don't belong to you."

"Oh, we'll see about that." He chuckled as he stepped closer, slow and deliberate.

"Hey, mister, leave my friend alone." It was Runt. She had somehow found her way out of the pit and now stood glaring at Shasta with a cat under each arm.

Fear spiked through Evazee. If anything should happen to Runt...

"Oh look, it's the runt. Smallest little reject of the bunch." Shasta examined the small girl as one would watch an ant before squishing it.

The dome caught Evazee's eye. With Shasta's attention elsewhere, his influence had slipped. Kai was rallying them. *Not at the cost of Runt's life. Please, Jesus.*

Elden staggered to his feet. Blood streamed down the side of his face. "Leave the girl alone. She's not yours."

Shasta sneered at him, "Oh, look, the boy of shifting loyalties. Here's an ancient proverb for you...those who straddle both sides will find themselves split in half."

Elden laughed, a deep hearty chuckle. "Look again, I was never yours. Nothing in me ever belonged to you."

Shasta tilted his head, studying Elden sideways. "Hmm. Do you think I didn't know that you were thoroughly sold out to the other side? You thought you were so clever, but it backfired, you know. It's a pity. You could have been great." He drew his hand back, and his palm spiked with electricity. The writhing snakes were back.

Runt threw herself at Shasta and bounced off him, barely budging him. She caught herself and held her two kittens right up in his face. "My cats want to meet you."

Shasta gaped, taken aback. Fury filled his features, and he drew himself up tall.

Evazee got up to throw herself between them, but before she could move, Shasta jerked forward with an enormous sneeze.

~*~

Kai stood alone on a hilltop with his eyes shut, his mind focussed on Tau.

If you believe in Me, rivers of Living Water will flow from within you.

I believe. He opened his mouth and started to sing words he didn't understand. They left his mouth and flew through the air, dancing in and around and through the serum that had been sucking the life out of his friends.

He kept singing. His voice swelled and grew, a living thing full of light and life. Words flew through the air like flaming arrows, landing deep in the hearts of kids tied up in black hopelessness. Burning through coils of deadly lies. Shattering the darkness of oppression.

He imagined Tau standing with him like a flaming tower of goodness.

One by one, they started to come.

~*~

Elden saw his opportunity. He flew at Shasta and punched hard. The man fell back, knocked his head on a chair, and toppled to the ground in a heap.

"Evazee, quick! The equipment!"

Evazee ran to the control table Shasta had been working at. She picked up a jug of water and upturned it over the laptop. The screen turned funky and went black. The dome flickered and shut down.

Kai's voice rang out clear and strong over the noise and confusion.

Evazee stood on the rim and picked up the tune of the song and sang too. She sang from a heart bursting with gratitude. Warmth and light. She sensed Jesus before she saw Him. He stood next to her, studying the crowd below with a tenderness that took her breath away.

Runt ran up and slipped in under his arm. He kissed her forehead, took the two cats from her and balanced them on His chest. They purred and rubbed against His chin, making Him laugh. "Here, these are yours. Well done for listening when I asked you to bring them with."

Runt giggled. "Yeah, they all thought I was nuts. But I knew."

Elden slid in next to Evazee, staring at the glowing man with wide eyes. His face was a mess of blood from the wound on his forehead, but his eyes sparkled. He pointed to the pit, "Look! I think they're ready."

There was a crowd around Kai, eyes closed, faces

upturned.

Evazee searched the crowd for her friends. She found them one by one, until only Bree remained unaccounted for. "Where's Bree?"

Evazee followed Elden's finger and found Bree, arms huddled around her knees at Kai's feet, leaning on his leg. She studied her hands, tracing the smooth skin of the one that had been damaged. With a sigh she leaned back and slipped an arm around Kai's leg. Kai's hand dropped and his fingers curled around a lock of her hair. The look on her face was something that Evazee had never seen there before. Contentment.

~*~

Kai watched the multitude press in close with their eyes shut. One by one, he watched their faces change, and he knew that Tau was weaving in between, shattering the amulets that held them captive.

He waited for Zulu, Zap, and Ruaan to be done and gathered them close.

"We need to go neutralize the serum. I know exactly where to go. Come on."

32

Kai sat on the edge of the couch in the office at the OS with a cup of coffee turning cold on the table next to him.

Elden sat opposite, looking like a war victim with his head wound bandaged tight, while Runt played with her cats on the mat.

"So are you telling me that you were never truly on their side?"

Evazee patted Elden's leg, and her voiced dropped to a conspiratorial whisper. "He knows Jesus and everything. I saw it with my own eyes."

Elden grinned at her, then his smile withered. "I know it looked like I was working for the other side. But who do you think kept reprogramming the Naviband every time you came back? Who kept giving you security access? I'm sure you didn't think it would be that easy to waltz in and out of a facility with such high-level security. Why do you think I let them mark Evazee? You were right about the amulets. The only way to take them out was to bring their owners in. So really it all worked out brilliantly. Should I go on?"

Bree sat in silence next to Kai, staring at her brother. Every now and then she'd shake her head but actual words were beyond her.

"And what do they call you again?" Kai's brain might have exploded from all the info he was taking in.

"A Seeker. We work undercover. We aid and assist wherever we're needed. Then you get Water Workers, and they are all about healing and restoring. You know some of them actually. Beaver and Shrimp?" He waited for Kai to nod before carrying on. "Liberation Crew...the Stone City rebels are Liberation Crew through and through. They lead rescue missions to free the marked ones out of the most dangerous situations. All of us are Spirit Walkers working towards the same goal. There are a bunch of different areas you can specialize in depending on your gifting."

"And there are some people who want to talk to us about becoming Spirit Walkers too?" Kai frowned deeply.

"They've been following you all over. The first time they tried to make contact was at TrisTessa's art gallery. They saw you go in, but there was no way she was giving them any information on you. She chased them away with her paintbrush swinging."

Kai sat up in shock. "I remember that day. She made me paint with her. I was terrible, but she made my clumsy attempt at art look good. She shuffled me out of there when they arrived."

"There've been other occasions too, but you just kept slipping from their grasp. Don't tell them I told you, but they've already got some tasks lined up. Getting rid of all the serum produced at the factory, that's way up on the priority list. Part of that is helping your dads adjust to their new mission. They are feeling very lost right now." Elden shot a quick glance at Bree, but she was boring holes in her hands with her eyes as she rubbed her palms together, tracing her fingertips over the healed skin.

"Fetching all Zulu's boys back from the testing

arch and training them. Also, the priests of Zulu's village are ready for a visit."

Kai laughed, "Are you nuts? They would string me up and feed me to their worms."

Elden looked puzzled. "Worms? I don't know about worms, but I know the priests are ready now."

Bree clasped her hands together and eyed her brother from across the room as if listening to a stranger talk. "You could have told me, you know. All I wanted to do was rescue you from being indoctrinated, sucked deeper into that whole mess, but you just stubbornly ignored me. I was worried sick." She shuffled a bit closer to Kai, close enough that he felt the warmth of her leg next to his. It was a feeling he could get used to.

Elden tried to glare at it her but failed. "And you should have listened to me. How many times did I tell you to go home? You are at least as stubborn as I am!" He shook his head with a laugh. "And yet that stubbornness and love is exactly why you'd make an excellent Spirit Walker. You two should think about it."

Kai curled a lock of Bree's hair around his finger, winding it tight before letting it slip off with a bounce. "What do you think, Bree? Should we do this?"

"Well, I'm only just getting to know Him. But you? I've watched you work with Tau. All the titles and tasks, it's all just a technicality. You're already doing the job. He calls, you answer."

"I don't know what I'm doing though. I'm like a kid with crayons, messing up the master artist's canvas."

Evazee laughed. "We've been through so much, but you still don't get it. All you have to do is be you.

That's enough. He does the rest. Ask me, I know."

"Like my painting with TrisTessa."

"Exactly like that." Evazee sat next to Elden with her eyes shining and her imprint sparkling between her collar bones. She was glowing much like the first time she'd slapped him in the desert.

Bree stared at Evazee as if she were an oasis in the desert. A slow smile tugged at the corners of her mouth. "You should listen to her, Kai. The girl speaks sense. Between you and Tau, you've got this down to a fine art."

Thank you...

for purchasing this Watershed Books title. For other inspirational stories, please visit our on-line bookstore at www.pelicanbookgroup.com.

For questions or more information, contact us at customer@pelicanbookgroup.com.

Watershed Books
Make a Splash!™
an imprint of Pelican Book Group
www.PelicanBookGroup.com

Connect with Us
www.facebook.com/Pelicanbookgroup
www.twitter.com/pelicanbookgrp

To receive news and specials, subscribe to our bulletin
http://pelink.us/bulletin

May God's glory shine through
this inspirational work of fiction.

AMDG

You Can Help!

At Pelican Book Group it is our mission to entertain readers with fiction that uplifts the Gospel. It is our privilege to spend time with you awhile as you read our stories.

We believe you can help us to bring Christ into the lives of people across the globe. And you don't have to open your wallet or even leave your house!

Here are 3 simple things you can do to help us bring illuminating fiction™ to people everywhere.

1) If you enjoyed this book, write a positive review. Post it at online retailers and websites where readers gather. And share your review with us at reviews@pelicanbookgroup.com (this does give us permission to reprint your review in whole or in part.)

2) If you enjoyed this book, recommend it to a friend in person, at a book club or on social media.

3) If you have suggestions on how we can improve or expand our selection, let us know. We value your opinion. Use the contact form on our web site or e-mail us at customer@pelicanbookgroup.com

God Can Help!

Are you in need? The Almighty can do great things for you. Holy is His Name! He has mercy in every generation. He can lift up the lowly and accomplish all things. Reach out today.

Do not fear: I am with you; do not be anxious: I am your God. I will strengthen you, I will help you, I will uphold you with my victorious right hand.

~Isaiah 41:10 (NAB)

We pray daily, and we especially pray for everyone connected to Pelican Book Group—that includes you! If you have a specific need, we welcome the opportunity to pray for you. Share your needs or praise reports at http://pelink.us/pray4us

Free Book Offer

We're looking for booklovers like you to partner with us! Join our team of influencers today and periodically receive free eBooks and exclusive offers.

For more information
Visit http://pelicanbookgroup.com/booklovers